FINDERS KEEPERS

Acclaim for Radclyffe's Fiction

"Medical drama, gossipy lesbian romance, and angsty backstory all get equal time in [*Unrivaled*,] Radclyffe's fifth PMC Hospital Romance…[F]ans of small community dynamics and workplace romance without ethical complications will find this hits the spot."—*Publishers Weekly*

"*Dangerous Waters* is a bumpy ride through a devastating time with powerful events and resolute characters. Radclyffe gives us the strong, dedicated women we love to read in a story that keeps us turning pages until the end."—*Lambda Literary Review*

"Radclyffe's *Dangerous Waters* has the feel of a tense television drama, as the narrative interchanges between hurricane trackers and first responders. Sawyer and Dara butt heads in the beginning as each moves for some level of control during the storm's approach, and the interference of a lovely television reporter adds an engaging love triangle threat to the sexual tension brewing between them."—*RT Book Reviews*

"*Love After Hours*, the fourth in Radclyffe's Rivers Community series, evokes the sense of a continuing drama as Gina and Carrie's slow-burning romance intertwines with details of other Rivers residents. They become part of a greater picture where friends and family support each other in personal and recreational endeavors. Vivid settings and characters draw in the reader…" —*RT Book Reviews*

Secret Hearts "delivers exactly what it says on the tin: poignant story, sweet romance, great characters, chemistry and hot sex scenes. Radclyffe knows how to pen a good lesbian romance." —*LezReviewBooks Blog*

Wild Shores "will hook you early. Radclyffe weaves a chance encounter into all-out steamy romance. These strong, dynamic women have great conversations, and fantastic chemistry." —*The Romantic Reader Blog*

In **2016 RWA/OCC Book Buyers Best award winner for suspense and mystery with romantic elements** *Price of Honor* "Radclyffe is master of the action-thriller series…The old familiar characters are there, but enough new blood is introduced to give it a fresh feel and open new avenues for intrigue."—*Curve Magazine*

In ***Prescription for Love*** "Radclyffe populates her small town with colorful characters, among the most memorable being Flann's little sister, Margie, and Abby's 15-year-old trans son, Blake…This romantic drama has plenty of heart and soul."—*Publishers Weekly*

2013 RWA/New England Bean Pot award winner for contemporary romance *Crossroads* "will draw the reader in and make her heart ache, willing the two main characters to find love and a life together. It's a story that lingers long after coming to 'the end.'"—*Lambda Literary*

In **2012 RWA/FTHRW Lories and RWA HODRW Aspen Gold award winner** *Firestorm* "Radclyffe brings another hot lesbian romance for her readers."—*The Lesbrary*

Foreword Review Book of the Year finalist and IPPY silver medalist *Trauma Alert* "is hard to put down and it will sizzle in the reader's hands. The characters are hot, the sex scenes explicit and explosive, and the book is moved along by an interesting plot with well drawn secondary characters. The real star of this show is the attraction between the two characters, both of whom resist and then fall head over heels."—*Lambda Literary Reviews*

Lambda Literary Award Finalist *Best Lesbian Romance 2010* features "stories [that] are diverse in tone, style, and subject, making for more variety than in many, similar anthologies… well written, each containing a satisfying, surprising twist. Best Lesbian Romance series editor Radclyffe has assembled a respectable crop of 17 authors for this year's offering."—*Curve Magazine*

2010 Prism award winner and ForeWord Review Book of the Year Award finalist *Secrets in the Stone* is "so powerfully [written] that the worlds of these three women shimmer between reality and dreams…A strong, must read novel that will linger in the minds of readers long after the last page is turned."—*Just About Write*

In **Benjamin Franklin Award finalist** *Desire by Starlight* "Radclyffe writes romance with such heart and her down-to-earth characters not only come to life but leap off the page until you feel like you know them. What Jenna and Gard feel for each other is not only a spark but an inferno and, as a reader, you will be washed away in this tumultuous romance until you can do nothing but succumb to it."—*Queer Magazine Online*

Lambda Literary Award winner *Distant Shores, Silent Thunder* "weaves an intricate tapestry about passion and commitment between lovers. The story explores the fragile nature of trust and the sanctuary provided by loving relationships." —*Sapphic Reader*

Lambda Literary Award winner *Stolen Moments* "is a collection of steamy stories about women who just couldn't wait. It's sex when desire overrides reason, and it's incredibly hot!" —*On Our Backs*

Lambda Literary Award Finalist *Justice Served* delivers a "crisply written, fast-paced story with twists and turns and keeps us guessing until the final explosive ending."—*Independent Gay Writer*

Lambda Literary Award finalist *Turn Back Time* "is filled with wonderful love scenes, which are both tender and hot." —*MegaScene*

Applause for L.L. Raand's Midnight Hunters Series

The Midnight Hunt
RWA 2012 VCRW Laurel Wreath winner *Blood Hunt*
Night Hunt
The Lone Hunt

"Raand has built a complex world inhabited by werewolves, vampires, and other paranormal beings…Raand has given her readers a complex plot filled with wonderful characters as well as insight into the hierarchy of Sylvan's pack and vampire clans. There are many plot twists and turns, as well as erotic sex scenes in this riveting novel that keep the pages flying until its satisfying conclusion."—*Just About Write*

"Once again, I am amazed at the storytelling ability of L.L. Raand aka Radclyffe. In *Blood Hunt*, she mixes high levels of sheer eroticism that will leave you squirming in your seat with an impeccable multi-character storyline all streaming together to form one great read."—*Queer Magazine Online*

"Are you sick of the same old hetero vampire/werewolf story plastered in every bookstore and at every movie theater? Well, I've got the cure to your werewolf fever. *The Midnight Hunt* is first in, what I hope is, a long-running series of fantasy erotica for L.L. Raand (aka Radclyffe)."—*Queer Magazine Online*

By Radclyffe

Romances
Innocent Hearts
Promising Hearts
Love's Melody Lost
Love's Tender Warriors
Tomorrow's Promise
Love's Masquerade
shadowland
Turn Back Time
When Dreams Tremble
The Lonely Hearts Club
Secrets in the Stone
Desire by Starlight
Homestead
The Color of Love
Secret Hearts
Only This Summer

First Responders Novels
Trauma Alert
Firestorm
Taking Fire

Wild Shores
Heart Stop
Dangerous Waters

Honor Series
Above All, Honor
Honor Bound
Love & Honor
Honor Guards
Honor Reclaimed
Honor Under Siege

Word of Honor
Oath of Honor
(First Responders)
Code of Honor
Price of Honor
Cost of Honor

Justice Series
A Matter of Trust (prequel)
Shield of Justice
In Pursuit of Justice

Justice in the Shadows
Justice Served
Justice for All

Visit us at www.boldstrokesbooks.com

FINDERS KEEPERS

by

RADCLY*ff*E

2023

FINDERS KEEPERS

ISBN 13: 978-1-63679-428-0

This Trade Paperback Original Is Published By
Bold Strokes Books, Inc.
P.O. Box 249
Valley Falls, NY 12185

First Edition: June 2023

Credits

Editors: Ruth Sternglantz and Stacia Seaman
Production Design: Stacia Seaman
Cover Design by Inkspiral Design

Acknowledgments

Thank you to the readers whose support and loyalty are the reason this and the many other books from BSB exist. Mega thanks to Sandy Lowe, whose input and encouragement on stories and whose firm hand on the wheel at BSB gives me room to write; to Stacia Seaman and Ruth Sternglantz for the past twenty years of care and editing of my books; and to Lee, for never doubting it would all work.

Radclyffe 2023

For all the readers, past, present, and future

Chapter One

Rome Ashcroft left the Four Seasons Hotel in Albany a little after five a.m. on an October morning that had dawned clear and crisp. Heading north on the interstate, she let the 911 climb to twenty over the posted speed limit. When her radar warned her of a speed trap ahead, she eased off the gas before passing the trooper tucked into a narrow space between the tall spruce and fir trees that filled the wide median separating the north- and southbound lanes. The red Porsche was easy to spot and a magnet for highway patrol, so she'd learned to be vigilant, figuring the radar detector evened the playing field. But with empty roads and good weather, she liked the speed and the hungry way the coupe gripped the road, like a hunter on the prowl. An old girlfriend—who hadn't been old at the time, they'd both been first year college students then—had told her she'd made love—the girlfriend'd used another word then too—like she drove. Hard and fast and smooth. Rome had chosen to take it as a compliment, as the woman in question had expressed her pleasure more than once that night, but she'd remembered the words and made it a point to let her bedmates set the pace after that. But behind the wheel of the highly responsive and powerful machine, she could indulge her desire to live out on the edge of control.

When she left the interstate, the abrupt change from straight, unfettered highway to narrow, uneven, and barely paved roads put an end to her speed. Forty minutes out of the city, she powered down to a sedate fifty, to both her disgust and that of her coupe, whose engine strained and throbbed and threatened to break loose if her attention wavered for an instant. And she couldn't afford *not* to pay attention, not given the heavy pockets of fog that appeared unexpectedly around curves in the twisting country roads, obscuring her vison for seconds at a time while she squinted into the murk without the faintest notion of where the shoulder—what there was of it—might be. She didn't expect road lights, or even shoulder reflectors, but didn't they believe in lane markings out here?

At least she was the only one on the road. If the sky had been clear—or even visible—the sinuous two-lane that climbed and dipped and swerved would have been a fun exercise in sports driving, but she really didn't want to arrive for the first day of work *in* the ambulance instead of waiting to meet it. Rounding a bend, she caught a glimpse of a faint red flicker in the wall of gray ahead, and her foot hit the brakes before her brain registered *taillights!*

Heart pounding and mentally cursing softly, she peered ahead as the rear of what looked like a pickup truck disappeared into the swirling mist. That could have been a disaster, and her own mistake for not anticipating someone else on the road. Careless. Careless got you, or someone you cared about, dead. She took a breath. Right. Proceed as if Grandmother was in the car. Rome smiled. Had Grandmother Ashcroft been aboard, she would have been urging Rome to *get a move on, dahling*.

Checking her mirrors, Rome pulled forward and just as quickly swerved to avoid a large dark shape half on the road and half in the bushes on the sloping shoulder, densely bordered by a thicket of trees that came right down to the road's edge. She pulled over as far as she could without putting the 911 in the weeds, put on her hazard lights, and climbed out to investigate. With every step closer, the taste of ash built in her throat, and she flashed back to the rows and rows of similar shapes awaiting the last flight home—body bags on the airfield at Ramstein, eight clicks from Landstuhl Hospital where she'd been stationed in the last days of the Iraqi conflicts.

She blinked and muttered, "Relax. It's just an old duffel bag. Somebody's trash, that's all."

Or maybe not. Maybe the thing had flown off the back of that truck that had just sped away. Could have laundry in it or a week's worth of clothes for some trip. She frowned and took a couple of steps closer. Or maybe not.

"What the…"

Something was off. Something about the bag raised an alert, a survival sense honed by a thousand trips in a Humvee over roads littered with IEDs. Her mind balked at registering what she *thought* she saw. No, she wasn't wrong. There was something *inside* that bag, all right. Something moving.

Her pulse spiked, and she ran. Running into the face of danger was second nature too. Time was everything in a crisis—seconds meant lives. Seconds meant soldiers—friends—bleeding out, limbs lost, brains forever damaged. She had to…

Rome skidded to a stop, her leather soles sliding on the dew-damp road surface. She had to slow down. Think. Her being dead or wounded saved no one.

And this wasn't a war zone. This was rural Upstate New York. Farm country. Not Baghdad. The war was over.

Focused now and totally present, Rome crouched next to the duffel, her hands steady even though her nerves were jangling and her stomach tensed into a ball. Gripping the pull on the big brass zipper cutting down the center of the worn, faded green canvas, she yanked. Something black came hurtling out and pain lanced through her palm. She rocked back on her heels—snake? Raccoon? Please don't let it be a freaking skunk.

The black body wiggled free and plopped onto the road. Rome stared.

She spread the edges of the duffel and peered inside. "You've got to be kidding me."

❖

Tally Dewilde parked her baby-blue VW Bug in one of the three slots marked for clinic staff. The cute little signs, cut into the shapes of a cow, chicken, and bunny, perched on posts crafted to resemble tree branches driven into the grass at the edge of the gravel lot. She chose the chicken. Seemed more…professional somehow. Chickens were enterprising and pretty smart, after all. Bunnies were kind of soft and helpless—not her, definitely. And cows—well, they could be sweet and had their uses, but…no.

She grabbed her lunch bag and took a second look at the sign, warmth spreading through her. *Staff.* She was staff, at last. A vet at the Upland County Animal Hospital. Okay, only on the job for sixty-two hours, but still. She had done it.

She walked around to the small, covered entry porch, accessible by either three steps or a short ramp, used the key she'd been given the Friday before when she'd met Sydney Valentine, her new boss, in person for the first time, and reached inside to turn on the lights. As she entered the empty waiting room with its functional gray tile floor, plain navy fabric chairs, and waist-high counter on the far side, another wave of satisfaction made her smile. Finally, *finally* she had a job, a job *she* wanted, not the one found to be acceptable by her family. Maybe not exactly *where* she'd expected to be, but she could get used to country living. Probably. Definitely.

Especially since it meant independence and escape from the critical opinions of friends and family, most of whom thought veterinary medicine one step up from menial labor—unless of course one ministered to the elite clients on the show ring circuit. As if she would ever want to be trapped in that world of competition and politics. She almost smiled, remembering her mother's disdain when she'd revealed her plans.

"But really, darling, *cows* of all things? What could you possibly care what became of them?"

Tally hadn't bothered to explain that she'd specialized in small animal care, which was specifically why Val hired her, although she'd cover farm call in emergencies. Or that farm animals were critical to a large portion of food production and the mainstay of many farming enterprises. Her mother didn't care about the details of what Tally planned to do, only that it wasn't what was expected of the daughters of families in their social circle. And by extension, how that reflected on her mother. As if Tally's success was somehow her mother's failure. That hurt, but she'd had eight years to get used to it. Her mother might not approve of her choices, but she'd stopped trying to please her—mostly.

Tally mentally shrugged aside the last frosty conversation she'd had with her mother, where she'd declined yet another contact her mother had found for her among her friends on the dog show circuit, and retrieved the printout of the day's appointment schedule from behind the counter. She was about to start her first full day of office visits and couldn't wait. She'd already asked to see the schedule on Friday afternoon when she'd stopped at the clinic before even picking up the keys to the small house she'd rented a few miles away. Val had laughed at her enthusiasm—in a nice way—saying she'd get over that excitement fairly quickly, but Tally didn't think she would. As Tally understood from their conversation, Val had worked in this same clinic when she'd first started out in practice but had left for a big-city boutique practice like the one Tally's mother imagined for her. That hadn't led to the life Val envisioned, and when she'd had the chance, she'd come back to her roots. So Val might not understand what breaking free of Tally's family's traditions to pursue her dream had cost her, but that was fine too. No one else needed to know. She knew.

And if perusing the list of clients and their pets put a little thrill of anticipation buzzing in her middle, what was the harm? She deserved a little happiness, a little pleasure, and work was certainly the safest way. Val had large animal farm call that morning and would be driving the mobile hospital van throughout the county from farm to farm, and Tally was on her own for patient hours at the clinic. She was fine with that too. At their one and only Zoom job interview, Tally'd gleaned after the first five minutes that Val's true passion wasn't looking after the small domestic or exotic animals that Tally preferred. She loved the connection between the owners and their pets—that special bond that came from living with an animal who loved and depended upon you. She'd always wanted pets as a kid, so maybe she was just making up for that now, but her passion for small animal care and Val's for farm animals made them perfect partners. She hoped that would be true as far as the practice went too, someday. Being part of the business she loved would be a bit like building a family.

She glanced up from the client list at the sound of tires squealing and gravel crunching outside. At five fifty a.m.?

Maybe it was one of the staff coming in early—although they'd be parking around the side where she'd parked, wouldn't they? Not a client, not unless there was an emergency. Automatically, she checked her phone as she'd done almost every hour all weekend. Val had welcomed her with a quick tour of the rambling single-story clinic, surgery, and boarding area that sprawled in an L on several acres of land nestled among slopes covered in evergreens and maples before saying, "Now that you're here, I can finally take the weekend off. You have my number, right?"

"Yes," Tally said.

"Good. Call me if anything comes up you can't handle."

"Oh, okay," Tally replied, as if she could say anything else. Who told the boss they didn't want to take call, after all. On the first day of work in a place she'd never been before. So much for her plans to settle into the house she'd rented, drive into the village, and explore. How tough could a weekend of call be in a practice like this, anyhow? She'd had plenty of ER experience in a busy urban clinic while in training. Still, she'd been nervous, understandably—she didn't even have a good idea of where anyplace was located out here—and uncertain of the cell service. Hence, the compulsive phone checking.

No missed calls.

So not an emergency. Tally relaxed. Someone just making a U-turn, probably. She replaced the day's schedule by the phone and headed down the hallway toward the treatment rooms and the small office she'd been assigned next to Val's slightly larger one. A pounding on the front door brought her turning back with a frown. When the knob rattled and the pounding resumed, she hurried back through the waiting room, only to hesitate before pulling open the front door. She was alone in the clinic.

The nearest house was at least a half mile away if she'd judged accurately when driving to the clinic. But half a mile or a few hundred yards hardly mattered. The closest person was well beyond shouting distance. Her stomach tightened. No peephole in the door.

"Who is it?" she called.

"Can you open up? I've got a problem here."

A woman's voice, low and forceful. That didn't necessarily spell safety. Tally slid over to see if she could get a glimpse of the person out the small window above the line of chairs. Years of city living had ingrained a sense of caution she couldn't ignore.

"Hello?" the woman called again. "You there? I could use a little help."

Tally chided herself for the knee-jerk suspicion. This was a rural community where everyone knew everyone, if her conversations with the Realtor who'd given her a verbal tour of the village had been any indication. Besides, whoever was outside had parked directly in front of the building, in plain sight of the road and any security cameras—did they even have security cameras? Well, at any rate, she wasn't in danger of a home invasion at the vet clinic, but just to be safe, she flicked her phone to the call screen and punched in 911. She could send the SOS in a second if she needed to.

"Just a minute," Tally called as she pulled the door halfway open, blocking the opening with her body as she peered out. A woman in a blue shirt, expensive-looking tailored black pants, and even more expensive-looking black ankle boots with narrow crisscrossing straps over the arch and a bronze buckle on the side stood on the porch, the rest of her body and part of her face mostly hidden by the large green canvas bag she carried in her arms. "Sorry. We're not open yet."

"I have a situation here," the woman snapped. "Damn it—cut that out!"

Tally frowned as the woman jostled the bag, as if about to lose her grip. "What's the problem?"

"Puppies," the woman said tersely and pushed a shoulder against the door, forcing Tally to give way and let her in. "At least I think that's all that's in here. I haven't taken a head count, but there's a bunch of the little buggers."

The stranger set the partially unzipped bag on the floor, and a black snout appeared. "That's the ringleader. Got teeth like a piranha."

"What?" Tally's voice rose as she stared first at the bag and then at the woman crouched beside it. A woman whose face she now recognized. Whose face she could never forget. Her throat tightened. She had to be wrong—it *had* been more than ten years. But there couldn't be two of them as damnably handsome, or as effortlessly entitled as to barge in without the slightest explanation.

One more look confirmed it. Disheveled collar-length jet-black hair, fuller on top than on the sides, cobalt blue eyes, and commanding features too strong to be called pretty. Arresting. That was the word, and Tally nearly laughed at the irony. God, she needed to get a grip. She wasn't a teenager any longer, and even when she had been, she hadn't fallen for the charismatic facade. The anger burned cold now, banked for so many years, but no less formidable. She embraced the rage, and her spine stiffened.

"Hello, Roman," Tally said quietly. "We're not open now. You'll need to call back after the start of business and make an appointment." She gestured to the still open door. "Our hours are on the sign out front."

Roman Ashcroft's head jerked up, and she frowned. "Do I...? Sorry, I don't recall."

"Talia Dewilde," Tally said and heard the ice in her voice. Probably not a good professional approach. Screw it. She didn't really care what Roman Ashcroft thought of her. She didn't need to pretend to be friendly.

"Ah," Roman said with a weary sigh. "Sheila's sister."

"Yes."

"Tally, I—"

"It's Talia," Tally said bluntly. Okay, now she was being needlessly unfriendly, but why, oh, why was Roman here? Possibly the last person she ever wanted to see again, and the one she most wanted to forget. The snout that had appeared through the opening in the bag became a furry black head with suspicious black eyes. A mixed breed puppy and, from the sounds of it, more than one. Her professional curiosity and sense of responsibility won out over her desire that Roman disappear—forever. "Do you want to tell me what this is all about?"

"Talia, right." Roman blew out a breath and indicated the bag with a tip of her chin. Her ridiculously sculpted chin with the sexy little dent. "Found these on the highway. I don't know what to do with them."

"You found a bunch of puppies..."

"No," Roman said impatiently, "not the *puppies*. The bag. When I opened it, the little bug—one of them, that one I'm pretty sure, poked its head out and bit me. I shoved it back in after a quick look, and here I am. There they are. And now I need to go."

"I don't think so," Tally said, wishing she could just open the door and Roman would be gone as if she'd never been there. "I have to file a report. I'll need some more information."

"Fine," Roman said as she stood and grasped the doorknob.

"I'll leave you my number. You can text me later, and I'll tell you what I know, which isn't much."

Tally, giving herself props for not pointing out that Roman was not the one in charge, said, "One of them bit you?"

"It's a scratch," Roman said and made a fist. Not quickly enough to hide the blood.

"Let me see."

Roman sighed that sigh again, the one that sounded as if she thought Tally was still fifteen.

Tally stiffened. "Are you trying to be difficult, or is that just your natural state?"

"Neither. Why do you want to see it?" Roman asked.

"First of all," Tally said, mustering every ounce of her professional patience when she really wanted to push Roman out the door, "it needs to be cleaned up—sooner rather than later. Secondly, I need to make a record of it, test the puppies for contagious diseases, monitor them, and follow up with you *and* animal control. The one who bit you will need to be quarantined."

"Lot of work," Roman muttered.

"Yes, thank you very much."

Roman had the grace to look contrite. "Sorry, I didn't know what to do with them. I couldn't leave them in the bag to starve, and I couldn't let them loose by the side of the road for worse to happen."

Tally softened, catching sight of the black noses—several more of them now, edging free of the bag. She had no idea the location of the nearest animal shelter, and likely no one would be in for at least an hour at any rate, with luck. Besides, she couldn't just send someone, not even Roman, off with a bag full of puppies who might be sick or diseased or injured. And Roman's hand *did* need treatment. "You did the right thing."

Saying that to Roman Ashcroft seemed surreal. Tally grabbed the strap and hefted the bag. Bodies shifted inside, and the cries of protest escaping the open top turned to indignant yelps. "Sorry, little ones. We'll get you out of there in just a minute. Roman, come back with me. I'll get a look at them after I check your hand."

Roman didn't move. "Look, I'm supposed to be on my way to the hospital. Could you just take them? I'm fine."

"No," Tally said tightly. "Why are you going to the hospital? Are you sick?"

"No, I'm not sick. But I *am* going to be late if this takes much longer." Roman's eyes actually sparked with irritation.

Tally hid a smile. Petty of her, but still—gratifying to know she was annoying Roman.

"Are you a doctor?" Tally asked.

"PA," Roman said tightly.

Oh. She *was* annoyed.

"Good. Then you can assist me with them after I'm done looking at you."

Tally marched off, not waiting for an answer, satisfied despite her displeasure at finding the last human on earth she ever wanted to see again at her door.

CHAPTER TWO

R ome clenched her teeth as Tally pointedly gave her the
literal cold shoulder by turning around and walking away—
expecting her, obviously, to tag along behind as bidden. For
half a second she considered just walking out and driving away.
But something kept her following Tally through a neat and
tidy waiting area with blue leather padded bench seats against
one wall and a row of matching chairs in front of the reception
counter. From the looks of the stack of folders sitting next to the
computer, the clinic would be busy later.

The puppies, that's what it was. She'd found them, so she
wanted to be sure they were going to be well taken care of. That's
all. But assist her?

Not likely. Five minutes—she'd give her five minutes.

The brightly lit hall took her into another part of the
building that smelled like an emergency room—antiseptically
clean and faintly medicinal, with the addition of eau du animal,
a not unpleasant odor of fur and fresh air. The framed posters
that marched down the walls on either side pictured various
domestic and farm animals in cute poses—kittens with balls of
yarn, dogs with plush toys clamped in their grinning jowls, and
cows regarding the world with doleful patience. If she'd had to
describe the offices of a family vet—a rural family vet at that—
this would be it.

Rome mentally shook her head. She couldn't fit Tally

Dewilde into a place like this, and as a vet no less. The last time she'd seen her, Tally had been barely fifteen. She'd been hanging around the fringes of the party Sheila had thrown at the Dewildes' summer house in the Hamptons while their parents were in Paris for some business function. That had been the summer Rome had turned nineteen. The summer the world as she'd known it had shattered.

Tally wasn't fifteen anymore, but not much else had changed. She'd grown into an older, even more stunning version of the model-beautiful teen she'd been then. Tally—blond, with moss-green eyes, fair skin, and classically sculpted arching cheekbones—didn't look anything like her older sister. Sheila had been dark to Tally's light. Thick, shoulder-length sable hair, smoldering dark eyes, and—in retrospect—a beautiful but cruel mouth. The lack of family resemblance was some small blessing now, at least. Just dealing with the storm of conflicting feelings aroused by coming upon Tally so unexpectedly was challenge enough without seeing Sheila every time she looked at her. Tally seemed to have Sheila's temperament, though. Frosty and fiery all rolled into one. That hadn't changed either. Rome could still hear the last words Tally had screamed at her. *I saw you. I saw you with my sister. I know what you did.*

Rome paused at the door to the room where Tally had deposited the duffel on a high, narrow stainless steel treatment table. A big overhead light enhanced the feel of an ER and reminded Rome of where she needed to be. She could just turn around and walk out—ought to do that right now. Tally obviously was just as unhappy about the situation as she was. What could Tally do? Physically stop her?

"Look…" Rome began just as Tally cried, "Oh!" and three small rockets exploded out of the bag. A furry black grenade skidded across the slick steel surface and launched into the air.

"Cover!" Rome shouted, and dove.

"Careful!" Tally said as Rome's shoulder hit the floor and her head slammed into the table leg.

"Ow," she groaned as she lay on her back, blinking slowly at the very bright light overhead. A pair of shining black eyes stared at her. The puppy she'd caught was still firmly in her grasp, cradled safely against her chest. "You again."

"Oh my goodness," Tally murmured gently, bending down beside her. "Are you hurt?"

The soft concern in her tone caught Rome off guard, almost as much as the sudden surge of pleasure at the unexpected attention.

"Not too…" Rome hesitated as Tally lifted the puppy from her with a tender *Hey, hey there. You're all right now. You're safe.*

With a definite afterthought, Tally glanced down at her. Her brow quirked. Amused, was she? "You're going to have a lump on your forehead."

"Great." Rome sighed and climbed to her feet. "Should make a nice impression my first day on the job." She checked the time. "And I really need to go. I'm already cutting it close."

"I'll get you out of here in ten minutes." Tally pushed the puppy back into her hands. "Hold this one. She's obviously the ringleader. I'll get the rest of them into the kennels."

"Her, huh?"

"Yes," Tally said absently as she carried puppies two at a time to one of the wire kennels arranged in three stacked rows along one wall.

Rome lifted the tight little ball of sleek black fur up to eye level. The puppy barely filled her hand. A white blaze shaped like an elongated diamond, the only patch of color on her otherwise midnight body, decorated the space between her floppy ears. The puppy regarded her warily, an unexpected depth of soulfulness in her solemn gaze. Rome's chest tightened. Small helpless creatures deserved to be protected, not dumped like so much trash by the side of the road. "I can't keep calling you *little bugger* now, can I."

The puppy tilted her head as if considering the statement.

Then she made a sound somewhere between a growl and a grumble.

Rome laughed. "Bravo. That's what we'll call you."

"There's no point naming them," Tally said as she lifted number six out of the bag.

Rome looked them over as Tally deposited them in the kennel. Bravo was the only black one in the bunch—the rest were an assortment of browns, tan, white, and black in all kinds of patterns. Gave new meaning to the term *mixed bag*.

"Why not?" Rome asked.

Tally sighed. "Give me that one. You're sure she's the one who bit you?"

"It's a scratch."

"So you said." Tally put Bravo in a smaller kennel by herself. The puppy immediately began to bark. More a squeak really, but her point was clear. She didn't like being separated from the rest.

"She's not happy," Rome said. "Why don't you put her with the others?"

"She'll have to be quarantined after I get her blood drawn."

"Because of this?" Rome held out her left hand, palm up. Two neat little punctures, each with a pinpoint of blood in the center, adorned the fleshy pad at the base of her thumb. "This is nothing. A little Betadine scrub and a Band-Aid will take care of it."

"She'll need to be quarantined until we can observe her for any abnormal behavior and test her for communicable diseases. CDC recommendations for any unvaccinated animal that bites a human." Tally grasped her wrist and tugged. "Come over here to the sink."

Rome followed, thrown by the strength—and unexpected heat—of Tally's grip. How long had it been since anyone had done that to her? She flushed, glad that Tally's back was to her. "I wouldn't even give a patient antibiotics for this."

"I don't think you need them either. Not right now at least."

Tally opened a disposable Betadine scrub brush. "Scrub it. But we'll see what her blood tests look like."

"How old are they, do you think?" Rome automatically scrubbed both hands and lower forearms, as if preparing to tend to a wound. Tally leaned a hip against the corner of the utility sink, watching her. Rome didn't even have to look at her to feel the scrutiny. She tried to imagine what she would see—beyond the sun lines around her eyes and the corners of her mouth that had appeared in the mirror one day after three years in the desert, or the fading scar on the angle of her jaw from the shrapnel that day on the road to Baghdad. Or would Tally only ever see the nineteen-year-old, full of confidence and plans of glory on the field, who Tally believed had ruined her sister's life?

"Not very old," Tally finally said. "It's difficult to tell because they look fairly malnourished, but I'd say no more than four weeks."

Rome smothered an oath and cast about for something to fill the cold silence. Tally obviously disliked her being there, bringing up a past they both wanted to forget, as much as she did. "That's really young to be separated from the mom, right?"

Tally nodded. "If they were ever with her at all. It's possible that some stray whelped the litter in someone's barn or back pasture and then left them."

"I thought the maternal instinct ran pretty strong in animals." Rome shook the water from her hands and looked around for something to dry them with.

Tally tore open the end of a sterile disposable towel pack and held it up so Rome could extract the towel. "Ordinarily, yes, the instinct to protect the young at any cost overrides every other, but once animals have gone feral and their survival instinct is all that keeps them going, that maternal drive falls away."

"Thanks," Rome muttered, retrieving the towel and blotting her hands dry. Anger roiled in her chest. She'd seen death in all its cruel and senseless shapes in war, and in countless other fickle, inexplicable forms in the ER. Death in the field held some sort of meaning, however fatalistic. On the battlefield soldiers fought for a belief, or a sense of duty, or for each other. And in the ER, death was simply a reality she would never stop battling, but one she knew she would not always defeat. But this was different. Abandoning these helpless creatures to a terrifying and painful death was a step beyond cruel. Heartless, in the truest sense. "Doesn't this kind of thing make you crazy?"

Tally's eyes widened, and for an instant her gaze searched Rome's face. Rome thought she read surprise. But of course Tally would think her incapable of any kind of feeling. The realization ought to have stung, but after seeing that look so often, she was used to it.

"If I let it, it would," Tally murmured, her questing stare still searching for something. "But I'd rather do what I can, about what I can."

Uncomfortable under Tally's probing eyes, Rome held out her palm. The bleeding had stopped and the punctures were barely visible. "See? Nothing to worry about."

Tally surprised her again by taking her hand in both of hers and bending slightly to study the bite. She smelled...good. Apples, maybe? Something sweet and a little tangy. The scent and the heat of her hands combined to send a shiver up Rome's arm.

Tally cleared her throat and stepped back quickly. "I'll get some antibiotic ointment and a Band-Aid."

"Right. Like I said—it's nothing." Rome resisted the urge to close her hand again, to hold on to the sensation of Tally's fingers brushing over her skin.

"Tell me when and where you found them," Tally said, her back to Rome as she opened a cabinet.

Rome said, "About two miles past the turn for the road that intersects this one, across from a big red barn."

Tally turned back to her, grinning. "Roman, there's a red barn every few hundred yards around here."

Rome caught her breath. Tally Dewilde was definitely not

fifteen any longer. When Tally wasn't bone-deep angry, when humor and maybe even pleasure lit her face, she was... Rome couldn't think of a word to describe how singularly extraordinary Tally appeared. Beautiful seemed too ordinary. Too inadequate. Luminescent? Ephemeral. Hell, she was no poet, and that's what she needed.

Tally cocked her head, and her hair fell forward to caress her cheek. Absently, she brushed the strands away with a delicate flick of her hand. "What?"

The heat brewing in Rome's insides ratcheted up a few thousand degrees. "I'll bring up the Google route on my phone and point out where I was."

"Good idea. Did you see the vehicle that dropped them off?"

"Just the back of it—it was foggy. A pickup truck of some kind."

"That helps—since everyone around here owns one." Tally sighed and secured the Band-Aid on Rome's palm. "You know what to look for in terms of problems. Make sure you don't ignore any."

"I'll keep an eye on it."

Tally took a step back. "That's it, then. You can text your number to the office number on the sign out front. If I need any other information, I'll contact you."

Dismissed.

Now that she was free to escape, Rome hesitated. "Ah—I was wondering what all the blood tests were for."

Rome followed Tally over to the kennel, kitted out with a clean paper liner and water bowl, where Bravo scrabbled at the cage door.

"Oh," Tally said as she opened the door and scooped the puppy up, "they'll have to be screened for distemper, parvo, and the usual infectious diseases before animal control can take them. Just the usual red tape with these kinds of abandoned animals."

Rome tensed. "Animal control? You mean like the pound?"

Tally must have heard the criticism in her voice. Her brows drew down into the expression of displeasure Rome seemed to inspire in her. "Yes, as I mentioned, it's the law. We'll have to turn them over within forty-eight hours of them having been found, assuming no owner appears on the scene to claim them."

Rome scoffed. "Well, that's not gonna happen. Whoever dumped them by the side of the road in the middle of nowhere won't even think about them again."

Tally shook her head and set Bravo down on the exam table on a clean puppy pad. "No, they won't. But at least they didn't drown them or leave them out in the woods somewhere where they wouldn't have had any chance of surviving at all."

"Nothing excuses their behavior."

"No, of course it doesn't." Tally kept a hand on the squirming puppy and opened a drawer and pulled out several small blood vials.

"Here—let me hold her while you do what you have to do." Rome slid her hand under Tally's on the puppy's back. A jolt of static electricity skittered over her skin, and she gritted her teeth. What the hell? She'd never been touch sensitive like this before, not even when she'd been intentionally intimate with someone.

"I thought you had someplace to be?" Tally set a lab form of some kind down next to the tubes.

"I do. I like to be early—I've still got time. Why do they have to go to the pound? There must be people around here who want dogs."

"It doesn't work that way," Tally said. "Hold her front leg for me. We can't keep them here. We're not set up to foster them. Besides, we'd have to interview and ultimately be responsible for transferring them to other individuals. That's what the animal care centers are for."

"They'll get adopted, right?"

"Probably," Tally said, but she wasn't looking at Rome. She

slid a tiny needle into the puppy's leg. The puppy stiffened but didn't make a sound.

"Tough one, aren't you," Rome murmured. "What do you mean, *probably* get adopted?"

Tally sighed. "They're malnourished, almost certainly have parasites or other infections, and may not all survive. The animal rescue sites don't have endless room or resources to care for the sick ones."

"So what, they just…" Rome clenched a fist. "Come on, that's not right."

"I don't know what world you come from…" Tally gave a short laugh. "Actually, I know *exactly* what world you came from, and in that world, no, these things don't happen because *these things*"—she gestured to the empty duffel bag on the floor—"don't happen. You're used to people who own boutique animals or fanatically bred and coddled show dogs. Animals like these don't exist in that universe."

"You don't know what world I come from."

"Oh, don't I? Did you forget I lived there too? I know quite a bit about you."

"You only know what you think you know, Tally," Rome said. "You don't know me at all."

"My memory is very clear," Tally said, meeting her eyes. "And forgive me if I got this part wrong, but isn't your grand-mother one of the top judges at Westminster? French bulldogs, isn't it?"

"That's right," Rome said, "but I don't see what that has to do with anything. That's my grandmother, not me. And she loves anything that barks, pedigree or not."

"What kind of dog did you have?"

"None," Rome said. "My father had severe asthma. No animals at all in our house."

Roman *almost* sounded sad about that, and for an instant, Tally *almost* felt a wave of sympathy. She hadn't had animals either, because her mother felt they were too messy. *Unclean* was the word she'd used. Tally'd always wanted one, but that didn't mean she had anything in common with Roman Ashcroft. Roman might believe the past could be erased, forgotten—or somehow forgiven. She didn't.

"The point still stands," Tally said while labeling the sample tube. "This is not the Upper East Side. Whoever abandoned these puppies was wrong, but they didn't kill them, and they could have. People around here sometimes have to give up animals they've had for years because they can't afford to feed them anymore. If the weather doesn't cooperate and crops fail, or if the markets change and no one wants corn or soybeans anymore, suddenly incomes can drop by fifty percent. Animals have to be fed and housed and given at least rudimentary care. It costs a lot of money. People can't afford to keep strays."

"I don't want them to go to the pound—or whatever name they're calling it now. However nice you make it sound."

"There are laws in this state—most states—about holding strays and how they're eventually…placed. You're not going to have a choice in that. They're going."

Rome picked up the black puppy who stood on the edge of the table watching them intently and glanced at the other five in the group kennel. Some were watching her, at least it seemed that way. Others had fallen into exhausted sleep in a jumble of small bodies, floppy ears, and limbs. "Not this one. Or any of the others. Not until they're healthy and have a chance to be adopted."

"I thought I just explained—"

"Look," Rome said impatiently. "I don't have time to negotiate. I'll pay for their care. You board here, right? It says so out front on the sign. Just bill me until they get homes."

"That's at least weeks away. And what if they don't?"

Rome shrugged. "We'll cross that bridge when we come to it."

"I can't make that decision without talking to the clinic owner."

"Fine. If there's a problem, I'll talk to them."

Exasperated, Tally snapped, "Has anyone ever said no to you, Roman?"

Rome met her gaze. "More times than you would believe."

"You're right," Tally said quietly as she placed Bravo back in the kennel and extracted another puppy. "I need to finish up here. You can let yourself out."

"You'll keep them, right?" Rome said.

"Forty-eight hours, until we're sure they're healthy," Tally repeated, already busy examining the next puppy, a scrawny brown and white male with one bent ear that flopped down over a suspicious brown eye. "After that they go to the shelter for the rest of their holding period."

"Hood," Rome muttered. "That one's Hood."

"Naming them won't change anything. This is puppy A, since B is already taken." Tally bent over the forms, rapidly checking boxes with a black felt-tip pen.

"I'll be back as soon as I can to make the financial arrangements," Rome said.

"Best to call first," Tally said. "We don't exactly have visiting hours."

"Right." Rome knew when she'd been dismissed and left without wasting more breath trying to get past Tally Dewilde's icy exterior. Those puppies were not going to be abandoned again—someone had to stand for them. Might as well be her.

CHAPTER THREE

Once outside, Rome programmed in her destination, checked the shortest route to the hospital—no surprise, there was only one route, so no choice there—and pulled out of the gravel lot. The road was clear of traffic and the fog had mostly disappeared, so she set the Porsche's cruise control at sixty and let it prowl around the curves and climb the gentle rises between rolling fields stubbled with the remains of corn stalks and furrowed with freshly turned earth awaiting spring planting. Thickets of forest dotted the hillside, cloistering the farmsteads and clusters of barns from wind and storms. The drive might have been relaxing if not for the fretful cries of the abandoned pups still gnawing at her and the cutting edge of Tally Dewilde's anger still burning. As she sped along, a kaleidoscope of images played through her mind, past and present intertwined in an uncomfortable embrace. Tally Dewilde as a teenager whose emerging beauty was already destined to turn heads, staring wide-eyed at her as she bent over Sheila's inert form, screaming *What have you done to my sister?* Sheila, coy and demanding, angry and accusing, so still in her silence. The flashing lights, the sirens, the endless questions. Choices thrust upon her by family and friends, and finally, the escape on her own terms. A choice she didn't regret, as the consequences had led her here.

Rome shook her head and concentrated on the road. She hadn't revisited those times—events from a different life—since she'd walked away from the world she'd known and joined the military. Two tours of duty had provided her with so many other images of far greater devastation to crowd out her small personal tragedy. The visions of war, monumental in their unfathomable horror, relegated her nightmares to a near-forgotten other life. Until today, when Tally Dewilde appeared out of her past to bring everything back into razor-sharp clarity. With a long breath, Rome worked the tension out of her shoulders and resolved to leave thoughts of Sheila Dewilde and the mistakes she'd made where they belonged—ten years in the past.

She'd started over before, more than once, and each time she'd come closer to finding a place to belong again. She had redefined herself at nineteen when she'd enlisted and was about to do that again. Soon she'd start her new job and a new life as a civilian. Still a medic, which she'd never imagined she might one day consider the most important aspect of her life. This place, this chance, might just be at the end of her search.

As to Tally Dewilde, they were strangers, after all, linked only by events that could not be changed. She already knew what Tally thought of her, and nothing was going to change that either. Everything that could have been said, that might have changed Tally's mind about her, had already been said.

At just after six thirty, farmland morphed seamlessly into the outskirts of a village, and with a wave of relief, Rome sighted the sign announcing *Pop. 3272*. The main street, lined by two- and three-story wood clapboard or brick homes set back from wide sidewalks by grassy front lawns, led her into the center of the morning activity.

A school bus pulled out of a cross street and made its unhurried journey from stop to stop where parents waited at the ends of driveways with their children to board. Rome didn't mind the crawl, taking advantage of the time to survey her new home. A row of pickup trucks and vans lined up in front of a storefront restaurant with an oversized stencil in the big front window of a platter of eggs and bacon next to a steaming mug of coffee. A little farther along, a steady stream of vehicles entered and exited the crowded lot in front of a corner convenience store that also offered four double islands of gas pumps. Clearly coffee and gas constituted the predominant orders of the morning.

A block past a pizza parlor, she found the street, Myrtle Avenue, that Brody had told her would take her to the hospital. Making a sharp right, she passed through two massive stone block arches flanked by stone walls leading off into thick stands of trees on either side of a single cobblestone lane and started to climb the winding private road. The stately approach, easily a quarter mile or more, shaded by dense forests of old maples and pines, ended in a grassy plateau bearing a building that might have been a private mansion a century or so before. From what she'd read, the place was built as a hospital by two wealthy villagers, one of whom was the patriarch of the family for which the place was named—the Rivers. This hospital was nothing like the sprawling urban medical complex at Fort Bragg or the windswept, sand-filled field hospitals of Iraq and Afghanistan. Two-story-high scrolled white columns framed the entrance to an ivy-covered central brick edifice from which sweeping wings curved around the knoll. Glimpses of recently constructed extensions sprawled beyond terraced beds of floral shrubs interlaced with flagstone walkways. Off to her right, as she followed the discreet signs indicating the staff lot where Brody had told her to park, the village she'd just driven through nestled in the depths of the valley below like a scene from a postcard. No, nothing in this oasis of tranquility and timeless elegance resembled anything in her prior life. But that was exactly what she'd wanted after all, even if she *had* had to work hard to convince Brody of it.

She'd seen Brody's Facebook post on one of those veterans' sites that kept popping up in her feed when she'd returned stateside, at loose ends with no idea where she was headed, other than *not* back to Manhattan. She and Brody'd caught up over the course of a few weeks, and when Brody had mentioned they were looking for more PAs in their ER, Rome had known, somehow, that's where she was destined to go.

"I'm interested, and my military certs should make the paperwork easy," she'd said.

"The place might be a little quiet for you, Rome," Brody replied with a hint of caution. "Not much nightlife, if you know what I mean, and the big highlights are usually sports or parades."

"Parades?"

Brody laughed. "Easter parades, Memorial Day parades, Fourth of July, Labor Day, Halloween—oh, and the Thanksgiving tractor parade, of course."

"You're making that last one up."

"Nope."

"Sports sounds entertaining enough."

"Ah…I should have clarified. *High school* sports—the folks around here follow them like they were the pros. And there's the hospital baseball league, of course."

"When can I start?"

"You sure?" Brody asked, uncharacteristically serious.

"I am," Rome said, knowing Brody was probably thinking about her reputation for being a bit of a wild card in the military. Always the first to volunteer to go beyond the wire on the tough missions, the last to leave the party after making it back one more time—and not always leaving alone. Mostly never, if she could manage it. "I won't let you down."

"Never doubted that. I'll put you in touch with the right people about the application and whatnot."

Six weeks later, Rome arrived.

She parked in a slot marked *staff* in a small, mostly empty lot behind one of the two-story wings with rows of tall windows that she imagined might be offices. That staff designation in front of where she'd parked her coupe felt pretty damn good. She hadn't expected to miss the rank or the hierarchy of the military, but the abrupt loss of the identity she'd lived with for so long proved uncomfortably disorienting. Now she was building a new identity, one she wanted to last. A big Suzuki bike occupied the space next to her, and a few other vehicles, mostly trucks and SUVs, took up other spots. As she climbed out of the 911, a familiar voice called, "Nice ride, Ashcroft. Didn't think you'd be giving up the Humvees so soon."

With a swell of pleasure, Rome spun around. "Brody. Sorry, I'm late. I got hung up on the way over."

Brody Clark hadn't changed much in the three years since Rome had last seen her. The wedding band was new, but Brody'd already told her she'd settled down, and her tone had made it sound as if she couldn't believe her luck. That was a side of Brody she'd never seen, but then none of them had been big on serious personal connections—not when every day could be the last. Maybe for some, like Brody—and unlike her—flying solo had just been situational. Still lanky and lean, Brody didn't look quite as wired as she used to either. But then, she wasn't flying rescue missions through STA rocket flak anymore.

"You're not late," Brody said, holding out a hand. She held a coffee cup in the opposite hand with a red scroll on the side spelling out *Stewart's*. That had to be the filling station-convenience store getting all the traffic at the corner.

"Decent coffee?" Rome asked.

"Two schools of thought on that," Brody said, gesturing toward a walkway that circled a flower bed adorned with fall mums, tight reds and oranges and yellows in dense clusters, to a side entrance. "Some swear by the espresso at the Breadbasket Café, and then others, like me, go for the sugar and cream high of Stewart's."

Rome winced. "Might try the café first."

"Before I forget, here's the key to the trailer." Brody fished a key on a blue plastic tab out of her pocket and passed it to Rome. "You have the directions, right?"

"Turn right at the post office, drive a half mile, and the trailer park is on the right."

"That's mobile home park."

"Ah, right."

"Didn't you tell me once you grew up in Manhattan? Bet you're the first to trade a brownstone for an Airstream." Brody grinned.

"I appreciate you letting me bunk in your place." If Brody noticed Rome didn't comment about where she'd grown up, she didn't let on.

"You're doing me a favor," Brody said. "Since Val and I bought the house, the trailer's been vacant. This way I won't have to worry about it. So thanks."

"I'm looking forward to moving in."

"Better wait till you see it." Laughing, Brody held the door, letting Rome enter a small foyer where a middle-aged white man in a khaki security guard uniform leaned behind a semicircular counter. He straightened as Brody came in behind Rome and nodded. "Hey, Brody."

"Paul. This is Rome Ashcroft—one of our new PAs."

"Good to meet you," Rome said.

"Morning," the guard said. "You'll want to hit Employee Resources soon as you get a chance—get your ID and all that."

"Will do. Thanks." As Rome kept stride with Brody, the sounds of jumbled voices, clattering equipment, and the ding of elevator doors opening grew steadily louder.

"If you need any help getting moved in out at the trailer, give a shout," Brody said.

"Thanks, but I don't have anything to unpack except my gear."

"Still traveling light," Brody said.

Rome hunched a shoulder. Why try to explain she hadn't had any other home since joining the military? She had nothing of her former life to reclaim. "Simpler. How's Honcho?"

"Happy. Maybe a mite lazy without steady work. She's taken to riding with Val—my wife—on her callouts. Seems to think she's on recon." Brody laughed. "Val says Honcho always checks the terrain before letting Val out of the vehicle."

"Hey, once a war dog, always a war dog."

Brody met her gaze. "Hard habits to break."

"Yeah," Rome said quietly. They were talking about a lot more than the constant vigilance and never-ending expectation of trauma, but neither had to say so. The image of Honcho geared out in flak vest and protective footwear searching out IEDs made her think of the duffel she'd found. Not meaning to, but unable to get the whole episode out of her mind, she went on, "The damnedest thing went down this morning. I was on my way here, and I came upon a bag full of puppies somebody had dumped by the side of the road."

Brody jerked to a stop and stared. Her expression went flat, the way a seasoned combat vet's face always did when faced with a bad scene. "A bag full of puppies? *Dead* puppies?"

"No, no. Not dead. Live. Wiggly little buggers too. Kept trying to get out while I was driving."

Brody glanced back in the direction of the lot outside. "Where are they?"

"What?" Rome chuckled. "Not in my 911, for sure. I took the bunch of them, bag and all, to the first vet clinic I could find."

"Whereabouts was this, did you say?"

"Ten, twelve miles from here, maybe? I could show you on the nav."

"Had to be Upland County Animal Hospital."

"Yeah, that's the one."

Brody frowned. "I didn't hear about it."

"Why would you?" Rome asked.

"Because that's Val's place, and she's halfway across the county doing antibiotic testing on a herd of organic dairy cows. So what did you do with the puppies?"

"I left them with the vet. Ah...Dr. Dewilde."

"Oh, right." Brody laughed and shook her head. "I'm not

quite used to the fact that there's another vet. Val has been solo for so long, and Tally just started. She must be pretty eager if she was there this early in the day."

"So she's a recent hire?" Rome asked carefully as they headed toward a set of double doors marked with a big red sign declaring *Emergency Room-Authorized Personnel Only*. She stopped short of mentioning Tally and she had met before. Getting into that history wasn't something she wanted to do—and revealing Tally's part in all of it seemed...wrong somehow. Not her story to tell. And Tally'd been just a kid, after all. No, Rome hadn't traveled halfway around the world to a war zone to escape the fallout, just to drag the whole thing out in the open at the first opportunity. Especially not here, where she planned a new start.

"Yeah, Tally just arrived," Brody said, swiping the entrance lock with her ID. "Val's practice exploded in the last few months—her previous boss retired, another couple vets nearing retirement quit early with the pandemic, and young vets starting out are looking for practices that don't involve emergency work."

"I'm guessing that's not the case around here? The emergencies."

"Mostly farm calls at night—but there's always the domestic pet that eats something they shouldn't or gets injured somehow. Val was really happy to find an associate as well-trained and eager as Tally to move here."

Rome wondered what had prompted a young heiress from the Upper East Side to move to a rural community too, but resolved to put her curiosity about Tally Dewilde firmly aside. "She got the puppies all squared away with no problems."

"Good to know." Brody led her through the ER, slowing at the central hub where staff worked at computers in a semicircle of stations that faced a digital wallboard with the names and room numbers of patients. "A little less chaotic than you're used to in here, and more paperwork. All the records are digital now—the patient will have a record in your tablet where you can access labs, make notes, enter findings, record treatment and follow-up. All pretty obvious. Patients are assigned by the doc or PA who's in charge of your shift. In an emergency, it's whoever gets there first."

"Trauma alerts?" Rome asked.

"You'll get a beeper when you're on the trauma team. Three bays just down that hallway to the right. Full complement of ER residents, plus whatever general surgery residents, PA trainees, and PAs are on rotation."

"Sounds busy."

Brody's grin returned. "In the last six months, we flew more air evacs in the surrounding three counties than all of Albany's five trauma centers."

"Just what I wanted to hear," Rome said, and she meant it. She wanted to be busy. She wanted to end the day feeling she'd made a difference, even if no one but her knew it.

"That's the nickel tour," Brody said. "If you're ready to get to work, let's find Glenn Archer, the head of the PA training program. She'll want to add you to the teaching rotation—we've got four PA students in each year. Then we'll track down Abby Remy, the ER chief, for your schedule."

"I'm ready," Rome said. More than ready.

Work was exactly what she needed to put the whole disturbing encounter with Tally Dewilde out of her mind.

❖

Tally slipped the last pup back into the kennel and gathered up the notes she'd made for animal control. When the clinic staff arrived, she'd have to ask which local animal control centers served their area, get the contact info for the animal shelter for the region, and ask where the forms were to report the strays. Probably the first of many assists she'd need until she actually had the chance to put all the theory she'd learned into practice. Asking for help didn't come naturally. She'd always tried to be the easy child, the one who never bothered anyone for attention or created problems. Her parents, especially her mother, always seemed so stressed taking care of Sheila during her many crises growing up. Or making Sheila's problems go away.

But Tally wasn't a child now, and she couldn't let her pride get in the way of her professionalism. If she needed help, she'd have to ask.

Tally took a deep breath. Right. That was then, this was now.

The chorus of barks from the kennel area brought the abrupt reminder that *now* had somehow deposited Roman Ashcroft at her door.

Roman Ashcroft. Who would've believed she could turn up here, two hundred miles from the Upper East Side and a universe away from the high society world where the Ashcroft family still managed to reign? Then again, she was here too, but she'd been trying to escape the same stifling social stratum for a decade. Roman didn't have anything to escape from. She'd managed to use her family's influence or money to avoid any consequences for her actions. Tally's anger at the injustice came roiling back, along with the memory of feeling powerless. She wasn't helpless any longer, not ruled by her mother's inflexible view of how she should live her life, nor trying to force herself into a stifling world where she was never really seen.

She was on her own. By her own choice.

"Damn right," Tally muttered. She would *not* be thrown by Roman's appearance out of nowhere or consumed by the rage she'd experienced when Roman had walked away from that night unscathed. She would focus on the now. On what mattered, and that definitely was *not* Roman.

"Hello, little one," Tally said, lifting a tiger kitten due to go home that day out of her holding pen. "Let's see how your incision is looking."

As Tally sat on a stool with the kitten in her lap, the tiny ball of fur emitted a soothing rumble, loud for such a little body, and worked its tiny claws into the fabric of her jeans. Good thing she wasn't addicted to designer clothes. That was another thing that had gone by the wayside. Jeans, plain cotton pants, pullover tops, and anything else that was easy to move around in and wouldn't be any great loss if it got smeared with various animal effluvia constituted most of her wardrobe. As always, the presence of the small innocent animal centered her. When she heard the back door to the clinic open and close, she got up to put the protesting kitten back in her pen.

"Don't fret, now. Your family will be here to pick you up in just a few hours." She closed the door and secured the latch. "You might need some more crunchies, though. I can see your appetite is back."

Tally spun around as someone announced, "I'll do that. I'll take care of everyone's food and water after I clean the runs."

Blake...Remy, that was his last name, smiled at her from the open door of the treatment room. They'd met long enough for quick introductions as she was leaving Friday afternoon. Val had mentioned he was one of several volunteers who helped out around the clinic.

"Morning," she said. Sixteen or seventeen, Blake was a typical good-looking teenage boy with dark hair and crisp blue eyes in a face that hadn't quite yet begun to get the heaviness of maleness that would be coming in a year or so. He wore dark jeans, Superstar sneakers, and a plain red T-shirt under a navy varsity letter jacket. "That's great. Is there anything I need to do?"

"Nope. Got it covered." His voice cracked just a little bit in the way that was common for guys his age. He pointed to the large holding area where the puppies slept in a jumble.

"Who are they?"

"Orphans," Tally said. "Rome...ah, someone found them by the side of the road this morning in that duffel bag over there."

"Someone dumped them?" He stared from the canvas bag to her, his gaze stricken. "Who would do that?"

She shook her head. "I don't know. But luckily, they got rescued."

"What do we do with them?"

Tally repeated what she'd told Roman about the holding period and the testing.

"Why is that one by herself?" Blake crouched in front of the little black female's pen. "She's awfully skinny."

The puppy put both front paws against the wire, eyed him seriously for a moment, and yelped. Indignantly.

Tally chuckled. "She appears to be the pack leader. She also bit the person who rescued them—not even seriously, and likely not even intentionally, more out of panic or stress. But I'm keeping her separate just to be safe."

"She doesn't look sick," Blake murmured. "But she does seem to think she's in charge."

Tally smiled thinly. Of course that would be the one Roman picked. "Apparently so. Goes by the name of Bravo."

Blake glanced at her, a curious expression on his face. "You named them?"

"Not exactly," she said. "The person who found them christened that one."

As they talked, Blake made his way through changing the water and food in each of the holding crates. He pointed to the cocker who'd been spayed the day before but hadn't emerged quickly enough from anesthesia to go home safely. "This guy ought to go home today, right?"

"Yes, when the front desk staff arrives I'll ask them to call and let the owners know."

"I can do that when I finish up here."

"It's still pretty early," Tally said. She didn't want to undermine his initiative, but most people wouldn't want to hear from their vet's before seven a.m.

Blake laughed. "Not for anybody around here, and I know the Romeros. They'll just be coming back from the morning milking."

Morning milking. Right. Clearly, she was going to need to learn the rhythms of the new world she lived in. "Okay, sure."

"Anything else that needs doing back here just now?"

"No, I think you've taken care of everything."

"Okay, I'll be back after basketball practice this afternoon for cleanup."

Tally cast about for something to say. She had no experience talking to teenage boys. She hadn't had any brothers, and she hadn't been interested in dating any of the guys in her social set—or anywhere else. Blake obviously spent a lot of time in the clinic, and she wanted to connect. Basketball. That explained the letter jacket. "So, ah, how is the team doing?"

A shadow passed over his face for an instant. Crap. Not the right question. Maybe she should have asked what position he played. As if she'd have a clue what the answer would mean.

"It's the best team in the division," he said seriously. "This is my first year, but the team usually makes it into the finals for the state championships."

"That's awesome," she said.

He nodded. "The first game of the season is coming up in a couple of weeks. Are you coming?"

"I don't know," she said, wondering if there was a right answer. She didn't know anything about basketball and didn't know any of the people, and couldn't imagine it was much of a thing. "I don't actually know much about the game."

"It's easy to pick up the basics. Besides, pretty much everybody goes, and anyone can explain what's going on."

"You mean parents?"

"Not just the families of the players. It's a town pride thing—our team's competing against those from other towns. Lots of people get into it. Val will be there for sure."

"Oh. That's…cool."

"I'm guessing you didn't grow up in a place like this."

"Not even close. New York City." And Sheila, not her, had been the one who liked dating the ones into sailing and golf or any sport that qualified in her mind as elite—like lacrosse. And there it was again—another reminder of Roman Ashcroft and why Sheila had found her attractive. All these memories coming back. Why now? Not just because Roman had unexpectedly appeared. Tally sighed. Just so many changes, that was all. She just needed a little time to settle.

"Manhattan for me too," Blake said. "Where I moved from, I mean."

Grateful to be pulled back to the present, Tally said, "Really. I didn't realize that. So it's a big change, huh?"

"Yeah, totally. It hasn't even been a year, but that seems like…forever ago."

"But you like it here."

He nodded sharply. "A lot."

Tally cocked her head, hearing something unsaid. "I guess it took getting used to, though."

Blake shrugged, his expression cautious. "I wasn't so sure when my mom decided to move us here, but she was right. About just about everything."

Tally nodded. Not really following, but sensing the conversation was going somewhere beyond casual. Blake seemed to be studying her, or maybe just considering what he wanted to say next. She recognized that fine edge between moving into unknown territory with someone or backing off to a safe, if less meaningful, distance.

His silence filled several long seconds as she waited.

"I'm trans," he said. "So she thought a new place and a new school would be easier for me."

"Oh." Tally'd known some trans individuals in her classes—not as friends, but just the kind of casual nodding acquaintance that developed in that setting. What Blake just told her was already more personal than any conversation she'd ever had with any of her classmates. "Was it? Easier than Manhattan, I mean?"

His shoulders relaxed. "Yes. Most of the time. At least here no one knew me before I transitioned."

"Was it like starting a new life?" Tally asked, then quickly added, "I'm sorry. Is that an offensive question? I guess maybe you get a lot of clueless questions. I realize that I can't really imagine how you felt. So...sorry."

"No, I disclosed, after all. And not exactly a new life—my real life, I guess. Life as I knew I should be living it."

Tally nodded. "That sounds like a good thing, a really big thing."

"The biggest. Even if sometimes it's hard, totally worth it."

"I know how it can be when people find out you're queer," Tally said. "People can be jerks. I lost a few friends when I came out."

Blake nodded. "Me too." He took a deep breath. "Well anyhow, if we hadn't moved here, I wouldn't have met Margie—you'll meet her today or tomorrow—and I wouldn't be on the basketball team, or realized I wanted to be a vet, and my mom wouldn't have married Flann and we wouldn't be a family. So it's all good."

"Actually," Tally laughed, "it sounds great."

He grinned. "You have to be who you are, right? To have a chance at the good stuff?"

"I hope so," Tally murmured.

Blake grinned. "I gotta get to school. I'll probably see you later."

"Have a good one," she called as he ambled out the door.

As Blake's footsteps faded away, the clinic grew quiet again except for the snuffling of the animals in their kennels. Maybe she'd get as lucky as Blake in this new place, the place she'd chosen where she could be herself. That's all she'd ever really wanted. A little bit of loneliness now and then was a small price to pay for that.

❖

Rome worked steadily from seven a.m. after a quick meeting with the ER chief, Abby Remy.

"Roman, good to have you aboard," Abby had said. "Walk with me—I have to see a patient with one of the residents."

Rome fell into step as Abby, a little above average height, blond, green-eyed, and with the quick step and firm voice of a woman in command, continued, "I was going to give you a day to get oriented, but one of my docs and another PA have both called out after testing positive for the damn virus again. I could use you today."

"I'm ready to go," Rome said. "I've nowhere to be except here."

Abby shot her a look. "Moved in already?"

"Brody is renting me her trailer." Rome suspected there was more to the question and added, "And there's just me. So I'm good with any kind of schedule."

"I can't say I'm sorry to hear that. Check in with Mark Gonzalez anyway. He's the ER doc who's got first shift today. He'll tell you where he needs you, unless Glenn Archer wants you in the PA rotation elsewhere."

"I already talked to Glenn," Rome said, "and she doesn't have me scheduled for anything today."

"Even better. Ordinarily, we try to coordinate our people beforehand, but today's a little chaotic."

Rome laughed. "Is there ever a day when it isn't?"

Abby shook her head. "Actually, no, but that's why we're all here, right? It wouldn't be so much fun otherwise."

"That's a roger," Rome said.

Abby pointed her in the direction she needed to go to find Gonzalez and left her with a brisk, "Staff meeting tomorrow at six thirty. See you then."

And Rome had felt her life settle into order.

Ten hours in a busy ER passed a lot faster than a day huddled under a camouflage awning in the stultifying desert air waiting for the next callout. Sometimes even an evac in a hot zone beat the hell out of another day of relentless boredom. Now at five p.m., even though technically she was supposed to have been off shift at three when the day shift ended, she was just finishing notes on the last patient she had to discharge. She'd already signed over two others to the next shift—a skateboarder whose definitely broken arm X-rays hadn't come back yet, and a brittle forty-year-old diabetic with a malfunctioning insulin pump who needed IV hydration and insulin.

"Sorry, Rome," said Pam Wendel, the evening charge nurse, "but Ms. Hermanos in three? She has another question. I tried to take care of it, but I think she really wants to talk to you."

"I'll be right there," Rome said, still typing on her tablet. "I just want to finish this one note. Do you know what the problem is?"

"I think it's something of a…personal nature."

Rome looked up and caught Pam grinning. Pam, Rome realized now that she wasn't running back and forth between patients and had a moment to connect, was a great-looking woman with warm bronze skin and brown eyes that regarded her with a hint of laughter and quite possibly something else. She hadn't been on the receiving end of an appreciative glance like that in so long she wasn't quite sure.

"Ah. Okay. Thank you," Rome said.

"Mm-hmm," Pam said as she turned around to view the patient wallboard. "Looks like another busy one ahead."

"Better than not," Rome said.

Pam turned back. "You're Brody's friend from the service, right?"

"Yep."

"Good. I like military medics. Quick and efficient. Just don't call me ma'am."

Rome laughed. "That is not the first thing that comes to my mind."

"I'm glad to hear that." Pam's smile took on a definitely sexy curl. At least Rome thought it might have—for a second.

"Right." Rome stood and slid the tablet into the rack. "Ms. Hermanos."

"You have a good night, now," Pam said. "I'll see you tomorrow."

"'Night," Rome said, still wondering if she'd imagined Pam had been flirting just a little. Not sure what that said about her that she couldn't even tell any longer. With a sense of relief at being on sturdier footing, she tucked the curtain at cubicle three aside a few inches and looked in at the middle-aged woman inside.

Consuelo Hermanos, married mother of five, was just pulling on a green sweater with orange pumpkins scattered over it that complemented her slim dark brown tights.

"Ms. Hermanos?" Rome said. "You had another question?"

"Yes," she said softly.

"What can I help you with?" Rome asked. She'd already explained to her that the ultrasound had revealed several large stones in her gallbladder that were the cause of her episodic pain and had accompanied the surgical resident who'd answered that consult and recommended surgery. That was a lot of information to take in, so not surprising the patient still had questions.

Ms. Hermanos motioned her in, and Rome entered, letting the curtain fall closed behind her, giving them the semblance of privacy.

"This thing the young surgical doctor says about my gallbladder. That I should have it removed. Do you think this is right?"

"Yes, I agree. The scans were very clear, and all the trouble you've been having after meals, with the pain and the nausea— that all fits." She leaned back against the counter, signaling she was happy to stay until Ms. Hermanos's questions were answered. "If you wait, it's possible you could get an infection, which could make you very sick. The surgery if you're not sick is very simple."

"And this Dr. Rivers—the surgeon the young doctor recommended. This is a good doctor too?"

Easy question. Flann Rivers was the chief of surgery. "Yes, a very good surgeon."

"So, does that mean no more babies?"

Rome took a breath. Not the question she'd been expecting. "No, the surgery shouldn't have anything to do with that. Is that a problem? Having babies or not having babies?"

"We have five." She smiled. "Two girls and three boys. We like children, and my husband would like another girl. Me, I don't care which, but six would be a good number."

Six. Great number—although she hadn't given children much thought, as a relationship of that kind really didn't figure into her future, but if it did, *two* was a nice number also. "Gallbladder surgery shouldn't have anything to do with number six. But maybe not for a little while after surgery."

"So, how long before we can start on making baby six?"

Rome worked at not smiling. "If you have your gallbladder out, your surgeon will talk to you about when you can resume intimate relations, but I don't think it would be very long. A week or two, depending on how you're feeling."

Her eyes widened. "That seems like a long time."

Rome wisely decided not to comment about that, although the thought did flash through her mind that four to six months hadn't even seemed like a very long time to her, and she'd passed that a while ago. "I think the time will pass pretty quickly."

Ms. Hermanos didn't look like she really believed her, but she nodded. "Yes, all right. If it is really necessary."

"It's not an emergency, but I do think it's something that you need to look into."

"Thank you very much."

Rome nodded. "If you have any problems or any more symptoms of pain like we talked about, you should come back to the emergency room."

"I will do that. Thank you."

Rome made a final note on her chart, with a referral to Flann Rivers, including the results of the ultrasound, and signed out. On her way out she stopped in the locker room off the staff lounge to retrieve the extra scrubs she'd been allotted that morning along with her duffel. Brody was just leaving as she came in.

"How'd it go?" Brody asked.

Rome hadn't seen her all day as Brody spent her downtime in the flight lounge with the pilots and other flight medics when she was between medevac flights.

"Good. Busy. Nothing out of the ordinary."

"Excellent. Listen, call me when you get out to the trailer tonight if there's any problem with getting the gas or power turned on."

"I will. Thanks again." Rome hesitated. "It's got a fenced yard, you said?"

"Yeah. I picked a lot where there was tree for shade that I could include inside the fence. Why?"

"No reason," Rome said, thinking about Bravo and the other puppies, and just as quickly dismissing the thought. The smart thing to do was pay for their care until they got placed. Over and then done.

CHAPTER FOUR

"We're closing up, Dr. Dewilde," Rita, the front desk receptionist, said as Tally handed her the last patient chart. "Another busy one, huh?"

"I'll say. And it's Tally, remember?"

"Right." The petite single mother of three, as Tally had learned over a quick lunch with the three clinic staff, grabbed a backpack and went to shut off the lights. As she reached the door, a man stepped inside with a bundle in his arms.

His broad ruddy face streamed with sweat, and he stared, breathing hard, from Tally to Rita as if not sure why he'd come.

"We were just about to close," Rita said. "Are you a client?"

"No—I mean, I am. Yes. Dr. Valentine is my...our...his... doctor." He held out the bundle as if that explained everything. "He's gone lame, and he won't eat."

Rita glanced at Tally with a look that said *What do we do now?*

"Rita, why don't you go on home," Tally said. "Blake is in the back cleaning up. If I need anything, he can help me."

"If you're sure," Rita said, clearly conflicted.

"We'll be fine." Tally smiled at the burly, distraught client, whose tan canvas pants, barn jacket, and calf-high muck boots said *farmer*. "I'm Dr. Dewilde. Who have you got there, Mr....?"

"Marco Polo. Him—not me. I'm Arnold Kojak." He drew back the edge of the striped beach towel, and a ginger head popped out wearing a decidedly annoyed glare. The accompanying yowl confirmed his supreme displeasure. "He's been fighting again, and his leg's all banged up."

"Why don't you bring Mr. Polo back and we'll get a look at him." As Tally led the way, she said, "He's a brawler, is he?"

"He likes to think so," Mr. Kojak said, "but he doesn't seem to win many of them."

Ordinarily Tally asked clients to step out when performing a procedure on their pets, but Arnold Kojak seemed far too anxious to leave his cat just then. Plus, Tally preferred not to wrangle with a grouchy feline if the owner could help calm him down.

"Let's put him up here." Tally spread out a towel on the exam table and washed her hands.

"Should I do something? He's just a little scared, you know. Usually nothing bothers him, but he doesn't like new places."

"You can hold him while I get a look at that leg. Yes, that's right. Put your hand just there, behind his head, and the other on his butt." After gently teasing the fur away from the long gash on the cat's foreleg to get a better look, Tally straightened. "That's a pretty deep bite and a fair amount of swelling. I'm going to shave the hair around the bite. It won't hurt him."

Blake, who'd come in to observe, asked, "Do you want to irrigate it with anything, Doc?"

"Let's see how deep the punctures are," Tally said as she shaved the tabby cat's foreleg. "It looks like he lost this fight."

Arnold sighed. "His sister. Half the time they're curled up together, and the other half they're biting each other."

"Mm," Tally said. "That's cats. He's got some redness here, a little bit of infection. We'll put him on some antibiotics. Do you think you can get pills down him?"

"He don't like it much, but I'll manage."

"Good. Blake, let's flush this with saline."

When they'd finished, Tally wrapped the leg lightly with some gauze and vet wrap. "I'll give you enough antibiotics for him tonight, and you can pick up the rest of the prescription at the

front desk tomorrow. If it starts to drain or gets more swollen—
you probably know what to look for."

"Not his first bite," he said, already noticeably calmer. He
bundled Marco Polo back up in the towel and extended a hand
that dwarfed Tally's as she took it. "Appreciate this, Doc."

"Glad to help." Tally's phone rang and she checked caller
ID. She recognized the number for animal control in Albany that
she'd called earlier. She'd been waiting all day for a callback
from the officer who covered her area. The answering service had
told her the officer was out on a call and would be in contact as
soon as possible.

"Sorry, I have to take this. You should be all set, Mr. Kojak."

"No problem. Thanks again."

Tally walked back to her new office, which presently
consisted of a desk, a wheeled desk chair, and a rather sad-
looking succulent in a terra-cotta pot. As she dropped into the
brown leather chair with her phone to her ear, she said, "This is
Dr. Dewilde."

"This is Angelo Catelli," a gruff but friendly voice replied.
"Heard you wanted to talk to me."

"I surely do," she said. "This is Tally Dewilde. I'm a vet out
at Upland County Animal Hospital."

"Your place is out on Route 342, isn't it? Syd Valentine's?"

"Yes, I'm a new associate."

"Good to hear. What can I do for you?"

"I've got a litter of what look to be three-and-a-half to four-
week-old puppies that somebody dumped by the side of the road.
A driver passing by brought them in. I wanted to let you know so
we could make arrangements to transfer them."

His sigh was audible. "Wish I could help you. But we don't
cover that area any longer. We're not going to be able to take
those puppies."

"Oh, I'm sorry. I guess I have the wrong information."
Tally frowned. Rita must not have given her the most current
referral number, but considering the plethora and repetitiveness

of bulletins from state agencies, Tally wasn't all that surprised. She didn't always read the details herself. "Do you happen to know what division is covering us?"

He laughed, but even over the phone she could tell there was no humor in it. "I guess I'm just gonna have to be the bearer of bad news, so don't shoot me. *We* are the only center serving the county, but not the *whole* county—that is to say, not every township—any longer. Too many strays and abandoned animals for us to handle. We're at ninety-five percent capacity, and to avoid needing to euthanize some of our animals just to make space, we had to cut out service to about half the townships in your area alone."

"Cut out service."

"I'm afraid so."

"What shelters are available?"

He sighed. "As of right now, none."

"Let me understand this," Tally said, really not sure she was interpreting all this clearly. Because none of it made any sense. "This area, actually half the county, you're saying, doesn't have any avenue for placing abandoned or abused or stray animals?"

"That's not exactly the case," he said. "Only dogs are mandated by the state to be sheltered. You just have to make local arrangements."

"I see. We're on our own, you mean."

"For the foreseeable future, yes."

"Okay then, well, thank you for the information."

He hurried to add, "Now, if you have any enforcement issues, we can take care of that. We've been cracking down on puppy mills as fast as we can, but they're cropping up all over the place. So for an enforcement issue, you're still covered, and of course, you can contact us or DEC for any wild animal problems that may turn up. But domestic animals…we can't house them."

"I understand. Thank you." She hung up and stared at the phone. How was that even possible? No facilities for housing abandoned, stray, or abused animals. The state law required it, at least for canines. She'd have to find out from Val about the alternative arrangements for their region. Fortunately, she really didn't have to do anything with the puppies until the lab reports came back, so that bought her forty-eight hours. Still, housing and caring for them cost money. Apparently Roman Ashcroft had been serious when she'd volunteered to pay for their initial care. According to Rita, who seemed equally stunned and thrilled that a stranger would be so generous, Roman had called with credit card details to cover the bill. Tally wasn't sure what the plan would be for them now, but of one thing she was certain. She didn't plan on involving Roman any more than necessary.

❖

With an hour of light left when Rome climbed into the Porsche, she figured she'd make it to the clinic before they closed. With more traffic on the road, she kept to the speed limit. She didn't want to risk being stopped and miss seeing the puppies. When she pulled into the Upland County Animal Hospital a few minutes before six, the front lot was empty, but a new-looking pickup truck and a Volkswagen Bug were parked around the corner. That and the lights visible through the clinic front windows suggested someone was still around. She tried the front door and, when it opened, stepped inside. The foyer was empty, but a dark-haired teen in a scrub shirt and black jeans peered around the corner a few seconds later.

"Help you?" he asked.

"Hi. I was wondering if Dr. Dewilde was still here."

"I think she's just finishing up on a call in the back. Is there an emergency?"

"Not exactly, but I brought in those abandoned puppies, and I was wondering how they were doing."

The teen grinned. "Oh. The Good Samaritan."

Rome lifted a shoulder, the image somehow uncomfortable. "I suppose. It was mostly reflex, though. I saw the bag in the road and it just…well, it didn't look right."

"I'll see if the doc can give you an update. Hold on." He paused. "I'm Blake, by the way. I'm a kennel assistant."

"Rome Ashcroft. Thanks for checking."

Five minutes passed, and Rome had a feeling Tally was going to avoid her. Debating whether to leave or not, she decided to give it another minute when the teen reappeared. "Come on back. Dr. Dewilde is in her office."

"Thanks."

The office was a ten-by-ten room that resembled a patient room at the hospital—gray tile floors, off-white walls, recessed overhead lighting. Tally Dewilde sat behind a dark brown wood-laminate office desk, looking mildly perturbed. She'd rolled the sleeves of her pale yellow shirt up to just above her wrists, revealing a sports watch of some kind and no other jewelry. No rings. Realizing she was probably staring a bit too long, Rome jerked her gaze up to Tally's face. "Hi. I thought I'd make it before you closed for the day."

"I didn't expect to see you again," Tally said by way of greeting. "One of the staff said you called in a credit card number to cover the cost of the testing." She paused. "Let me grab the paperwork, and I can go over the details of the bill."

Rome shook her head and relaxed into a stand easy position, seeing as Tally didn't offer her a seat. "No need to bother. I can see everyone is gone. Just give me the basics."

Tally frowned. Did Roman think she had a calculator in her head—even if she was familiar with the charges for the various tests and exams, which she wasn't. "I'm only going to be able to give you a ballpark figure. They all need their first set of shots—an initial set of distemper shots, parvo, the usual dose of dewormers. We might be a little early on those, but I'm worried about what they might have been exposed to already, and I can't be entirely certain of their age. Given their uncertain parental background, weights don't really help us all that much. So just to be sure, I'd rather get them started."

"Right, fine."

"And then there's the blood tests, boarding fees, and miscellaneous charges. You should approve the initial charges, and then we can call you if there's anything we need to add."

"I already told Rita to just bill me for whatever they needed while they're here."

Tally sighed. "Don't you want to know how much it's going to cost?"

"Not really."

"No, I suppose it doesn't matter to you."

Rome caught the insult but preferred not to engage. Maybe if she ignored the barbs, Tally would eventually tolerate her presence. "Like I said, whatever they need."

Tally shook her head and *almost* smiled. "Thank you. That's very generous. You really didn't need to come all this way again, since you've covered it all with Rita."

Rome hadn't really expected Tally to be glad to see her, but she hadn't expected to be bothered by her cool look either. A day for surprises. "I was just passing by. I wanted to see them."

And you. The thought blindsided her. She *did* want to see the puppies. She'd been thinking about them whenever she hadn't been occupied in the ER or busy getting her new quarters squared away. And she'd been thinking about Tally Dewilde too. About the woman she'd become—a woman who, under vastly different circumstances, she'd be interested in getting to know better. Not that even casual friendship was a possibility, given what Tally believed about her. But the thought had been there, all the same. Of getting to know Dr. Tally Dewilde.

"I doubt you were just passing by since we aren't—as far as I can tell—on the road to anywhere other than a dozen farms. And I know you're not a farmer."

Rome laughed. "Got it in one."

"I suppose since you're paying for them, you're officially their owner."

"Ah, not really what I signed up for, but I'll stand in until they get settled. Can I see them?"

"Sure. Come on."

Rome squatted down in front of Bravo's kennel. "How is your day going, huh?"

Bravo yipped and pushed a paw through the wire cage. The other five scrabbled at their door a few pens away. Rome's stomach tensed. She pretty much hated seeing them all caged up, even though they were clean, warm, and fed. She glanced over her shoulder. Tally stood behind her, her arms folded across her middle, an unreadable expression on her face. "Can I take her out?"

Tally shook her head. "I know she looks fine, and chances are she is, but I can't be responsible for you being bitten again."

"She won't," Rome said. "She was just guarding her pack. And probably terrified."

"No, I'm sorry."

"Fine." Rome stretched out with her shoulder against the cage and rubbed the protruding paw with her finger. "We'll just visit a while, right, Bravo? I'll go when you're ready to close up, Tally."

"Talia," Tally said automatically. She stared as no words came into her head other than *Who are you? Because I know you're not Roman Ashcroft.*

The Roman Ashcroft she'd known—the woman her sister had been obsessed with—had been bold and brash with the carefree sense of entitlement that wealth and privilege bestowed. Tally recognized the traits since most of her friends acted the same way. Her old friends, she should say. They would not be found sitting on the floor talking to an abandoned puppy as if they had nowhere better to be.

"Talia," Roman said, glancing up at her as she shoved a hand through her hair. "Do you think we could call a truce here?"

"Sheila and Aron Sipowicz got married, you know. After all the gossip died down and Sheila...recovered."

Rome tensed. "I didn't know that. Aron and Justin were best friends, I remember."

"Yes, well, Justin broke things off after that night."

Rome sighed. She hadn't known, hadn't *wanted* to know, what had become of any of the friends she'd run with back then. Tally—*Talia*—seemed determined to remind her. "It's good about her and Aron, then."

"They were together about fifteen months, and then it ended."

"Ah. That's rough."

"Yes, it is," Tally said. "My sister's life would have been different, except for you. So no—I don't think a truce is likely."

"Then I'll try to stay out of your way while they're here," Rome said. "If there's a good time for me to visit when it won't disturb you, I'll try to arrange my schedule to accommodate."

"So you can visit a stray puppy."

Rome rubbed a thumb over Bravo's paw, who had stopped barking and lay against the front of the kennel. "They had a tough start. And I'm not doing anything else."

Tally sighed. "Unfortunately, I'm not sure when we'll be able to move them to an animal shelter. Primarily because there isn't one."

Rome frowned. "What do you mean?"

"There isn't one available." Tally explained about the lack of capacity for new animals, particularly in smaller and, as it turned out, more rural areas. "So I'm not sure where we go from here, but I strongly advise you avoid getting attached. Or feeling responsible for them. You've done more than almost anyone else would."

Tally sounded both surprised and mildly annoyed.

"Well, something has to be done to find them homes, right?" Rome narrowed her eyes. "Right?"

"As I said, I'll have to talk to Val—the clinic owner—about where we go from here, but maybe there's some system to find fosters for them."

"You mean split them up?"

"Probably. I'm sure it would be easier to find a couple of families or individuals who were willing to take one or two of them. But an entire litter of puppies?" Tally shook her head. "That's entirely different."

"They're gonna be really unhappy if they get separated."

"They're going to be separated, sooner or later," Tally said, and this time, she actually sounded regretful.

"How are our new boarders doing today," a voice said from behind them. "They look better already. What a bunch of cuties."

A thirtyish blonde in blue jeans, farm boots, and a cocoa-colored cable-knit sweater, her hair pulled back in a loose ponytail, leaned down next to Rome to peer into the kennels. "Hi there, babies." She turned to Rome and smiled. "Hello. I'm Sydney Valentine. Most people call me Val."

Rome got to her feet and held out a hand. "I'm Roman—Rome—Ashcroft. A friend of Brody's."

"Ah—of course." Val's smile widened. "That's great you've joined the Rivers. How is that going?"

"So far can't complain." Rome grinned. "I haven't had much time to get out to see the squad until now."

"The squad. That sounds about right." Val laughed and glanced at Tally. "We've all been waiting for reinforcements, it seems. Couldn't wait to get you all to work."

Tally murmured assent, watching Roman and her easy way with Val. Roman hadn't lost that effortless confidence, no matter how much she tried to pretend she'd changed.

Roman smiled as a big Belgian Malinois with a muscular black and brown body and sharp, inquisitive eyes edged up against Val's leg. Rome made no move to touch the dog but said warmly, "Honcho. Hey. How are you doing. Remember me?"

Val's dog, for the animal was clearly her dog from the way it seemed to read Val's body language, cocked her head, ears up, and looked from Rome to Val.

"Of course, you two have met," Val said. "Honcho, at ease. You can pet her, Rome."

Honcho wagged her tail and took several steps forward.

Brody squatted and held out a hand. "How you doing, Lieutenant."

"They have rank?" Tally asked.

"They do," Roman said, glancing over at her. "They usually rank one notch above their handlers. Honcho here was trained to find IEDs, and part of the medic team." She grimaced. "For obvious reasons, I guess. Chief Warrant Officer Brody was her handler." She gently touched the dog's head. "This one, she's a legend. You're looking good too. Still working a little bit, I hear."

"Honcho still thinks she's always on duty." Val ran a hand down the dog's back. "We're working on getting you to relax, aren't we, girl."

Rome stood. "I understand how that is. She's a working dog, right? That's her nature."

"Oh, that will never change, and I don't see any reason for it to." Val turned to Tally. "Did I catch something about fostering these puppies? You've probably heard that we don't have any recourse in terms of sheltering right now."

Tally nodded grimly. "Actually, yes, I had that lovely conversation earlier today. I was about to ask you about the next steps."

Val smiled. "We start making some calls."

Rome cleared her throat. "I…uh…might have an idea. It's a little out there maybe, but…"

"Around here we just call things like that inventive," Val said. "Let's hear it, Rome."

CHAPTER FIVE

Rome took in Val's curious expression and Tally's exasperated one. Tally seemed set on not liking anything Rome had to say, even before she'd heard it. Rome almost backed off. Another confrontation with Tally really wasn't where she wanted to go. But, not being a coward or easily intimidated, she stood her ground. Besides, Bravo Company was counting on her. A little diplomacy might be a good idea, though, so she focused on Tally as she spoke. She could give away a little power to win in the end. Even though her sports career had gone up in flames before it had ever really started, the competitive lessons of a youth spent on the lacrosse field remained. Let the opponent think they had the upper hand—overconfidence often made people careless. She'd learned the hard way not to be careless.

"You said placing them in an animal shelter wasn't likely, right?"

"I haven't had a chance to call all the possible places yet," Tally said. "I might be able to find somewhere locally that has space."

"For all of them," Rome said.

Tally winced. "Possibly."

"So that's plan A. But if you can't find somewhere, then you need a plan B."

"Obviously." Tally suppressed a glare. After not laying eyes on Roman for over a decade, now she couldn't seem to be rid of her. The gods must be laughing at her now, considering the two of them ended up in the same small town in exactly nowhere, Roman showed up with a problem on the first full day of her new job, *and* Roman turned out to be good friends with her boss's wife. In what universe was that fair? "Is this going somewhere? Because I really do need to make some calls."

Rome smiled. "Just thinking out loud. In case shelters aren't a possibility, then what next?"

"We certainly can't keep them here for long," Val said. "Just feeding and housing them is expensive, and even though we've got a couple of excellent kennel volunteers, the extra work would be a problem." Val shook her head. "I hate to say it, but if the little biter shows no signs of illness, which is highly likely, we'll have to consider shipping them out of state or sending them to whatever places we can find locally as soon as the mandated isolation period is up. We just can't keep them here when we need the kennel space for our own clients."

"The kennel expenses are covered," Tally said quietly. "Roman has already agreed to pay for their boarding once we can move them out of isolation and over to the boarding kennel."

Val's eyebrows rose. "You understand that's going to be very expensive."

"Then I'll be highly motivated to figure out what to do about them," Rome said. "I know I don't understand all the protocols here, but sometimes you have to improvise."

"You mean disregard the rules, don't you?" Tally said. Typical, coming from someone who'd never had to worry about the repercussions of their actions. Possibly the statement from anyone else would have sounded innocent enough, but she'd grown up in a world where rules often applied only to other people. Get a speeding ticket? A friend on the bench would fix that. Have some underage friends over for a little party—no problem, everyone does it. She'd seen it in her own family, where Sheila always seemed to escape the restrictions levied on Tally.

Rome gritted her teeth. Patience was something else she'd

acquired in the military, *hurry up and wait* being one of the ten commandments. Just the same, she needed to get this done before Tally's resistance eroded what little control she had left. "I was thinking *alternatives* might be the better word for it."

"All right," Tally said after a long moment of silence. "Let's hear your idea."

Rome relaxed a fraction. Tally might not be happy about where the help was coming from, but she cared about the puppies more than her personal objections. "We all agree the best thing for them short-term is to find a nice stable home for them while they're growing up and waiting for their final placement. Fostering, as you mentioned."

"Yes, of course that's ideal. And we'll use our local resources to try to find places for them," Tally said. "We've been over this."

"I'm talking about all of them. Fostering all of them together would be best, right?"

"What's best isn't always possible," Tally snapped. "We don't live in a perfect world."

Val interjected, "One problem we face in a community like this is that both parents and often the older children all work, either on the family farm or second jobs. That's not such an issue with family pets, who are often bred from animals who already live there. The mothers provide for the young." She shook her head. "That's the problem with finding foster families when we don't have a shelter. It's very difficult. Even one puppy can be a challenge—but an entire litter? Highly unlikely."

Some rational part of Rome's brain told her to shut up, but her mouth wasn't listening. "I was thinking I could take them."

Tally laughed. "You? You've never even had a dog!"

"Half the population has dogs," Rome said. "And I've been around dogs all my life, even if I couldn't have one."

"In the show ring," Tally said. "Most of those dogs aren't even pets."

"My grandmother's dogs were pets," Rome said, "but that's beside the point. I'm offering a solution."

Tally turned to Val. "This is a crazy idea. Forgetting that Roman hasn't ever raised a dog, let alone six puppies, she's a PA. I'm sure her schedule prohibits her from doing something like this. It's not just a question of feeding them—even though that's a three-times-a-day chore. You need to clean the pens, socialize them, bring them in for vet visits. And what if no one adopts them? Then what?"

"I'm afraid Tally's right, Rome," Val said gently. "I...we... appreciate your efforts and your generous intentions here. You've already offered to do more, believe me, than ninety-nine percent of the people who might have driven past that bag lying on the road. But taking care of one puppy is a major undertaking. A litter of them at this age, even if you have help, is practically a twenty-four hour a day job. I know what Brody's schedule is like, and you're likely to have very erratic hours, especially at first when you're probably going to be picking up extra shifts for people who've been waiting for a chance to get some time off. I can't see any way you can handle this."

"What if I found some help and set up a rotation schedule of some kind?"

"Believe me," Val said with a laugh, "trying to schedule three adults and a couple of volunteers for twelve hours a day at the clinic here is a headache. Even if you could find some willing hands, organizing people to take care of puppies would be an enormous headache."

"But it's not impossible," Rome said, refusing to give up. Maybe she would have let it go, if she could forget the way the puppies had looked when she'd opened the damn duffel bag. Scared, defiant, helpless. Hopeful.

She didn't believe in fate. She couldn't, not when she'd had to watch her whole life destroyed in one night. She'd had to believe she could take control of her future, create a life she wanted—and keep that life safe. She might not have been destined to find Bravo Company, but she had, and now they were hers. At least for now.

"Do you think people would be interested in helping out if they knew they were going to get one of the puppies at the end?"

"Sure, a few people would be willing to come by for an hour a day," Val said, "but you'd still need to organize and supervise the whole process."

Rome shrugged. "I've had plenty of experience doing that in the Army. Maybe one of your staff who knows the people in the community could help put together a group of people who wanted to take care of the puppies."

"I could do that," Blake said as he joined the group. He flushed. "Sorry, I just overheard the conversation, and I think it's a really good idea."

Rome nodded in his direction. Finally, an ally. "Thanks."

"Where exactly are you gonna put these puppies?" Tally asked, not even bothering to hide her incredulity.

"Well, I've got a fenced yard."

Val laughed. "Brody fenced that yard for Honcho, who wouldn't leave her post if a bomb went off a hundred yards away. Literally. But puppies—you'd need some serious puppy-proofing before you could let them out there."

"But Honcho was okay out there—right? Safe?"

"Honcho is an extremely well trained, intelligent animal, who has been conditioned to survive in extreme conditions." Val curled her fingers through the ruff at the back of Honcho's neck. "That's a far cry from a litter of puppies. And even when they're big enough to go outside, which won't be for a while, you'd have to keep a close eye on them. The temperature changes rapidly this time of year, and predators would be a problem even during the day."

"What do you mean, *predators*?" Rome asked flatly.

"The kinds of things that like to eat small animals," Val said. "A coyote could jump the fence, a fox could burrow under it, even a raptor hunting during the day could pick up one of those puppies."

"Seriously? A bird?" Rome clenched her jaws and glanced

back at Bravo, who stood, small snout pressed against the wire of the cage. She could swear Bravo was watching her.

"A full-size eagle can take a fox," Val said matter-of-factly.

Rome's brain wouldn't even make the image of a bird grasping Bravo in her claws or talons or whatever they were. "By the time they're ready to leave here, I'll make sure the yard is safe." She glanced at Blake. "You probably know some people that are handy with construction, right?"

Blake laughed. "Oh, only about a dozen."

Rome grinned. "Well, see, there you have it."

"What if one of your volunteers can't show up. What then?" Tally asked.

Roman blew out a breath. If she hadn't believed that Val had been simply trying to point out some of the difficulties with the decision, rather than knee-jerk rejecting it, she would've been frustrated. Maybe even a little angry. But Val had been a good sounding board, and now Tally made a good point. She needed to keep her feelings under control. "Reinforcements."

"Sorry?" Tally said.

"A few people willing to come in at short notice."

"What you need," Blake said, "is a...project manager. Somebody between you and the actual care and feeding of the puppies. So that if one of the volunteers can't make it, they contact that person who then either finds a substitute or fills in until someone else can get there."

"That sounds like a good idea," Rome said. "Obviously if I'm in the middle of a shift at the hospital, I won't be able to leave right away." She glanced at Blake. "Are you volunteering to take point on this?"

He grinned. "If you're taking applications."

"You're hired."

Blake laughed. "I can probably find at least four other people who are willing to take a shift."

Rome glanced at Tally. "There, see? We're halfway to having the problem solved."

"We're halfway to creating more problems for you than you ever could've realized," Tally said.

"I doubt that's true," Rome said quietly.

Tally flushed. "It's worth exploring. I don't think we should make a hasty decision until I've exhausted every possibility for local placement."

"I don't want them split up," Rome said.

"Why?" Tally asked, clearly frustrated. "Why do you care?"

Rome thought, *Because they're mine now.* Instead she said, "Because they've only known each other, and they still feel safest with each other. When they're bigger, it will be easier for them to be separated." She held Tally's gaze. "Right?"

"Possibly," Tally said. "But first we try it my way. Yours is…extreme."

"All right. But in the meantime, we plan for an alternative action." She turned to Blake. "So, what do we do? Interview people? Although I guess that's probably not necessary around here. You probably know everybody."

"You'd be surprised how even in a place this small," Val said, "there are groups within groups. I think putting up notices at the café, at school, and on the town Facebook page ought to give us enough exposure to put together a reasonable list of volunteers. But Tally's right," she hastened to add. "It's a lot more work than you realize, and I have concerns that volunteers will be called away for some emergency of their own. And young puppies like this simply can't be abandoned."

"No," Rome said, glancing down at Bravo. "They can't be."

She straightened and faced Tally and Val. "We won't do it if you don't find everything, including the volunteer schedule, in the best interest of the puppies. But this gives them a chance." Her gaze swept over Tally but didn't linger. "And everyone deserves a chance."

Chapter Six

The day had slipped away, and the night outside the window behind Tally's desk was as dark as Tally had ever seen. No streetlights, vehicle headlights, or hazy glow of city skylines punctured the inky blackness. She suddenly felt very small and very alone in this strange new world. And obviously very tired, given that she wasn't prone to flights of fancy.

With a sigh she leaned back, closed her eyes, and rubbed her temples. What a day. What a week—or almost two. Anything she might have imagined on the job wouldn't have come close to what had actually transpired since she'd started. Thankfully, the office visits had all been routine—puppy shots, lab tests on dogs who hadn't been eating well or weren't behaving normally, vaccinations, and surgical follow-ups.

What she hadn't anticipated was starting the new job with a duffel bag full of puppies delivered by a woman from her past she'd never expected to see again. She'd never forgotten Roman, but she'd finally stopped thinking about her and Sheila and that night as she dealt with the challenge of forging her own life against the tide of her family dynamics.

So ending every day—or most days—with a visit from Rome, who stopped by more frequently than Tally expected, kept her constantly off stride. She never quite got her balance back after every encounter—snippets of her exchanges with Roman kept coming back to her, along with images of her that didn't quite mesh with the memories. But then, her memories had been of a privileged nineteen-year-old college student, not a woman who'd seen war and death. Or one who would throw herself halfway across the room to catch a puppy who'd fallen off the exam table.

Worse even than being thrown off stride, which was something she'd thought she'd gotten over when she'd finally developed some immunity to her family's constant criticism and her mother's disdain, were the emotions she hadn't anticipated. Begrudging admiration for Roman's insistence on trying to help a litter of puppies for which she really bore no responsibility. Her obvious affection for the little leader of the pack. And the patience Tally wouldn't have expected from someone who had grown up being able to make a request or, more often than not, give an order and have it fulfilled.

Despite all that, she'd managed all her clinical duties with no major problems, but she wasn't certain she'd made a very good impression on her new boss. She'd been more than a little curt with Roman initially, and she wasn't entirely proud of her behavior. Still, remembering Sheila's devastated cries and descent into self-destructive despair brought back some of the edge to her anger.

"Am I interrupting?" Val said quietly from the door.

With a jolt, Tally sat forward and opened her eyes. "No, of course not." She looked around the room, which held only another somewhat bare-bones office chair, and started to rise. "Do you need me?"

"No, sit, sit." Val motioned her back down as she came in and took the matching chair that faced Tally's desk. "I was just wondering how you were doing. Pretty busy day. And there've been a few of them lately."

"Fine," Tally said automatically. "We had a few add-ons, but I think everything went well."

Val chuckled. "I saw that Marco Polo was back. That cat must be the worst fighter in the county. He's always showing up with bites and tears."

"A sweetie, though."

"Mm, so's his owner. He dotes on those animals." Val smiled fondly. "Any luck with the shelters?"

Tally sighed and shook her head. "I'm afraid not. The list of possibles was pretty short, and I called every local shelter in a twenty-five-mile radius." She paused. "Is that far enough, do you think?"

"Twenty-five miles out here is practically our backyard," Val said, laughing a little, "but anything beyond that is probably too far away. Those places are going to be filling up, if they're not already, with animals from even farther away than here."

Tally looked at the list she'd made, and the names she'd scratched out. "Of the places I was actually able to reach, only one possible, and they wouldn't have room unless they moved out some of the animals they're already holding. They're saying at least a couple of weeks, but we're on their list. The others are full and can't say when they might have a vacancy. I still have two to check."

"Well at least there are a couple of maybes." Val frowned. "I'm a little skeptical that they won't need to give those spots to animals in their districts, but as it is, we're getting to the point we need to place them somewhere. I'll reach out to some of the contacts I have in Saratoga and Albany tomorrow. We're not in their catchment area either, but I might be able to call in a favor."

"I don't understand how we're going to be able to handle this kind of thing in the future," Tally said. "What if we get more strays?"

Val said quietly, "We don't see that many strays being brought in—feline or canine. The barns around here are filled with cats, some feral and others that are actually being cared for as sort of outdoor pets. Puppies are a bigger problem because they really can't live independently, but we're not seeing large bands of roving feral dogs. People take them to shelters—or used to. I'm afraid we might see more canines being abandoned."

"I can't quite imagine what the people who dropped these puppies off in a bag by the side of the road expected to happen to them."

Val's expression darkened. "I expect they thought the bag would roll down into the ditch and stay there, and no one would ever notice it."

"That's horrible."

"It is. These puppies are extremely lucky that someone bothered to check the duffel, let alone bring them in."

"I'm beginning to see that."

"And to have someone who's willing to assume some of the expense, and even try to provide a place for them." Val shook her head. "I can't quite believe it myself."

"Yes," Tally said as evenly as she could, "Roman is definitely the Good Samaritan in all of this."

"Roman," Val said softly. "Brody has only ever referred to her as Rome. I got the feeling you weren't too happy with her."

Tally winced inwardly. "I suppose I have been a little resistant to her solution. It's just…really, I don't think she has any idea what she's volunteering for."

"I think you're probably right. Didn't you mention that she's never had a dog?"

"Yes, she told me that. She's been around dogs, of course. Her grandmother was…is…a well-known bulldog breeder and judge on Long Island."

"You seem to know her pretty well."

Tally stiffened. "Actually, no. We were never…friendly. Our families knew each other."

"That's quite a coincidence. You didn't know she was coming here, then?"

Tally laughed ruefully. "Not in my wildest imaginings. I never expected to see her again."

"Is it going to be a problem, working with her? One of us should schedule a stop or two on the mobile route for puppy shots and routine puppy care. It's easier than dragging them in here, especially since Rome's schedule is likely to be unpredictable. I can do it, if you'd rather."

"Of course not," Tally said quickly. "There's no problem."

"All right then. Great." Val stood. "I've got a couple of surgeries scheduled tomorrow morning. Why don't you plan on being here for those. Then we can do farm call together, so you can get to know some more of the clients."

"Sounds great."

Val paused at the door. "We're having a get-together after the first game at the end of the week. I hope you'll come, get to meet some of the folks from the village."

"The game?" Tally asked.

"The basketball game at the high school. Blake will be playing in the varsity game. Starts around seven."

"Oh, right. He did mention that. I guess I'll be going?" She tried to make it not sound like a question. Would it be terribly rude if she said she hadn't the slightest interest in watching a group of teenagers play basketball?

"It's not required, but you might find it turns out to be fun. It's something of a community event. But please come by after, even if you don't make the game. Around eight thirty. I'll text you the directions."

"All right, thank you. I'll try to be there."

Tally sagged back in her chair after Val left. That was uncomfortable. Obviously, she'd let her personal feelings for Roman show just a little bit too much. And of course, Roman had to turn out to be a friend of Val's wife. She'd have to work at being more sociable when they were together, or at least keep her real feelings to herself.

A basketball game. There was something else to add to her list of unexpected events. In a very short time, her life had taken a very strange turn.

❖

Brody's trailer, tucked in a large grassy back corner of a sprawling mobile home park a few miles out of town, was a lot homier than Rome had expected. She stood just inside the aluminum door and tried to figure out where the hell she was going to put puppies—a long silver bullet, with a bedroom at the far end, a small serviceable bathroom with a surprisingly large shower, and a tiny kitchen area with a microwave, two-burner stove, and a sink adjacent to a sitting area big enough for a table that would accommodate a visitor or two for a game of cards. Playing cards had become something of an addiction in the service, there not being a whole lot else to do while waiting for the next mission. As she didn't know anyone other than Brody, she wasn't likely to have visitors—cards or no cards.

She hadn't thought she'd miss anything about being deployed, even though there'd been times when the adrenaline and the fear morphed into something near euphoric when she saved a life—when she beat the odds. She could live without that rush, but she missed her unit, the friends she'd made there, the sense of belonging. Ever since she'd been back, she'd felt a little aimless, a little unmoored, not quite sure where she belonged. She hoped that feeling would disappear now that she was part of another team.

She'd always been part of the team, it seemed. Lacrosse had been like that. Her teammates had been her best friends, and without siblings, they'd stood in for family. She'd been lucky, losing one family but finding another in the Army.

When a knock came on the door, she tensed and automatically reached for a weapon she no longer wore. She sucked in a breath and spun to peer outside. The narrow unpaved road that meandered between the trailers was unlit, and only the moonlight illuminated the figure standing there. The features were swallowed by the ink-black night, but the stance was unmistakable.

"Yo, Brody," Rome said as she pushed the door open. "Come on in."

"Sorry I didn't call," Brody said as she entered and gave a quick glance around. "Everything been working out okay?"

"Yeah. It's great." Rome grinned. Hell, she was glad to see her. Brody brought a little bit of normal back into a life that had gotten a little weird—starting with puppies, a busy shift at a brand-new posting, and everywhere she turned, Tally Dewilde.

"Excellent," Brody said. "So, Val tells me you might be getting some company."

Rome laughed. "News travels fast. I was gonna talk to you about it next time I saw you. Are you okay with it?"

"Sure."

"Where am I gonna put them?"

Brody laughed. "I guess you didn't think to check out the facilities before volunteering."

"I forgot the part about never volunteering," Rome said dryly.

"You don't need a lot of room for them right away. Just a little barrier that you can put in one corner over there," Brody said, pointing to the far corner. "A baby gate will do it—you can pick one up at the hardware store next to Stewart's in town. An old blanket, and they'll be good in there for a few weeks. By then, maybe you'll get them placed."

"Would you be opposed to me putting some kind of shelter outside if they're still here when they're a little bigger? Like a shed?"

"I'm okay with it, but you'll have to check with the park manager. They're pretty easy about letting you do whatever you want with your own lot. Especially if it enhances things."

"I wouldn't leave them out there, you know, twenty-four hours a day or anything, but if the weather's good, I thought it might work to make a small run for them."

"A good idea." Brody leaned a hip against the edge of the table. "So, Val mentioned that you and Tally knew each other."

Rome kept her expression neutral. "I knew her sister, her family, but Tally was a little younger than me."

"Must have been a surprise when you ended up at the clinic that first morning and saw her," Brody said.

"Yeah, heckuva one. This is the last place I'd expect to see her."

"Huh. Why is that?"

"Oh, you know, city girl—well, not a girl any longer—but I would have expected her to have a practice in the city or the suburbs. Way the heck out here seems a world away from Manhattan."

"It is that," Brody said and grinned. "But then again, you're here."

Rome shunted that aside easily and grinned. "So are you."

"I grew up here."

"Yeah, I guess you're lucky," Rome said softly. "You came home."

"I did," Brody said with rare seriousness. "I never thought I would."

"Thanks again for the trailer," Rome said, needing to change the subject. She'd already gotten closer to her past with Tally Dewilde than she'd wanted. In the service, no one asked questions about another soldier's past. What mattered was the here and now. That had worked just fine for her and plenty of others whom she suspected would just as soon forget what had led them to the desert and a war whose purpose had been nearly forgotten. It sure had been what she'd wanted—a place to start over.

As if recognizing an off-limits topic, Brody said, "So, I went by to see the puppies. They're looking good. Val says they'll need a couple more days of isolation, but if everything looks good, and they haven't placed them yet, you're gonna become a foster parent."

"Man, don't put it that way."

Brody laughed. "Hey, by the way, Friday night at our place.

A get-together after the basketball game. Food, drinks, casual. I'll give you directions."

"Um…"

"Come on, no arguments."

"Do I have a choice?"

Brody shook her head. "Nope."

"Thanks, then. I'll be there, I guess."

"Good." Brody paused at the door. "It's good you're here."

Brody let herself out, and Rome set about unpacking the few groceries she'd picked up on the way back and sliding them into the minifridge. Seemed like she was going to be part of the community, whether she was ready for it or not.

CHAPTER SEVEN

Blake heard footsteps coming toward the kitchen and said without turning from the fridge, "Do you want half an English muffin?"

"Sure," Flann said. "You know we have electricity, right? So, you know, you could see what you're doing in here?"

"You're just used to all those bright lights in the OR. There's enough light," Blake said, repeating the conversation he had almost every morning with either Flann or his mother. Unlike his parents, who both started the day in high gear, he liked to ease into the day with coffee and the quiet, with no light in the room except the gray of early morning. Flann was already dressed in scrubs and would probably be out the door before Blake had finished half his coffee. "I like taking my time with my coffee before I start the day."

Flann grunted and reached for the coffee that Blake had put on when he got up. "You could always just stay in bed if you don't want to be all the way awake."

"I'm awake. I'm just easing into it." Blake smiled. "Besides, mornings are the best time, so why rush through it."

"You sure you don't want to be a surgeon? Morning people."

"Vets operate."

"True," Flann said, settling at the table with her coffee. "You're still sure about vet school, huh?"

"More every day." Blake brought his coffee over and slid half an English muffin across the table to Flann as he sat down. "Mom still asleep?"

"Yeah, she's catching a little extra," Flann said with that slightly evasive tone that suggested things that Blake didn't really want to think about his parents doing first thing in the morning.

"Right," he said. "So, do you mind?"

Flann frowned. "Mind what?"

"You know, that I'm not continuing the family tradition and going into people medicine?"

Flann grinned. "Close enough, and seriously, whatever you want to do would be good with us if it makes you happy."

Blake wrapped his hands around his coffee cup and looked down, hiding the sudden totally embarrassing moisture in his eyes. "Yeah, I get that. Thanks."

"So, how was practice yesterday?" Flann asked in that super casual way she had that said she was trying not to be too probe-y.

"It was fine. Coach worked us hard."

"Did you get much play time?"

"He had me switching between point and shooting, so yeah, I took a lot of shots. It was good."

"That's excellent. How do you feel about the two positions?" Flann finished off her English muffin and carried the plate to the sink. "Have a choice?"

"Well, you know, I'd be happy to play anywhere, but yeah, point feels pretty natural to me."

"It helps to have quick hands and fast feet and good basketball IQ. And you've got all of that."

"Yeah, maybe." Blake teetered between grateful Flann cared about what was going on for him and wishing he didn't have to talk about it. Didn't really matter what he wanted. Coach would decide if he even got to start on Friday night. Or anytime.

Flann turned and gave him a look. "But?"

Blake sighed. "You know how it is. The point guard is

supposed to lead the team—relaying the plays or calling them, getting the ball to the right player, keeping the team working together."

Flann took a slow swallow of coffee, a sure sign she was searching for the right thing to say.

Blake leaned back and met Flann's gaze. "You want to, you know, just ask outright?"

Flann blew out a breath. "Right. I'm not real sure where the line is between invading your privacy and doing the good parent thing."

"How about if we make a deal. You ask what you want, and I'll tell you if it's something I don't want to answer."

"That works for you? Works for me."

"I'm good."

"So, playing the number one position—you don't think you can do that?"

"*I* think I can, but I don't know if Coach does. Besides, it's more than just playing good basketball. The guys have to be down with me playing there too, or it won't work. The team won't gel."

"Has there been any problem with them—at practice or… anything?"

"Things are a little weird," Blake said. "I got bumped to varsity even though I'm new at school, so there's that."

"You're the right age for the team, and you earned it in tryouts and practice up until now. Right?"

"Yeah, but you know that doesn't really matter if you're taking the place of somebody who's been there the whole time."

"I get that," Flann said. "Some of them will resent you for jumping into first string. You're the new guy."

"Yeah, the new trans guy," Blake said flatly.

"That too." Flann didn't hesitate now. "Is there trouble over that? Hazing or anything?"

"Nothing physical," Blake said quickly. "I would have told you if that happened. More…attitude, I guess. Just letting me know I don't really belong. There might be a little resentment about me actually being good at it—for the ones who don't see me as one of them."

"Guys," Flann muttered. "Always have to prove who's the alpha."

"Hey, I'm a guy!" Blake laughed. "And you seem pretty alpha to me—Chief of Surgery Rivers."

Flann grinned. "Totally different."

"Uh-huh."

"I'm sorry you're getting that attitude," Flann said, suddenly serious again. "And that you keep getting it every time you're in a new situation."

"I'm okay. It's gonna happen on a team, right? Everyone has to show they deserve their place." Blake shrugged. "It's not like I didn't expect some of them to pretend I don't exist."

"As long as that's all it is, and you're all right."

"I'm good."

"Okay. Just so you know we're here." Flann rinsed her coffee cup and put it in the sink. "So why *are* you up a half hour early?"

"Oh, I'm picking Margie up, and we're gonna swing by the clinic."

"I thought you had the morning shift there yesterday."

"I did," Blake said. "But there's some extra work with the new puppies, so I'm giving Margie a hand."

"Still haven't placed them?" Flann asked.

"Not that I know of, but we've got the volunteer list set up for the move to Rome's trailer."

"How do you think that's going to work out?"

"It should be fine. We've got plenty of people to cover six shifts a day—to feed, clean, and play with them."

Flann laughed. "I'm thinking the last part is the real draw."

Blake shrugged. "Come on—puppies."

"Uh-huh," Abby said as she walked in. Like Flann, she

was dressed for a day at the hospital in navy-blue scrubs and black Crocs, her shoulder-length blond hair still damp from the shower. "Sounds like Rome is going to be busy between the ER and rescuing strays. Is there coffee?"

"Here," Flann said and handed her a mug. "How's Rome doing?"

"Fine. She settled in like she'd been here a year—probably comes from being reassigned so frequently in the military. I might talk to Glenn about moving her out of the ER and assigning her permanently to the trauma unit or the flight team. She's got more trauma experience than some of the new trauma surgeons."

"Hey!" Flann protested. "Those are my people you're talking about."

"And truth is truth." Abby smiled and sipped the coffee with a contented sigh. "So, Blake, you're going to be raising some puppies. Do you have time, with school and basketball and volunteering in the ER and the clinic?"

Blake looked from Flann to his mother and figured now was as good a time as any. "I'm thinking I should drop the shift in the ER—not because of the puppies," he said quickly, "but I've got to start prepping for SATs and stuff."

Abby nodded. "If you hadn't already decided, I would have suggested it. If you have to give something up, it should be the ER. Your experience with Val at the clinic will look very good on your applications for vet school."

"Good. Thanks," Blake said.

His mother took the toast Flann handed to her, muttered an absent thanks, and raised a brow to Blake. "Are you thinking about one of these homeless pups for us?"

Blake grinned. "You guys did say that when we moved into the new place, you know, pet time."

"It's for you to decide, but we're okay with it. Having a dog around will be nice," Abby said. "And you're sure you'll have time for this rotation thing?"

"It shouldn't be a problem. Margie and I already worked out

between us the schedule at the clinic. Fitting in a couple more stops won't be a big deal."

"All right, but you've got a lot on your plate."

"I'm handling it."

"Good enough." Abby finished off her toast and said to Flann, "You ready?"

"Yep."

Abby ruffled Blake's hair as she passed by. "Have a good day."

"Be careful driving," Flann said as she always did every time Blake left the house.

Blake figured that was an occupational hazard. Both his parents worried about a lot of things he never thought about. Accidents, weird illnesses, and all kinds of other hazards. Now that he had his very own vehicle, paid for with the money he'd been saving up forever, the cautions had doubled.

"See you later," he called and grabbed his backpack to follow them out. He didn't really mind. Secretly he was pretty sure he'd lucked out in the parent department.

❖

Margie was waiting for him, leaning against the colonnade of the porte cochere texting as he drove down the long drive to the Rivers Homestead. When they'd first met, they'd been about the same height, but he'd had a growth spurt and now had half a head on her. She looked taller, though, in the tight skinny jeans with the knees torn out. The baby-blue pullover hoodie perfectly matched her eyes too. Blake smiled to himself. Margie probably didn't even think of that—she just liked the hoodie. She didn't look much like Flann, whose eyes were dark brown and her build a lot more muscular, which sometimes struck Blake as weird when he remembered they were sisters—also kind of weird, but he was used to that by now. Of all the Rivers sisters, Margie's wild blond curls and fair complexion were unique. As Blake pulled up beside her, Margie pocketed her phone and shouldered her way-too-small-looking backpack with the rainbow patch on the front.

"Hey," Margie said as she jumped into the front seat. She leaned over and kissed his cheek before settling into her seat and buckling up.

"Morning." Blake swung back down the drive and headed toward the clinic. He was getting used to—sort of—the new direction their friendship had taken since they'd become more of a thing, but Margie still took him by surprise with how easy she was about it. He had some worries about what might happen if they got more serious. Worried enough he'd mentioned it in a roundabout way to his mom when she'd started up on the safe-sex talk.

She'd given him the same straight in the eye look she'd given him when he'd told her he was sure he was trans. He could always trust his mom to treat him like he had a brain.

"Honey—everybody worries about what it will be like the first time. And plenty of times after that too. What matters is that both of you are thinking about what the other person feels just as much as you're thinking about what you want. If you care about them, then make it about showing them. Bodies are just bodies, Blake. The pleasure comes from paying attention to what feels right."

He still worried some, but for now he sure wasn't complaining about things just the way they were. "Anything happening?"

Margie said, "Taylor texted that Annika got the go-ahead to help with the puppies. So we're six."

"That's excellent."

"We might have to shift things around when you and Dave have practice or Tim has to tutor someone. But we can cover it."

"You've got practice too," Blake pointed out.

Margie made a face. "I was going to talk to you about that. I've decided not to play on the team. I'll have to tell Coach today."

Blake shot her a look. "Why?"

"I've got the ER and the clinic shifts, and now we have the SAT prep classes. Those are more important. To me, I mean."

"I was going to talk to you too," Blake said.

"You're not quitting the team!"

"No," he said. "The ER. Same reasons."

"Oh," she said quietly. "Yeah, I guess that makes the most sense."

"So I guess we're decided?"

Margie grinned. "I'm okay with it if you are."

"Glad we talked." Blake laughed and Margie joined him. "Anyhow, the puppies won't be a long-term thing. Hopefully they'll get adopted."

"I can't believe somebody did that," Margie said sharply.

"I can."

"Yeah," she sighed. "Me too. But it really sucks."

Blake reached over and squeezed her hand. "They're safe now. And taking care of them will be cool."

"Are you thinking to get one?"

He grinned. "The thought crossed my mind. There's six of them, you know."

Margie sighed. "I wouldn't mind a puppy, but you know, Baggly is getting older and sort of cranky. I don't know how he'd feel about a puppy."

"Having a puppy for him to teach how to herd would probably be good for him."

"If any of the puppies have the instinct." She glanced at her phone. "That was Taylor. Her mom said there's a thing at Brody and Val's after the game Friday. You want to go?"

"Sure. Is she telling Dave and Tim?"

"Already did. So, are you ready for the game?"

"I hope so," Blake said, pulling into the side lot at the clinic. "Guess it depends on the last practices this week. I still don't know if I'll start or ride the bench."

"You should start—you know you're good enough." Margie huffed. "But that doesn't always count."

"I know."

"That sucks too."

He looked at her, grateful as always that she got him without him needing to say it all out loud. "Yeah."

"The other guys," Margie said carefully, "they're cool around you, right?"

"No problems." He flushed but figured Margie wouldn't ask. "The first couple of times I was pretty uncomfortable in the locker room, worrying about getting hassled, but nobody…um… walks around showing all their stuff. So it's okay."

Margie squeezed his hand. "There go all my fantasies out the window."

He laughed and relaxed. Yeah, she got him.

She slid a little closer to him and rested her cheek against his shoulder. "So just play your game. You know what to do, and when the rest of them see that you can help them win, nothing else will matter."

"I feel like I have to keep winning my place every time I play. Every time I do anything, really."

"I know. And it sucks. It sucks that you have to. But you can do it."

"Thanks." He leaned his cheek against the top of her head. "So, you ready to go play with some puppies?"

Margie tilted her head up and gave him a look. "When aren't I?"

Remembering now why his life mostly didn't suck, Blake kissed her quickly. "Thanks, by the way."

Margie gave him a quizzical look. "For what?"

"For being terrific."

"Oh that." She laughed. "Ditto."

CHAPTER EIGHT

Tally jogged toward the center of town, following the activity focused on the block with the Breadbasket Café, which served excellent coffee and breakfast sandwiches. That discovery had cemented her decision to rent in the village despite the Realtor's warning she'd have a twenty-minute drive to the clinic—ha ha, as if driving along scenic country roads was a chore compared to the same trip in a cab or subway in the city. Since she'd rather eat after a morning jog than before, she had the perfect excuse to indulge in something special from their menu.

She entered the café, a happy swell of anticipation lightening some of the worry she hadn't been able to shake. Images of those puppies and the few options she had for solving the dilemma of how to keep them together that didn't involve Roman plagued her. The lightness dissipated almost as quickly as it had sparked when she realized the person at the end of the line was Roman Ashcroft. Was there nowhere in this village she wouldn't run into her?

Roman glanced back as Tally joined the queue, smiled, and said, "Morning."

"Morning," Tally said, withholding a sigh. That ought to be polite enough. She checked the handwritten menu above the small counter that displayed a variety of pastries as she reached into the side pocket of her running tights for her twenty. "Damn."

"Problem?" Roman asked.

"No," Tally said quickly, holding up the credit card she pulled out. "I wasn't thinking when I left this morning and grabbed this instead of cash." She laughed despite her annoyance. "I don't know why I can't remember that."

"Maybe because you almost never need cash for anything. I have the same problem, but I've got enough on me today. Go ahead and order. I'll cover it."

"Oh no, absolutely not."

"There's no obligation attached," Roman said quietly. "Just being neighborly."

Tally hesitated. Why did she find it so difficult to have a civil conversation? She'd had plenty of practice growing up being civil with people she hadn't cared for very much. One of the necessary social graces she'd learned early when forced to attend her mother's numerous dinner parties. "I'm not that far away. I'll just go home and get...coffee."

She obviously wasn't coming back here for it.

Roman grimaced. "Tally...*Talia*...I'm just offering to buy you a cup of coffee and a breakfast sandwich. If it makes you feel better, you can buy next time."

Tally's chin came up. As if there would ever be a next time. The line behind her was growing, and half the people in it were undoubtedly listening. Wonderful. Just the way she wanted potential new clients to meet her. "Thank you, Roman. I'll Venmo you what I owe you."

"You're welcome." Roman grinned as if she'd won some kind of victory. "And it's Rome, by the way."

"I—"

"Help you with something?" a blond teenager behind the counter asked, her brilliant smile and casual confidence something Tally didn't think she'd ever actually had at that age.

Before Tally could reply, Roman said quickly, "Yes, thanks. I'll have an Americano with an extra shot of espresso and one of those egg and cheese sandwiches on a croissant. And Dr. Dewilde will have..." She turned to Tally. "Doctor?"

Tally resisted rolling her eyes. She didn't enjoy being maneuvered into doing something she didn't want, but she actually really desperately *did* want coffee and wasn't going to look like an idiot by turning around and walking out. "Actually, I'll have the same thing."

"Great. Are you a new doctor at the Rivers?" the blonde asked.

"Ah, no, I'm a vet."

"Oh, hey, that's so cool. You're taking care of the puppies, right?"

Why was she surprised? The puppies were clearly a popular topic, and news seemed to travel very quickly around town. She really needed to remember that if she wanted to have any kind of private life—although that was not exactly on the top of her list. "Along with Dr. Valentine, yes."

"Awesome. I'm going to help when they get moved to Rome's. I'm Taylor Richelieu, by the way."

"Um, hi Taylor." Tally glanced at Rome, who was clearly a regular at the café. She might have to adjust her run time if she didn't want to run into her every morning. But that was silly—she wasn't going to change her life for anyone any longer. "That's great that you'll be helping out."

"I know! I can't wait. Just a few more days, right?"

"Well," Tally said, "it's not settled yet, but—"

Someone in line called out cheerfully, "Pretty hungry here, Taylor!"

"We'll know soon," Tally finished.

Taylor grinned and handed Tally a little flag with the number *3* written on it in red Magic Marker and said, "Just take it to your table. Someone will bring it out to you in a few."

"Oh, I…" Before Tally could say she wanted the sandwich and coffee to go, Taylor had turned away to give the order to the kitchen, and a polite cough from someone in line behind her suggested perhaps they should move on.

"I'm not having breakfast with you," Tally said quietly as

she followed Rome to a round wrought iron bistro table in front of a wide front window that reached to the vaulted ceiling. A counter with additional seating gave a view to Main Street. From the looks of the interior, the café had once been a bank. Of course, the huge brass vault standing open in the far corner, which now held bric-a-brac on shelves inside, was a fairly dead giveaway.

"You're certainly welcome to join me," Rome said, pulling out a chair for Tally before settling into one on the opposite side. The table was so small they'd practically be bumping knees beneath it. "But of course, that's up to you."

Tally could either stand awkwardly by the table and provide yet more entertainment for the half dozen people seated nearby, most of whom were unabashedly watching, or sit. She gritted her teeth and sat down, carefully avoiding bodily contact. "I don't actually have time to sit and eat. I need to get out to the clinic."

"I thought you didn't open until nine," Rome said.

"Clinic hours start then, but I've got animals to check, and I like to review the charts for the day."

"So," Rome said, "a veterinarian. Where did that come from? Why not a doctor?"

Tally laughed and tried to keep the bitterness from her tone. "Bingo. You sound a lot like my mother."

Rome grimaced. "Ouch. I'm sorry. So not a popular choice. Why did you decide to do it despite the family wishes?"

"I like animals better than people," Tally said and immediately wondered why she was answering.

Rome laughed, a genuine laugh that lit up her eyes and made those little gold flecks Tally had noticed before dance. Her smile, one that brought out a captivating little indent in her cheek, was full and inviting.

Inviting? Oh my God. That was so wrong on so many levels. Tally immediately squelched the reaction.

"What?" Rome asked.

"I'm sorry, what?" Tally said, suddenly losing track of what they'd been talking about. Rome couldn't possibly have known what she was thinking. *She* couldn't even believe what she'd been thinking.

"You looked, I don't know, kerfuffled there for a moment."

Tally sat up straight. "I don't get kerfuffled."

Rome laughed again, and Tally teetered between indignation and amusement. She finally gave in and laughed. Even she could admit when she was being ridiculous.

Rome leaned across the small table, her gaze fixed on Tally's.

Tally couldn't look away. She wanted to. She really did. Didn't she?

"You realize," Rome said intently, "we're having a conversation. This might be our first that doesn't center on puppies."

"I'm very good at having polite conversations, even when I don't want to," Tally said automatically. "Didn't you find that necessary to survive the tedium sometimes?"

"I wasn't too worried about what people thought, so I didn't bother," Rome said.

"I wasn't so daring," Tally said. "Not then, anyhow."

"I guess bucking the family about vet school was tough to do."

Tally shrugged. "I can't imagine joining the military was a popular decision either."

Rome's expression darkened, the gold highlights in her eyes eclipsed by a storm of indigo clouds.

Tally wondered if Rome realized her eyes revealed every emotion. Somehow she was certain she didn't. Rome did not strike her as a woman who let her vulnerabilities show. Until that moment, Tally would have sworn she didn't have any.

"Believe me, they were more than happy to see me go."

Of course Tally knew why. And why she kept forgetting that reason every time she and Rome interacted, she didn't know. Because she couldn't ever forget.

"Why a PA?" Tally asked, searching for a change of topic, and immediately regretted it. Yes, she was curious. Nothing about the picture she had of Roman Ashcroft, the callous entitled people-user, quite fit with that. But could she really believe any other picture?

"I was young and angry," Rome said, "and I enlisted mostly because I didn't have much in the way of choices." She met Tally's gaze straight on, but Tally couldn't find any anger or resentment in her expression now. Resignation, maybe. Even sorrow?

What did Rome have to be sad about? She hadn't suffered, not the way Sheila had—not the way *she* had, watching her sister spiral into self-destruction. Why couldn't she see the woman who caused all that unhappiness sitting across from her? Why was everything about Rome so confusing?

"After I lost my scholarship," Rome went on as if Tally had asked to know more, "I just wanted to get out from under… everything. I didn't have a lot of choices. I think I took the first exit door I could find. Then once I was there, I had to ask myself what I was really going to do." She shrugged and for the first time seemed a little self-conscious. "I wanted to make some kind of difference, so I trained to be a medic. Lucky for me, I was pretty good at it. I like what I do, despite how I got here. I guess you know how that feels."

Tally resisted the immediate sympathy she'd felt. She hadn't known about Rome losing her scholarship, although, really, was that such a terrible price to pay? No matter what Rome thought, their experiences were not the same. "I guess you were lucky, then."

Her sarcasm must have struck home. A spark of the Rome she remembered flared in Rome's eyes. Frustration, anger even.

Tally didn't flinch. She wasn't fifteen any longer.

"You know, Tally," Rome said in an unexpectedly gentle tone, "there was a lot more to that night than you think. And not everything happened the way it seemed."

"Yes, I know you said that. It was in the police reports. Sheila remembers that night differently."

"I know that too. And it was Justin's word against mine as to who was with her when…whatever happened happened." Rome leaned back as the server put their food down and removed the little flag from their table. "So I understand why you think what you do. Why a lot of people think what you do."

"I don't see any point in us discussing this," Tally said abruptly. She'd heard it all before—from her sister, from the lawyers who'd counseled her parents not to pursue charges with a weak case that would only bring unwanted media exposure— as if justice was secondary to the court of public opinion. She already knew all there was to know. She'd been there. She'd *seen*.

Tally stood and wrapped her food into a paper napkin. "I'm going to take this with me. I'm late already."

Rome nodded, her jaw tight.

Tally turned abruptly and nearly collided with a woman in scrubs carrying a coffee and Danish.

"Oh, sorry!" Tally said.

The woman laughed. "No problem. I was just trying for the last seat at the window." She laughed again, a full, warm sound. "Too late, anyhow."

Tally eased her way between the nearby tables on her way to the door, catching the sound of Rome offering the seat she'd just vacated to the other woman. She didn't look back as she left.

She hurried up the street toward the little converted schoolhouse she'd been lucky—as the Realtor had cheerfully advised her—to get after the previous residents had recently moved out. The caffeine helped clear some of the brain fog that seemed to descend every time she saw Rome—every time she struggled to fit the conflicting realities together, like forcing two mismatched puzzle pieces to somehow link. Turning through the white picket fence, a metaphor at the moment that struck her as sadly ironic, she reminded herself she didn't need to question what she already knew.

❖

"Thanks," Pam said as she settled into the seat Tally had just vacated. "I didn't expect it to be so crowded this early."

Rome glanced around the café. Nearly every seat was taken, at barely after six in the morning. The line for coffee and eats stretched to the side door. She hadn't noticed much of anything while Tally had been sitting across from her, except Tally. Spending any time with Tally ended up being a roller-coaster ride of surprisingly easy conversation that careened into the dark morass of old history from one moment to the next. Why she thought anything would change Tally's mind about the night Sheila had been drugged at the house party escaped her. The only one who could possibly do that was Sheila, and Sheila had no reason at all to change her story.

Rome made an effort to put the past aside—something she'd done successfully for most of the last decade, and what she definitely needed to do from then on—and smiled at Pam. "I haven't tried the coffee at the other place. I guess I probably should sometime. What do you think?"

Pam laughed. "Around here, people take sides on just about everything—more for the sake of having something to compete over than anything else. But yes, you should try the other brew at least once before deciding if you're a café or convenience store fan."

Rome liked Pam's easy humor, and the interested way Pam's gaze traveled over her face. Her appreciation was a welcome change to the cold disdain she received from Tally. "How about dinner choices—any recommendations there? I've mostly been grabbing something at the hospital after my shifts."

"Oh, don't tell me you're eating out of the vending room. There's a great tavern, Bottoms Up, that makes burgers to die for. Unless you're vegetarian? Then I recommend the pasta place two blocks down from here—Pellini's."

"Which camp are you in?" Rome asked.

"I'm flexible," Pam said, her tone subtly sultry. "It all depends on the company. What's your preference?"

"Ah." Rome grinned. The conversation was moving fast, but she got the general direction. At least she *thought* she did. Pam's dark eyes glinted with amusement. She was enjoying Rome's consternation. "Help me out here."

Pam laughed. "Oh, I don't think you really need any help. How about a burger after work one night soon?"

Okay, she'd been right about where they'd been headed. Rome hesitated. A date? Was she really looking for a date? Well, dinner, at least. With an attractive, interesting woman who seemed to enjoy her company. What else did she have to do besides spend the night doing what she'd done the night before—reading in the trailer? Dinner could just be dinner.

"Sure," Rome said. "This week sometime?"

"Tomorrow or the next night sounds great."

Right. Okay. Rome appreciated clear mission objectives. "Tomorrow then. Is six good? Too early?"

"Around here?" Pam snorted. "It's never too early for dinner. Six is fine. I'll meet you there—if something comes up and you can't make it, just text me."

Rome took out her phone. "What's your number? I'll text you mine."

When they'd exchanged numbers, Rome said, "I'm sorry, but I need to run. There's somewhere I need to stop before my shift."

"No problem," Pam said. "I'll see you in the ER."

"See you later." Rome hurried out. With luck, she'd just make it.

CHAPTER NINE

Tally expected to be the first one at the clinic, as she liked getting there an hour early. After her encounter with Rome at the café, all she'd wanted to do was get her nice, normal day started. Being around animals soothed her, and when they were ill or injured, taking care of them filled her with a deep sense of satisfaction and meaning. She'd showered and dressed quickly while steadfastly refusing to replay a single moment of the tumultuous interlude with Rome. Thinking about her had already occupied too much of her energy. To her surprise, Blake's shiny black pickup truck already occupied a space in the staff area of the lot. The vehicle wasn't new, but unlike many she passed on the highway or noticed in the village, his didn't have rusted-out spots or a montage of decals declaring for one side or the other of the gun debate or the political divide, or announcing a love for a particular sport, animal, or military affiliation.

She entered through the staff door at the rear of the building and followed the sound of laughter to the light slanting out into the hall through the open kennel doorway. Margie Rivers sat cross-legged on the floor with five of the puppies cradled in her lap. She looked up as Tally walked in and gave her a blazing smile. She was pretty in the way that many teenage girls were— smooth skin holding a hint of natural blush, bright blue eyes, and enviable lustrous shoulder-length hair. But for all of the teen's natural beauty, it was the animation in her eyes that really caught

Tally's attention. She radiated confidence, amusement, and curiosity. And something else Tally envied her for—simple joy.

"Hi," Tally said. "How are our boarders doing?"

Margie laughed. "They're all looking good."

Blake came in from the adjacent mudroom carrying a stainless steel tray that he wiped with a towel as he walked in. "Hi, Dr. Dewilde."

"It's Tally," she said for at least the tenth time. "Morning, Blake."

"So, Margie has been keeping them occupied while I clean the kennel."

"I won't make any comment on how you decided on the division of labor," Tally said, smiling back.

"Oh," Margie said, grinning at Blake, "that was easy. He already got to play with them yesterday."

Blake said, "They look better every day, but Bravo is very unhappy to still be isolated."

Tally knelt down in front of Bravo's cage, opened the door, and drew her out. The squirmy puppy made a quick study of Tally's face and apparently decided that she was not the enemy, and quieted as Tally petted her.

"Let's look at you first," Tally said, taking her over to the table. "I've got good news for you. Today is your last day of solitary."

A quick look in her eyes, a temperature check, and a brief feel of her skin tone indicated she was well hydrated, showed no signs of infection, and had no evidence of any incipient illness. The puppy made a break for the end of the table, clearly intent on joining her littermates on the floor. Tally made a grab for her, immediately thinking of Rome's instinctual dive to catch her that first day. Now, as the moment flashed through her memory, the image of Rome's intense expression and her voice shouting *cover* came back to her. What had Rome been thinking? That there was some imminent danger? And Rome just threw herself headlong into it without an instant's hesitation? The idea of Rome's automatic selflessness, and her total disregard for her own safety, left Tally uncomfortably distraught. She did not want to wonder, much less worry, about what had instilled that kind of reaction. She held the puppy up to eye level. "No more escape attempts. Wasn't going airborne once enough for you?"

The puppy tried to lick her nose, and Tally laughed. "Oh, we should have named you Trouble."

"I can put her back. If you want," Blake said. "Can she go in with the others now?"

"One more day, just to be on the safe side," Tally said, handing Bravo back to Blake. "She looks good, though."

"The rest of them seem to be doing really well too," he said.

"Who's next?" Margie asked.

"Let's have the brown and white one next. The one with the floppy ear—Hood."

"Oh, good name," Margie said. "Did you name them all?"

"No, I..." Tally paused. Was Rome going to occupy every one of her thoughts for the rest of the morning? No. She was not. "Ah, they're just temporary names."

"Good ones." Margie handed over the puppy.

Tally quickly worked her way through the other five, finding them all looking much improved over the day before.

She was just finishing the last puppy's exam when a familiar voice called, "Am I too late for the party?"

Tally slipped the stethoscope from her ears and tucked it into the side pocket of her joggers, gazing at Rome across the table, the squirming puppy between them. "Do you always show up places before they are actually open for business?"

Rome grinned, clearly unconcerned. "Only when the door's open and I've got an extra half an hour before I need to be at work."

She'd strolled in as if she owned the place, which was so like her, and so not the case. Annoyed, Tally still couldn't think of a good reason to protest.

"I see you've got some of them out of the kennels. Can I see Bravo?"

"Strictly speaking," she said tightly, "as I explained every other time you've asked, no."

Tally pointedly ignored the stares from Blake and Margie. She would not think about providing entertainment for the local teenagers at the moment, even if she couldn't pretend the situation wasn't just the slightest bit entertaining. Rome at least seemed to be enjoying being a nuisance, as if she knew her showing up here at odd hours was annoying and not caring even a little bit.

"Is she sick?" Roman asked with a note of real concern in her voice, the humor leaving her eyes.

Now annoyed with herself for verging on churlish, not to mention nearly unprofessional, Tally sighed and surrendered. "No. She looks absolutely fine. Five minutes' visitation. And I mean that. We have work to do here and you're...out of order."

Rome grinned, and damn her, the grin was so genuine, so filled with pleasure, Tally felt an odd twist in her chest. She recognized that zing as attraction, even though the reaction was so rare as to have become a distant memory. Oh no. Oh, no no no.

"Like ICU visiting hours. Every five minutes on the hour?" Rome stepped over to the table opposite Tally, all that separated them the steel surface that glinted in the bright light from the big overhead lamps. So close, Tally could almost count the tiny green flecks in Rome's eyes. Not just blue, but blue like the ocean when the sunlight picked up the aquamarine reflections from beneath the surface and made them shimmer.

"You can't possibly have the kind of schedule to make that possible."

"You're right about that," Rome said, "but I can come back tonight."

Blake and Margie had gotten very quiet, and out of the corner of her eye, Tally caught their avid expressions. Really. Nothing of interest was going on here. Abruptly, she turned away and said to Blake, "Would you get Bravo, so Roman can see her for a few minutes."

"Sure," Blake said.

"Thanks," Rome said.

Margie said, "I can put that one back if you want, Dr. Dewilde." She nodded to Rome. "Hi, I'm Margie Rivers."

"Hi," Rome said. "I'm Rome Ashcroft. New in town. I work at the Rivers. I guess you're related?"

Margie grinned. "You could say. Flann, Carson, and Harper are my sisters."

Blake handed Bravo to Rome and added, "And Flann is married to my mom. But you know that." He flushed. "Very recently married—I mean, Margie and I aren't related, that way. In any way."

"Small towns, huh? Weird." Rome laughed.

Tally handed Margie the last puppy. "Here you go. Thanks."

Margie cradled the puppy and said to Rome, "We've got six of us lined up for rotation to look after these guys out at the trailer."

Rome blinked. "Six already?"

Margie nodded. "It wasn't any trouble."

Rome nestled Bravo against her shoulder, and the puppy, her eyes still alert and checking everyone out, settled, as if that was the place she'd been trying to get to all along. Rome absently scratched behind her ears as Margie explained about her friends and their plans to create a text tree for emergency coverage.

"We met Taylor at the café this morning," Rome said. "Good work getting it all together. Thanks."

Margie shrugged. "Everybody loves puppies."

"Unfortunately, that's not always true," Rome said.

Margie's expression darkened. "Yeah, I know."

"So are the two of you planning on vet school?" Rome asked, gently brushing Bravo's face away as the puppy tried to chew on her earlobe. "Cut that out, you little bugger."

"I am," Blake said.

"I'm for med school," Margie said.

Rome shrugged. "Same diff, pretty much."

Blake said, "That's about what Flann said!"

Margie and Blake glanced at each other and grinned, the kind of looks that said *parents, go figure.*

Tally appreciated their amusement and envied the way they obviously valued their families. How different that was from the world where she'd grown up, where parents, and sometimes siblings, wielded their power to control everyone within their sphere. She didn't really know what Blake's and Margie's lives were like, but she could see they were confident, intelligent, and just...nice. The way they took care of the animals told her a lot of what she needed to know.

The same thing could be said of Rome, as Tally watched the casual comfort she offered the scared little animal. Her hand curved protectively over the puppy's back as it rested on her shoulder. Bravo's eyes had closed, and she slept, apparently safe and secure. Tally resisted giving Rome the credit that perhaps she would have given to anyone else, but then Rome wasn't anyone else. She was someone who had hurt her sister and changed her life, perhaps irrevocably. That was every bit as true, truer perhaps, than the compassion and affection she showed now for a helpless, homeless animal.

"Time's up. Visiting hours are over," Tally said.

"Thank you for saving these puppies," Margie said, as she reached out for Bravo.

Rome swallowed. She'd been thanked by hundreds of earnest strangers for her service, service she had been grateful to be able to provide. She'd been thanked by soldiers in the midst of battle for not leaving them behind, as if she'd be able to live with herself if she'd abandoned them. She couldn't leave anyone— anything—alone and helpless, could she? "I was there."

Tally said, "I'll leave you to finish up. Margie, will you get Bravo back in the kennel?"

"Sure," Margie said.

"Assuming I don't find a placement for them today, tomorrow on the outside," Tally said to Rome, "we'll move them over to the boarding kennel tomorrow. I still might be able to find a few places here and there to place them."

"Please don't split them up. You call me," Rome said. "Call me before you do that. I'll come get them."

"You can text me or Margie," Blake said quickly. "We'll make sure someone is at your place to help out tomorrow night. Just in case."

"You're sure about this?" Tally asked. "You two must have a lot going on at school."

Margie said, "Shouldn't be a problem. We're all together for SAT prep after practice."

Rome said, "I appreciate it. Thanks."

"Then it seems to be settled." Tally said to Rome, "You might want to think about getting some supplies on hand, just in case."

"Supplies. Right. I'm on it."

As Tally walked out, she heard Rome say, "So, about these supplies. I need a list."

She smiled despite herself.

CHAPTER TEN

Pam tapped Rome on the shoulder as she sat at the central station completing her chart work at the end of her shift. "The medical consultant is down here to see Mr. Thompson. I thought you might want to talk to them."

"Oh, thanks," Rome said, closing the file of a thirty-year-old carpenter with a hand infection. She'd started him on antibiotics after extracting a half-inch splinter from his palm that he'd told her he'd been sure would just work its way out. She swiveled on the stool to look up at Pam. "Did we get the results of the CAT scan yet?"

"They just came in. You ought to have the digitals on your tablet about now. I put the films by the rack next to the cubicle. I think Dr. Rivers has them now."

Rome frowned. "Dr. Rivers? We didn't ask for surgery."

Pam grinned. "As in Harper Rivers?"

Rome stood up. "The chief of medicine is down here doing a consult?"

"I know, strange, isn't it? But that's how things go around here."

"Right." That was akin to the brigade commander showing up for a fireteam maneuver. Rome shook her head. Not hers to reason why. "Well, I guess I better get to it, then."

Pam laughed. "Don't worry, Harper is the mild-mannered one."

"I'll bet." Rome doubted any chief of service got to that position without being plenty tough, Rivers or no Rivers. She hurried down to cubicle ten, brushed the curtain aside, and stepped inside.

"Hi, Mr. Thompson," she said to her patient, a grizzled sixty-five-year-old man whose sallow features and sagging muscles indicated he had been much stronger at one point in his life. He'd come in that morning, after his wife insisted, complaining of progressive weakness and shortness of breath. His answer was a weary nod as she turned to the other occupant of the cubicle.

She'd been trying to recall the Rivers family rundown Brody had given her when they'd first talked about her joining the staff. Brody had all the details, since she'd casually admitted she'd lived with the family for half her youth. That little fact had been a surprise to Rome, but then, Brody knew next to nothing about her past either. Edward, the father, was still chief of staff, and Harper the heir apparent. The next in line, Flann, was chief of surgery, and a third sister—Carter, Carson?—was in administration. Oh, and not to forget, Harper's wife Presley happened to be the hospital CEO, while Flann was married to the ER chief, Abby Remy.

None of which explained why Harper Rivers was performing the duties of a first-year medical resident. "Dr. Rivers, I'm Roman Ashcroft, a PA. I've been looking after Mr. Thompson here."

No doubt as to the identity of Harper Rivers. She looked a lot like Flann, almost the same age, but her eyes were blue, not brown, and her hair dark brown instead of sandy blond. The same sturdy jaw and strong features, though. Her smile blazed like Flann's too as she held out her hand.

"Good to meet you," Harper said. "Brody told us that you were coming. That's terrific. How's it going?"

"Great, thanks."

Harper rested a hand lightly on Mr. Thompson's shoulder. "Mr. Thompson tells me he's feeling a little bit better since you ordered some medicine for him."

"Do you feel like your breathing is easier?" Rome asked, pulling her stethoscope from her back pocket.

An oxygen catheter that ran from a valve on the wall behind the stretcher sat on his upper lip, and he wheezed a little as he pulled in air to answer. "That tight feeling is easing up some. Won't be running any races right away."

"How about I take a listen to you." Rome listened over several areas of his chest for a minute or so and glanced at the chief. "Clearing up a little, but still has a ways to go."

"Yes, I agree. So I think," Harper said, addressing the patient, "that you had better stay with us for a day or so while we adjust your medication and get your breathing under control."

Mr. Thompson grimaced but shook his head as if he'd known what was coming. "Okay, Doc. If you think I ought to."

"I think that'll be a good idea."

Harper tilted her chin toward the hall, and Rome followed her out. At a distance where their voices couldn't be overheard, Harper said, "The diuretics are helping, but his PO2 is in borderline intubation range. What do you think?"

"His congestive heart failure is pretty advanced." Rome pulled his chest CT up on her tablet and angled it toward Harper. "His heart's significantly enlarged, and there's a lot of fluid buildup in both lungs. I'm not entirely certain there's not a pulmonary lesion hiding somewhere in there. I think he needs to be in step-down for monitoring and possibly ICU transfer if his gases worsen."

Harper sighed. "He's probably not a candidate for a transplant, and with that degree of cardiac compromise he's going to be hard to manage medically. I'll give his primary a call and let them know we're keeping him. Then we'll get Irene Zelinsky from cardiology to see him."

"I can take care of all that," Rome said quickly. Really, the chief of medicine didn't need to be doing the scut work.

"I don't mind. It makes me feel useful."

Rome laughed. "Somehow I doubt that's a problem."

"All right, I'll leave it to you." Harper paused. "Listen, when you finish up here, why don't you come on over to Bottoms Up. A few of us are getting together for burgers and brew. Brody will be there, and some of the other family. It's my sister's birthday."

"Oh, I don't want to intrude."

Harper shook her head. "Not possible. You're a good friend of Brody's, which makes you a friend of the family. It's a spur-of-the-moment thing—nothing fancy, and you have to eat, right?"

Rome laughed. "Well, then yes, I'd be happy to."

"Excellent. See you around six."

Rome hesitated, calculating the time. Forty-five minutes, and she still had calls to make and to see that Mr. Thompson got transferred upstairs. She wouldn't have time to get out to see the puppies. There was nothing she could do about them tonight, but she always felt better after seeing them, safe and sound and just being carefree puppies. She wanted to see Tally again too, and missing that chance bothered her even more. Despite Tally's seeming displeasure every time she showed up out there unannounced, Rome sensed the barest glimmer of the ice starting to thaw. Tally actually talked to her now and then, when she apparently forgot that she disliked Rome. Even though she knew better, Rome was encouraged. Tally was a link to her past—a connection that she never knew she wanted. And more, Tally was becoming a presence in her thoughts every day.

Hastily she said, "Thanks. I'll be there."

She'd miss seeing Tally, who would not, she was certain, miss her.

❖

Tally gave the ragdoll kitten her scheduled shots, scratched behind its ears, and was happy to elicit a purr.

"There you go, Dumpling," she said and passed Dumpling back to her anxious owner. "She's fine, a real trouper."

The elderly woman cradled the kitten to her chest. "She's so little. You're sure she's not underweight?"

"No, she's absolutely perfect. Let's go over what you're feeding her again, but I think she's right on schedule." After she assured the new owner that everything was in order, Tally made a quick note of the kitten's weight and the shots that had been given and said, "Eight weeks for the next round of vaccinations. I'll see you then, but if you have any concerns before then, just call. All right?"

"Yes, I will. I never wanted an animal, you know. So much trouble—but my son insisted I needed the company." She slipped the kitten into a little pouch on the front of her hand-knitted sweater that she had undoubtedly made for just that purpose. The kitten peeked out, completely at home. "I suppose he might have been right. We'll be here."

Tally walked with her out to the front desk and asked Rita, "Is that it, then?"

"Everyone's done," Rita said. "Val just texted. She's on her way back too."

"Oh, good. I'll wait, then."

Tally checked her watch. Five fifteen. If Rome was coming, she'd be there soon. When she missed a morning visit, she invariably came in the evening. Not that it mattered, of course. Margie was in the back doing the nightly feeding. She could see to Rome. If Rome came at all. Rome probably realized she had better things to do than visit a litter of strays. Whatever, she wouldn't need to see her at all. When the door opened at just past five thirty, she wasn't the least bit disappointed to see Val walk in and not Rome. Not at all. By then, she was fairly certain Rome wasn't coming, so she ought to be glad. She *was* glad. Although the odd sensation of regret was unmistakable. And where could that possibly have come from?

Walking to meet Val, she said, "Hi. How did everything go today?"

Val shucked her barn coat onto a wall rack and eased her shoulders. "Good, although I think every single animal I saw today leaned on me. I feel like I've been carrying a Volkswagen around on my back. How was your day?"

"Great. The post-ops all went home on time—no issues. And the clinic cases were all routine. I think I might have gotten the better part of this deal," Tally said lightly. "I *am* capable of doing farm call alone, by the way."

Val grinned. "Be careful what you wish for. And you will, not to worry. I wanted to give you a chance to get settled into the routine here first. And the new place to live—all a lot to get used to."

Tally laughed. "Somehow I expected life here to be…quiet. Fewer people, and all that. Every time I walk into the café for coffee in the morning, I feel liked I've walked into a barista bar in Manhattan—although a much friendlier one."

"Our population is smaller, but we make up for it by being incurably sociable." Val grinned.

Tally had a fleeting memory of how easily she'd fallen into conversing with Rome the day she'd run into her in the café, the most unnatural thing she could have imagined. And how… natural it had seemed. Until she'd remembered. She sighed and brought herself back to the safe and familiar. "I'm going to ride along tomorrow, right? So I can meet some more of the farm clients."

"Yep. That's the plan. I—hold on…" Val held up a finger as she answered her phone. "Hey you. No, I just got in…Actually, it sounds great…I will. I'll see you soon." She put her phone back in her pocket and said, "That was Brody. A few people are getting together at the local tavern. Why don't you come with me."

"Oh, I don't know." Tally had to resist physically backpedaling. She was tired, in a good way, but mostly she wasn't sure she had the energy to socialize. She much preferred talking to animals. "I mean, I don't know anyone."

"Well, that's the general idea," Val said, pulling her barn coat off the peg on the wall. "Now you will. You know where it is, right? Bottoms Up?"

"I think so. The village isn't very big. Down Main a few blocks from the café?"

"That's the place. Just follow me."

Tally couldn't think of a reasonable way to say no. Besides, she didn't have anything else to do, and meeting some of the people in town would probably be a good thing. Most of them would probably be clients sooner or later, and refusing would just seem rude.

"All right then. Yes, that would be great. Oh, but shouldn't I stop home to change?"

Val pointed to her work pants, boots, and long-sleeve Henley top. "I'm not changing, so you are going to look fabulous, not that you don't anyway."

Tally laughed. "Good save, Dr. Valentine."

"Well, I'm a little rusty, but I haven't lost all my social graces. You're great as you are."

"This is the first time I'm going out in public," Tally protested. She didn't expect to meet anyone she needed—or wanted—to impress but didn't intend to meet Val's friends and family covered with a variety of animal hair and quite possibly drool. "Give me five minutes at my place. I promise, I'll be fast."

Val laughed. "Believe me, you don't need to dress to impress this crowd, but okay. I get it. We'll stop at your place. You can leave your car there. I'll drive us down. That will be simpler."

"Great." Tally knew from experience that looking like you had everything under control was a good way to hide a multitude of uncertainties. And so far, nothing—and no one—she'd encountered since arriving had been what she'd expected.

❖

As she'd expected, Rome ended up in the midst of the scions of the Rivers family—Harper and her wife Presley; Flann and Abby; the third Rivers sister, Carson, and her husband Bill; Brody; and family friends Glenn Archer and her partner Mari. Someone had pushed a couple of tables together, and three pitchers of draft beer sat at intervals down the center along with several big platters of wings. Within minutes of Brody introducing her, she'd been absorbed into the group. If she didn't know better, she'd think she was in some watering hole off-base with a bunch of other boots. Conversations rolled easily from local news to hospital anecdotes to plans for the upcoming weekend. Rome didn't need to do anything except lean back and relax for the first time in a very long time. She was halfway through her first beer when a vibration in the air brought her to alert, and Brody, sitting next to her, shot to her feet, announcing cheerfully, "Good. Now everyone's here."

Rome swiveled in her chair and immediately tensed. Tally and Syd Valentine threaded their way toward them through the tables grouped in front of the bar. She hadn't expected to see Tally, and she definitely hadn't expected the twisting pulse of anticipation that hit her fast in the midsection. Tally looked great as usual in a pale yellow button-up shirt tucked loosely into slim jeans and her hair pulled back in a wide gold clasp. Rome hadn't recognized Tally when she'd first seen her at the clinic, but she would never mistake any other woman for her now. She made the simple look elegant.

Val went directly to Brody and kissed her. "Hi, babe."

"Hi." Brody grinned as if she'd just gotten the world's best present. She motioned to a chair on her other side. "Saved you a seat."

Before anyone could shuffle chairs, Rome slid down one place to make space for Tally in the single remaining empty seat beside her. "Here you go."

"Thank you." Tally sat, careful not to touch her as she did.

After Val introduced Tally to the rest of the group and the

conversations started up again, Rome leaned closer but kept space between them. "Couldn't say no?"

Tally's eyes widened, and she suppressed a grin. "How did you know?"

"It's contagious. I caught it too."

Tally laughed. The sound, so rare, was light and airy, like music drifting on a warm summer breeze. Rome's breath caught. She'd give a lot to hear that laughter on a regular basis. As if realizing who she was talking to, Tally quickly looked away, and the music faded along with Rome's pleasure.

"Any further word on placing the puppies?" Rome said into their little cocoon of silence.

"Nothing definitive," Tally said quietly. "I have one last potential place for a group placement that I should hear from sometime tomorrow."

"I don't understand how this can happen," Rome said. "I mean, I know there are lots of homeless animals, but I'm not sure why we're not equipped to take care of them. Other countries have laws to provide for animal welfare."

Tally huffed. "Quite a few countries place more value on humanitarian things than we do, although in fairness, we're far from the worst. But it costs money, and that means people have to be willing to pay for it. That means taxes."

Rome blew out a breath. "I guess everything comes down to that, doesn't it—what people value the most. Even lives."

Tally looked surprised, maybe even interested. That was new. So was the pulse of heat it stirred in Rome's midsection.

"Unfortunately, yes." Tally took a breath. "If more people took half the interest you did, we wouldn't have this problem."

"I didn't really have any choice," Rome said. "They were there, and so was I. What else could I do?"

"Any number of things," Tally said with a bitter laugh. "You could've left them. You could've dropped them off anonymously at our door and driven away. I've certainly seen that plenty of times. You definitely didn't have to offer to take care of them."

Rome shook her head. "Not viable options. Leaving them wasn't even a possibility, and dropping them on your doorstep would just have been…cowardly."

"Cowardly," Tally said. "I would've said irresponsible, but I wouldn't have thought of cowardly."

"Aren't they part of the same thing? Refusing to take responsibility is cowardice at its worst."

"I wouldn't expect to hear that from you," Tally said flatly.

The barb struck hard, but Rome didn't flinch. "I know."

Tally flushed and took a quick breath. "I'm sorry. You've gone above and beyond being responsible for these puppies, and I'm…thankful. Please accept my apologies."

"Not necessary," Rome said easily. Tally had reasons not to trust her—reasons Rome knew were false, but nothing she could say would alter what Tally believed. Constantly reopening old wounds helped neither of them.

"I know I haven't been very supportive of your plan for fostering them," Tally said, as if wanting to stay in the present as well, "but I am responsible for their welfare too."

Rome nodded. "So…might we have a truce while we take care of our shared responsibilities?"

Tally looked up as Val leaned over and put a frothing mug of beer in front of her. "I got one for you. I hope draft is okay."

"Oh, thank you," Tally said. "That's perfect."

Val glanced at Rome. "Hi. Getting ready for the new room-mates?"

"Working on it. I have a list of supplies to get on my way home tonight."

"If you're stopping at the hardware store, they close at seven," Brody put in.

Rome glanced at her watch. "Thanks. I've got a few minutes yet."

Tally sipped her beer. "Let's see this list."

Rome handed her a handwritten list on the clinic stationery.

"Which one of them did this?" Tally asked as she reviewed it.

"Margie."

"Looks good." She handed it back to Rome and caught her gaze. "You're really set on this, aren't you."

"I wouldn't have offered if I hadn't intended to follow through."

Tally sighed. "Then we have a temporary…alliance. I'll go with you to get these things."

"You just got here," Rome said, although she wasn't really trying to dissuade her. Spending a little more time with Tally beat anything else she could imagine doing.

"My responsibility too, remember? And you'll have an easier time finding some of these things with a little help." She leaned closer, her thigh brushing Rome's. "Besides, I really don't much like beer."

CHAPTER ELEVEN

The hardware store is a couple of blocks down," Rome said as she and Tally left the bar. "Why don't I drive us down, and we can load the stuff up. Then I'll drop you back here to pick up your car. More efficient that way."

"Oh damn," Tally muttered.

"What?" Rome asked.

"Val brought me over. I don't actually have my car." She probably should have thought of that earlier when she'd agreed to come out to the tavern. She was never one for social gatherings and always planned a way for an early exit. She hadn't really minded the idea of getting to meet more of the Rivers clan, but she wasn't one for sitting around chatting, even with people she knew really well. Somehow solitude had become her default from adolescence. She had friends, of course, because social activities were requirements at school and in her mother's expansive sphere of acquaintances, but she'd become expert at conjuring excuses to avoid them when she could. After Sheila's *accident*, as they'd come to call it, she'd been even more wary of groups where someone could always be counted on to bring it up in some way. College had been a bit of a sanctuary, but this move was the true break in the trail of gossip that seemed to follow her.

"Well, it doesn't matter," Tally said briskly. "I'll walk back here when we're done and wait for Val."

"She could be gone by then—or you'd be stuck waiting."

Rome hit the alert for her car and the lights flashed. "If you really want to come back and hang out here, I'll bring you back. But I can just as easily drive you home."

"I think I'm done socializing for the night, so yes, thanks, I'll take you up on a ride."

"I'd say we're making progress, then," Rome said. "You didn't even argue about it."

Tally halted. "I don't argue."

Rome grinned. "Right, and you don't get kerfuffled either."

"I don't. Except when you're around."

"Ah…so I'm the instigator."

Fortunately the parking lot wasn't lit well enough for Rome to tell she was blushing. Or that her immediate thought had been that Rome stirred up a lot more than the urge to resist her every suggestion and perhaps make her a little…kerfuffled. And she *really* didn't want Rome to have the slightest inkling of the way her heart raced just a little whenever they were alone like this. Just two people in the moment, with no past and no plans. Refusing to reveal feelings she had no control over and didn't want to think about, Tally went on the offense and pointed to the Porsche. "Can you actually get anything bigger than a loaf of bread in there anywhere?"

Rome laughed. "If I'm very efficient, I can get all my worldly goods in there." She shrugged. "Although they'd fit in that duffel bag with all six of the puppies."

Tally paused. "That's not really true, is it?"

The look Rome gave her was cautious, something she wasn't used to from her. Uh-oh. She'd asked a personal question. Why had she done that? Everything would be so much simpler if she could just draw a stark line in the sand where getting to know Rome in any way was on the far side of that line and she didn't cross it. Unfortunately, her line wiggled hither and yon, and she kept stepping over it to find out more. She really needed to stop doing that.

"You travel pretty light in the military," Rome said. "Your

gear, your personal kit—which doesn't amount to much more than a toothbrush—and everything else is provided."

"Yes, but you're not in the military anymore."

Rome laughed, an interesting laugh that sounded half self-deprecating and half amused. "Technically that's true, but my mindset is still pretty much there. Travel light, don't get attached, don't plan beyond the moment."

"And yet here you are." Tally gestured toward the tavern. "Look at where we just came from. I can practically see the roots stretching out the door and headed this way. In the hospital, it can't be any different. Not with the history it has and how many of the townspeople work there." She huffed and ran a hand through her hair. "God, look at the café. Wasn't half the village there and watching us the day we had breakfast?"

"You felt that way too, huh?" Rome said as she walked around and opened the passenger side door. "I didn't actually notice until you were leaving that the entire room was full and we were getting a fair amount of attention. And we only *almost* had breakfast."

"Yes, well," Tally said, eager to move away from the uncomfortable conversation they'd been having that morning, "I'm sure being new in town is worthy of discussion, and it is natural for people to be curious."

"Do you mind the idea of putting down roots?" Rome slid in behind the wheel, and Tally settled into the passenger side and buckled in. "Or…are you planning on this job being a temporary thing?"

Tally hesitated. Now the tables had turned and Rome was asking personal questions. How that had happened she couldn't begin to guess. She should just shrug it off with some vague reply and stay far on the safe side of the line. Instead she said, "I've only been here a couple of weeks, and maybe Val won't want me to stay on." She took a deep breath. "But I hope she does. Somehow this place feels…right."

"Strange," Rome murmured, "you feel it too." She glanced

at Tally. "You know, I've been looking for a place to settle my whole life, I guess. When I got this job, I hoped this would be it. I still do."

Tally caught the reference that Rome carefully didn't make. The incident...the *accident*...they didn't talk about. The one that had cost Rome her scholarship, apparently her place at the Ivy League school, and—if Tally could read between the lines, and she thought she could—Rome's relationship with her family too.

"Why didn't you stay in the military? Isn't that another kind of family?"

Rome sat with her hands curled lightly around the steering wheel, looking pensive and, outlined in moonlight, impossibly handsome. The line of her jaw angled strongly down from her arched cheekbone to a broad strong chin. A classic profile. Tally had never really been drawn to overly attractive people, who in her circle tended to be overly aware of it and often insufferably egotistical. She had automatically put Rome in that category, but now she wasn't quite so sure. Rome gave the oddest impression of not actually being very aware of herself at all. At least not what made her attractive.

And there it was again, the unmistakable twist of attraction. As if her body somehow short-circuited her brain, making her forget the many reasons why attraction was absolutely impossible. The biggest one, Rome was at the center of an event she was mentally and emotionally exhausted from revisiting, a habit that had been with her for a decade, like the unconscious worrying of a hangnail until she drew blood.

"The service is a family for sure," Rome said at last, "in the sense that your ties are closer to the soldiers in your unit than even to your family at the time. The world becomes just the stretch of safe ground outside your tent to the wire, metaphorically most of the time, that marks the danger zone, the boundary of your universe. Your unit becomes the brothers and sisters who you'd die for. And yet, I'm not sure any of us really knew each other, not completely." She shrugged. "In a way, that was probably the way most of us preferred it. We were, for all intents and purposes, no one beyond fellow soldiers."

"That sounds oddly dehumanizing as well as incredibly... connected. What a contradiction," Tally murmured.

"It didn't mean we didn't care if we lost someone, because everyone felt the loss like a part of the body," Rome said. "But we also were prepared for that to happen, as if the perpetual amputation was expected."

"You know, that sounds horrible."

"I'm sorry. This is a weird conversation." Rome blew out a breath. "I think we should stick to puppies."

"There's no need to be sorry for being who you had to be to survive and to help others do the same." Tally impulsively squeezed Rome's forearm. When Rome tensed, she pulled her hand back and said lightly, "Now, puppies are certainly the total opposite of what you've been describing. They indiscriminately love and trust you from the first moment they see you. They place their life in your hands and are happy to do it. And for them, you're the entire world."

"Okay, maybe I need to rethink puppies," Rome said, her shoulders relaxing. "That sounds like parenthood times six."

"Well, it is, in a way. And you certainly can reconsider. Actually, I think you should."

"I wasn't serious about minding," Rome said, turning in the seat to face her.

The coupe was very small inside, and only the narrow console between the seats separated their bodies. When Rome stretched out her arm across the back of the seats, her fingertips almost touched Tally's shoulder. The few millimeters of air that separated them practically vibrated. Tally resisted hunching forward. Really, she did *not* intend to telegraph how acutely aware she was of Rome's body.

Rome added, "I'm completely serious, and I'm totally willing to do whatever it takes to look after them."

Tally shook her head. "Why? I just don't quite get why."

"Because I found them. Because I picked them up and brought them to you. That makes them mine until they're safe and secure, and they're not yet."

"You're still living the way you were living in the military," Tally murmured, suddenly understanding why Rome threw herself forward without thought to catch that puppy. If that had been a grenade threatening her fellow soldiers, she would've done the same. The idea was frightening, horrifying, and deeply compelling. "All right then. If you intend to go forward and we have no alternatives, which I will know first thing tomorrow, then you need a crash course in puppy fostering."

Rome grinned, and the shadows that hadn't been from the moonlight, but from something far less ethereal, disappeared from her face. Tally caught her lip between her teeth, determined not to let her feelings show. The last thing in the world she wanted to acknowledge, or certainly to have recognized, was the simmering compulsion to reach out and touch her. To just trace her finger along that jawline and brush her thumb against the corner of that wide, beautiful mouth.

"We better get to it before the place closes," Rome said, her voice oddly husky.

"Yes," Tally said. She really needed to get out of the car and out of range of whatever Rome projected that kept her on edge, physically and emotionally. "That's a very good idea."

❖

"So, what do you think of this?" Rome said, coming around the end of the aisle where Tally studied the puppy food stacked on three-tiered metal shelves below a sign helpfully labeled *Dogs*.

She glanced at Rome and gave an exasperated sigh, perhaps for the tenth time. "They don't need tennis balls yet. The balls are bigger than their entire heads."

Undeterred, Rome placed them in the basket along with

half a dozen squeaky toys that resembled flattened animals, which Rome had cheerfully dubbed roadkill. "They'll grow. And they're going to be bored hanging around all day. They have to have something to do."

"They're puppies," Tally pointed out, for perhaps the fiftieth time. "They sleep all day."

"Still, they need something to keep them interested besides chewing up the furniture or whatever."

"What I suggest, initially, is a big crate for them to sleep in that you can put inside a penned-off area. It's good to get them used to being in a crate for when they're larger."

"Can't they just be loose when they get bigger?"

"That depends on whether you want your entire house destroyed when you're not there."

Rome grimaced. "That would be a problem, because I don't have a house. I'm living in Brody's trailer."

Tally cocked her head. "A trailer? Like something you hitch to the back of your car?"

"Well, not *my* car," Rome said, clearly aghast. "It's not that kind of trailer. It's, you know, a mobile home that you can take around the country. Brody brought it with her when she moved here and lived in it before she and Val got together."

"And this trailer has a yard? Were you making that up?"

"Fabricating, you mean?" Rome pressed a hand dramatically to her chest, and Tally laughed. "No. The lot the trailer is on has the yard, and yes, it's fenced. Brody did that so Honcho could be outside when she was at work."

"Oh, of course. She moved here with Honcho. What a gorgeous dog."

"She is. And unbelievably brave." A shadow passed over Rome's face. "She suffered for what she had to do over there. But she seems much better now."

"You love her."

Rome shrugged. "Everyone who knew her loved her. She would have died for any of us."

Tally's heart clenched. She was certain Rome would've done the same. She swallowed the sudden swell of emotion in her throat. For what the dog went through, of course. "She seems to be very content with her new life."

"She's found a new family to take care of. And at least she's not looking for bombs anymore."

"I'm sorry," Tally said.

Rome's brows drew down. "What are you sorry for?"

"What you experienced."

"I appreciate that, but it's okay. I can't say that I would ever want to do it again, but I would if I was needed. And I think the time I spent there, the people I spent it with, helped me find... what I needed to find." She wasn't going to say *herself*, because she didn't think that would make any sense to anyone but her. Or maybe someone else who'd gone through the same thing. "And besides, I learned to do what I do, so I've got no regrets."

Tally let it go. Rome had said all she'd wanted to say, or needed to say, and probing for more would very likely be probing a wound. She had no desire to do that. In a lighter tone, she gestured to the overladen cart. "This is very likely to teach you a little bit more about who you are."

"Like what?" Rome said in the same light tone as they pushed the cart toward the checkout counter.

"Infinite patience, for starters."

"Well, I could probably use that," Rome said.

"Who couldn't," Tally muttered, and Rome laughed. The sound eased her worry that they'd treaded too close to memories Rome didn't want to revisit.

"So you think we got everything?" Rome said as they pushed up to the counter and began to unload.

"We've got more than enough." Tally glanced at the cashier. "Are these items returnable if necessary?"

"Sure," the ruddy-faced man in the red and black checkered shirt and dark green work pants said as he began to scan items. "Don't have the dog yet?"

"Oh, I got them," Rome said. "And I won't be returning any-thing."

"Looks like you got a houseful."

Rome laughed. "Six of them."

He paused, studied her, and nodded as if a question had been asked and answered. "You must be the new doc who found the puppies."

"PA," Rome said automatically. "I guess you heard, huh?"

"My nephew Tim is going to be helping out with them." He shook his head and scowled. "Hell of a thing, treating animals that way."

"Tim Brown, right?" Rome said, remembering the names on Blake's list of volunteers.

The man smiled, his eyes warm and friendly. "That's the one. My sister Katie's boy."

"I'm very grateful for the help," Rome said. "I'm sure I'm going to need it."

"I'm Ed Wayne, but go by Scooch," he said, holding out his hand. "Good to meet you."

"Rome Ashcroft," Rome said, "and this is Dr. Tally Dewilde."

"Oh, you're the new vet, right?"

Tally smiled and shook his hand as well. "That's me."

"Heard you took care of Marco Polo right smartly last week."

"Ah…" Tally quickly considered patient confidentiality and then realized he already knew the story. "I did. He's a scrapper."

"He thinks so," Scooch said and laughed. "You want some help taking this out to the car?"

Rome surveyed the packages. "I can get it there, but I don't know if I can get it in."

"That your 911 out there?"

"Yep."

"Pretty machine that. I bet it's got some go in it."

"Always got plenty of that," Rome said.

"I can deliver this stuff tomorrow morning. If you want."

"I appreciate it," Rome said, "but I'm pretty good at fitting things in. I think we're good."

"Well, good luck with those puppies," Scooch said as they turned to go.

"Thanks," Rome said.

"Good night," Tally called out as they left. Once outside, she said, "Does it feel weird to you?"

"Which of the many weird things?" Rome asked, rearranging items to fit into the minuscule trunk.

Tally laughed. "The fact that people know everything you've done practically before you did it?"

"Surprised me at first," Rome said. "I mean, I'm used to not having much personal space or personal privacy, but you know, I guess the community is like a big beehive. Information moves fast."

"Apparently, and we're part of it now."

"I guess we are." Rome glanced at Tally. They might be a lot more connected than Tally realized. They shared a past. Even if it was one both wished had been different.

"It will take some getting used to," Tally said as she buckled in. "Being so…visible."

"Not what you were hoping for?" Rome asked as she started the engine.

"I didn't know what I was hoping for," Tally said quietly, "other than to get away."

"From what?" Rome asked just as quietly.

Tally met her gaze, her smile both whimsical and sad. "Some of the same things as you. A disappointed mother that still insisted on trying to change me. The feeling I was just a placeholder rather than a person." She grimaced. "Wow, that sounds really self-indulgent and kind of pathetic now that I say it out loud."

"Not really," Rome said. "We all had roles to play, even when we didn't know it. I guess we just sucked at it. Doesn't mean it wasn't hard to live through."

"Why aren't you bitter?" Tally asked.

"I was. Now I don't have the energy for it. Now I just want a life."

"Such a simple thing to want," Tally murmured. "And so hard to recognize."

Rome brushed her fingers over Tally's shoulder. "Maybe just take it as it comes."

"Right." Tally let out a breath and laughed. "Spontaneity is so not my thing."

"Oh, I don't know. You showed up at Bottoms Up, a place I will wager you never dreamed of going before tonight."

Tally nodded and Rome's fingers lightly brushed her cheek as she drew her hand away. Her heart jumped, and a shiver ran down her spine. From an absolutely innocent and meaningless gesture. "I'm at the east end of town, at the corner of Myrtle."

If Rome noticed her abrupt withdrawal she didn't show it.

"That's the street the hospital is on. You have the school-house?"

"Yes."

Rome pulled out of the lot and started down Main. "Pretty place."

"It is." When Rome pulled up in front of her house a few minutes later, Tally released her seat belt and turned in the seat to face Rome. "Thanks for the ride."

Rome gave her a wry smile. "Thanks for the help shopping."

Seconds passed, stretching into what felt like an hour as Tally watched Rome lean slowly toward her. Rome's gaze held hers, questing and questioning. The rush of heat to Tally's throat and the tight ball of need growing inside whispered *yes*.

Tally caught her breath and blinked, blindly pushing the door open behind her. Rome froze as the cold November night flooded in. "Good night."

"It was. Sleep well," Rome said as Tally firmly shut the door.

CHAPTER TWELVE

Tally did not sleep well, which did not help when she rose earlier than usual so she could unpack the rest of her clothes and dig out what she needed for another morning of farm call. Of course her second pair of boots were in the last box, helpfully marked *miscellaneous*. Once dressed in serviceable khaki pants she could move around in and wouldn't mind getting dirty, a T-shirt, and a light pullover sweater, she had a quick breakfast with two cups of coffee and was on her way. Her Bug handled well on the twisting roads, and her thoughts drifted back to the night before. In hindsight, the whole evening felt like an episode of *Stranger Things*. Never would she have guessed she'd end up shopping in a hardware store with Rome Ashcroft. And having a good time. Rome was funny and complicated and, when she talked about her time in the military, unnervingly honest and undeniably unaware of just how much she revealed about herself when she did.

And then there was what she'd thought was about to happen that couldn't possibly be happening that had kept her awake half the night. Because if Rome had actually been planning to kiss her, and she'd actually been about to let her, then she had totally lost her mind. There could be no other explanation. But she'd come to her senses in time, and now she'd be on guard against any further moments of insanity.

Tally clung to that very rational thought as she pulled into the clinic lot.

She'd wanted to be early, but the mobile unit was in the lot next to Val's red pickup truck, and the lights were on in the rear of the building. She found Val inside in the kennel area examining an elderly dog they'd admitted the day before to hydrate and treat his newly diagnosed diabetes.

"Hi," Tally said. "Sorry, I thought I gave myself plenty of time."

Val looked over her shoulder and smiled. "No problem. You *are* early." She closed the kennel door, made a quick note on the chart, and said, "This one looks much better than yesterday afternoon."

"Hey, Hector, who's a good boy?" Tally crooned, walking over to the dog's pen. The aging white pitbull mix raised his blocky head and wagged his tail. "Mm, yes, he looks much more alert today. That's great."

"It is. Mildred Porter would be lost without this dog. Wherever she goes, he goes, including the bank, the hairdresser's, and the IGA. I think everybody in town knows them both."

"You think she'll be able to manage his medical treatment?"

"We might need to check in on her a little bit at the beginning, but I think she'll manage the insulin injections just fine. Anything for Hector." Val laughed. "Although getting his weight down a little might be a challenge. I think he and Mildred eat a lot of the same foods."

Tally laughed. "I'll make sure to go over the diet plan and the new food options with her when she comes to pick him up."

Val asked, "Ready to get started?"

"Absolutely."

As they turned out the lights and headed out, Val said, "Listen, I'm sorry if I left you in the lurch last night. I completely forgot that you didn't have a car until I was leaving."

"Oh," Tally said. "No problem at all. If I had wanted to walk,

I certainly could have. Nothing's very far in this town, and the streets feel very safe at night."

"They are, but still, you're new to town, after dark, and all of that."

"I probably should've let you know that I was with Rome and not to worry."

"I *did* see you leave together, and then I got distracted and forgot I was driving you home." Val opened the mobile van and climbed in as Tally went around to the passenger side. "My sister-in-law...I think of the Riverses that way since Brody is part of the family...anyhow, Harper announced she and Presley just heard they'd been approved for adoption. They should be getting the baby very soon now."

"Wow, no wonder you were distracted," Tally said. "They must be ecstatic."

"The whole family is. Carson said it was the best birthday present ever—a niece for her and a cousin for her son." Val shook her head. "Still, I feel badly for inviting you out and then screwing up."

"I was the one who left early—Rome invited me to go shopping for the puppies with her, and it seemed only fair since she's taking on their care. She took me home. Right home." Tally realized she was sounding rather defensive and added more calmly, "After we finished at the hardware store."

Val grinned. "I bet that was fun."

Tally laughed. "I can tell you that these puppies are going to have more toys than a two-year-old on Christmas morning."

"I think they're going to be one very lucky bunch of puppies, and Rome is going to be a very, very busy person."

"I've told her that more than once," Tally said, "but I doubt once she's set her mind on something that anyone could change it."

"You know her pretty well, don't you."

"I thought so," Tally said slowly as the gray mist of morning swirled around the van, feathering into a cottony strand as they climbed the hills and lying thick as wool batting over the road in the dips. "I'm not so sure now."

"I can tell there's a story," Val said casually, watching the road, "but I'll leave it to you to tell if and when you want."

"It's not just my story—it's hers too." As she said it, Tally was struck with the realization that she had never heard Rome's story from Rome. Oh, she'd heard the details from the police reports the attorneys had given her parents, but there'd been no trial—no public statements from anyone. She had Sheila's version. And Justin's. But never Rome's. Tally let out a long breath. "There were some…problems…a long time ago between Rome and my older sister. They weren't exactly resolved, I guess you could say."

"Oh, that sounds complicated."

Tally laughed shortly. "That's the simplified word for it."

"That tangled up, huh?"

"Tangled up is exactly how I feel about her right now," Tally said, struck by being at once relieved and unhappy to admit her confusion. She didn't know what to think about Roman Ashcroft anymore. The woman who was suddenly everywhere in her life barely resembled the one she knew, or thought she knew. And she had a hard time believing that someone who would go out of their way to take responsibility for a bunch of animals that she had no real claim to could be the cold and calculating person who had misled her sister and attempted to seduce her with drugs. "Sometimes I wish we'd never met again."

"I'm sorry," Val said. "I don't know her, of course, but I know she's good friends with Brody. Which doesn't have any bearing on whatever your experience with her might be."

Tally shifted a little bit to watch Val's face as they spoke. "I'm not so certain Brody doesn't know an entirely different Rome Ashcroft than I knew."

Val cut her a quick look before turning her attention back to the road. "People change."

"Do they?" Tally shook her head. "I'm not really so sure. Oh, sometimes we adjust or learn to camouflage some of the behaviors that other people find problematic. But do we really fundamentally change? Can we change those patterns of behavior and beliefs that were formed before we even had awareness?"

"Heavy questions for first thing in the morning," Val said. "I'm not sure that we are the same people for our whole lives." She shook her head. "No, I'm sure we're not. I know that I'm not the same person I was when I left here for Manhattan, certain that the life I wanted was something...anything...completely different than what I'd grown up with here. I even believed that my cousin and I were enemies, or at least in enemy camps. That's another long story I'll tell you about sometime. But I know I'm not that person now."

"I'm not sure it's possible to give up a belief you've held your whole life."

Val looked at her again. "No matter that there's evidence to the contrary?"

"Maybe not even then," Tally said softly. Was that true for her? Was she irrevocably forged by her sister's experiences and not her own?

"I think you'll know," Val said at length, "where the real truth lies, in the present, or the past, given time."

"I hope you're right." Tally sighed. "I'm not so sure I'm happy to have met—remet, I guess—Rome, but I do know I'm glad to be here."

"I'm glad you are too. Now let's go have some fun." Val turned down a single-lane dirt road that ran between two cornfields toward a rambling yellow clapboard house on a hillside. A big red barn and fenced horse pastures sat beyond it. "Biff Washington's got a mare he's worried might have foundered. He's an experienced horseman, so I'm taking his concerns seriously."

"I'm kind of surprised, given the time of year," Tally said. Founder—a severe condition that began as laminitis in the hoof that could result in severe pain, chronic lameness, and eventual bone destruction—was most commonly caused by large quantities of high protein food, either grain or lush pasture grass. "Unless you think it's tick borne?"

"Could be, but my money's on the grass. The weather's been too warm for the summer grass to die off, and when they put the horses out to the winter pasture, the grass is still way green and, of course, horses being horses, they're overeating." Val pulled over behind a gray Ford pickup in the turnaround by the barn. "It could be something else, of course, and we'll run the usual tests, but I want to get a handle on how bad the physical problem is. Their farrier is supposed to be here too, so we can talk about management long-term."

"Is that usual?" Tally asked. "The farrier coming out, I mean."

"It is with this one," Val said. "Dan Sanchez is extremely responsible and reliable. He's the one who suggested they get a vet out here to check out this mare instead of trying the usual treatment of keeping her off the grass for a week or so."

Val got out and opened the side doors of the van. "We'll get the X-rays and go from there."

"Did he say it's both front legs?" Tally reached in and grabbed the equipment box.

"Yes, so it's not likely to be an abscess or some foreign body that's embedded in the hoof."

"Walks like a duck, quacks like a duck…" Tally murmured.

Val hauled out the portable X-ray unit and another tackle box filled with meds. "Yep. Laminitis if we're lucky. Hopefully the X-rays won't show any bone collapse."

"Detomidine to tranq her?"

"My drug of choice," Val said lightly. "You can go ahead and inject her once we get her in the crossties."

"No problem." Tally didn't think the suggestion was a test, but she wasn't worried if it was. She'd had enough large animal experience to be comfortable with intravenous injections in an animal as big as a horse. Finding the vein was pretty easy after a little bit of practice. She hadn't done it in a while, but she didn't expect any problems.

A tall, thin man in a dark green work shirt and blue jeans came out of the barn and sauntered over to meet them. "Morning, Doc. Let me give you a hand there."

Val handed over the X-ray machine. "Hi, Biff. How's Marigold?"

He shook his head. "She's mighty uncomfortable. And mighty upset to be in the stall while the others went out this morning."

"I'll bet she is. Is Dan here?"

He turned and glanced toward the road. "Looks like that's him coming down now."

"Great. This is Tally Dewilde, my new associate."

Washington gave her a friendly nod. "Doc."

"Good to meet you," Tally replied as they walked into a spacious barn with a center aisle and five single stalls on either side. The place smelled like fresh hay and apples. All the stalls were empty except for one, where a chestnut mare fretted and paced, snorting impatiently and eyeing them suspiciously.

"Hello there, you beautiful girl," Val said before turning to Biff. "Let's get a look at your girl while we wait for Dan."

"Oh now, don't be such a princess," Washington crooned as he opened the stall, slipped on a halter, and led her out to a wash stall at the back of the barn where he could secure her in crossties. She immediately displayed her displeasure by backing up and trying to twist free of the lines.

"If you'll just told her head there, Biff," Val said, "we'll get a look at her hooves."

Biff tightened his hold on the halter, and Val managed to get first one foreleg and then the other up for a quick look at each hoof.

Val glanced at Tally. "What do you think?"

"The laminae are separating on both sides. Might still just be severe inflammation, but we'll need the X-rays."

Val straightened. "It may not be as serious as we think. Let's get the X-rays and find out."

"Hope you brought some good tranqs," Biff muttered. "She's feeling ornery."

Val laughed softly. "First order of business. How much does she weigh?"

Biff told them, and Tally drew up the appropriate dose in a long-needled syringe.

"If you'd just keep her head up, Mr. Washington," she said and ran her hand down the mare's neck, searching for the pulse that indicated the location of the artery and the accompanying vein she wanted. "Okay, girl, this is not going to hurt, but I'm going to have to have you hold still for a minute."

She glanced at Mr. Washington, who nodded. Without hesitating, she inserted the long needle, angled to slip through the underlying muscles, and aspirated as she went until blood spurted into the syringe. Sure she was in the vein, she injected the drug. "This won't take long," she warned as she withdrew the needle.

"Whoa," Biff exclaimed as seconds later the mare's head drooped and she staggered.

"Steady there, Marigold," Val said, putting her shoulder against the horse's withers. "Got her, Biff?"

"Yep, she's not going anywhere. Amazing how fast that works," he said.

"Let's get her up on blocks and get the films," Val said.

Tally and Val worked quickly to set the wooden blocks under each of the horse's front hooves. She was so docile now that she'd been tranquilized, she was easy for them to maneuver. Without too much trouble they had her situated in good position for X-rays.

"I haven't used this machine before," Tally said as Val positioned the image plate on the far side of the mare's lower leg and hoof.

Val explained the mechanics as she dialed in the parameters

and held the plate to shoot the image. When she'd made the exposure, the digital impression was relayed wirelessly to the monitor they'd brought with them.

"Let's get a look," Val said. Using software specifically designed to analyze angles on the images, Val and Tally were able to determine the degree of bone rotation and judge just where the hoof needed to be trimmed to alter the forces placed on the underlying bones.

Val turned to Washington. "The good news is the rotation of the coffin bone isn't at a critical point, but she's going to need some aggressive hoof trimming."

"What do you think, Dan?" Biff looked at the dark-haired, husky guy in a jeans jacket, navy T-shirt, and jeans who'd joined them as they were taking the X-rays.

"I've been having a really hard time trimming her back. Her hooves are just so damn hard."

"Why don't you try this," Val said to Washington. "The night before Dan is going to show up to do her hooves, wrap her up in wet diapers and leave them on all night. The hooves should be soft enough for him to trim as much as he needs to in the morning."

Washington nodded. "I can do that. We've tried booties with baby oil and whatnot in them, but this sounds like it might be better."

"That's a good idea, Doc," Dan said.

Tally added, "You'll probably have to come more frequently and trim them back in stages."

Dan nodded. "Figured on that."

"All right then," Val said. "In the meantime, let's put her on some anti-inflammatories, keep her off the pasture grass, and for the next five days, keep her on hay inside."

Washington flipped off his ball cap and rubbed his forehead. "She's not gonna like that."

Val patted the horse's neck. "Sometimes we all have to do things we don't like to do. You'll be better for it in the long run."

As Tally gathered up the gear, Val gave them some last-minute instructions and the prescriptions.

"What do you think?" Val said as they drove out.

"That was great," Tally said.

Val laughed. "Spoken like a true greenhorn. Wait till you've had to do that in the middle of January when it's twenty degrees below outside and not much warmer inside the barn."

Tally laughed. "Can't wait."

Val rolled her eyes. "Okay, who's next on our list?"

The morning passed quickly, and Tally had the dubious pleasure of having lunch, consisting of a half-decent bean burrito wrapped in tinfoil, from the hot case at one of the ubiquitous convenience stores. She even tried the coffee, which was better than expected, if a tad too sweet. When they got back to the clinic in the late afternoon, she was ravenous, wanted a shower, and had visions of a very large plate of pasta with red sauce. Before she could ask about decent take-out places, Rita handed her a message slip.

"I think these are the people you've been waiting to hear from."

Tally glanced at it. "It is, thanks."

She called from her office, identified herself, and listened for a few moments as the earnest woman on the other end of the line told her how very sorry they were that they didn't have room for the puppies.

"Thanks anyhow. I really appreciate your efforts," Tally said.

She disconnected, leaned back, and closed her eyes with a sigh. Well, that was it. She was out of options. She studied her phone on her desk for another sixty seconds before picking it up and texting Rome.

CHAPTER THIRTEEN

Rome ended her PowerPoint and turned the conference room lights back up. "Okay, let's talk about abdominal pain now that we're all squared away on infectious disease in kids."

The four PA students seated around the oblong table gave her assorted looks of bafflement, surprise, and notably, eagerness.

"I know," she went on, "that's not the topic of today's session, but you already know all about evaluating children with fevers, rashes, ear pain, coughs, and other signs of viral or bacterial syndromes since we just talked about it. Let's talk about one of the most common things you're going to evaluate in the ER. Abdominal pain—this time in adults. Where do you start?"

The students glanced at each other, still getting used to each other at the start of a new rotation and judging the level of competitiveness. Eventually Jim Chang, one of the older students Rome knew had been a Navy corpsman before starting the PA program, similar to her own path, raised his hand.

"Jim?" Rome said.

"The history."

"Pretty safe answer." She paused for a second, then laughed and felt the tension in the room drop. "Of course, you're right. Almost."

These students all had exceptional academic records, or they wouldn't have been accepted into the program that Glenn Archer had put together. She didn't need to fast-forward their clinical

• 141 •

skills the way she might have if they needed to be ready for deployment at any moment. She could take the time to let them enjoy the process without the pressure. "We'll get to specifics in a minute. How about something else first?"

"Vital signs," he said, shaking his head. "Duh."

Rome nodded. "Chances are you'll have that info on the intake form along with a list of meds, possibly even copies of past ER visits. Before you walk into the patient's room, get all the info you can. Patients in pain or uneasy about their surroundings may very well forget to tell you something important. In fact, I can pretty much guarantee it."

She walked to the whiteboard on the wall and wrote down a set of vital signs. "Let's say this is a twenty-five-year-old woman with a temp of 101 and diffuse abdominal pain. What do you want to know? Claudia—want to take this?"

Claudia, a first year who'd graduated from an accelerated premedical science program and was younger than the others, nodded and took the time to think for a moment. Rome liked that—newbies too often tended to jump to obvious conclusions based on scant data. That might be essential in battle, where seconds might be all the time you had to make a decision and administer treatment, but in the ER—except in the midst of an acute trauma alert—a few extra minutes putting the puzzle pieces together might avoid an incorrect diagnosis.

"Onset of the pain, duration, is it constant or intermittent... um, had she ever had it before. Location of the pain, if it had changed since onset." Claudia paused, then added quickly, "Any previous surgery. Gyn history—could she be pregnant."

"Good. Anybody else?"

As another student answered, Rome's phone vibrated. Technically she was no longer on duty as her shift had ended with her obligatory lecture in the PA teaching rotation. She flicked a glance to it and saw a text from Tally. Her pulse jumped about 100 bpm, and the familiar tightening in her midsection followed. Just seeing the message brought back the wild urge she'd had to just lean over and kiss her the night before. The desire to kiss a woman wasn't new, but the twist in her chest as she'd been about to give in to the impulse had been. Hunger. Need. Wonder. All wrapped into a tangle she couldn't escape. She'd been trying all day not to think of the why of it or what might have happened if Tally hadn't withdrawn so abruptly, and couldn't afford to now.

She glanced away from the phone and refocused on the discussion. Fifteen minutes later after the students had filed out, she read the text.

Call me when you can. Not 911

Smiling at the notion she wouldn't respond to a message from Tally ASAP, she closed the door to the conference room and pulled up the number she'd gotten from Tally the first morning they'd met. Tally picked up on the second ring.

"Hi, it's me," Rome said and then on second thought, added, "Rome."

"I know, your name came up when my phone rang."

"Oh. Right. It would do that, wouldn't it."

"Am I interrupting anything? I'm sorry to bother you if you're at work."

"No. It's fine. Anytime. I mean, I *am* at work, but I'm done now. So now is…good." Rome laughed, amused by her own befuddlement. She wasn't only reacting like a teenager to a perfectly ordinary text from a woman, she was actually *acting* like one. "I'm free. What's up? Is everybody okay?"

"Is that always your first thought? That someone is in danger or something bad is about to happen?"

"That's a weird question," Rome said. "I don't know, does it seem that way?"

"I do get the feeling that you're always expecting a disaster."

Rome leaned back and closed her eyes. "You realize we have the weirdest conversations routinely, right?"

"I have to admit I have wondered about that." Tally laughed, and the sound was free and warm, and the tightening in Rome's stomach turned to heat. "You don't have to answer, you know."

"I don't mind." Rome didn't add that she liked talking to Tally about anything, even subjects she avoided with everyone else, even old friends like Brody. Tally's interest was as exciting as any physical advance she'd ever experienced. That probably should have set off blaring alarms and shouts of *incoming*, but she ignored the warnings. She was getting good at that where Tally was concerned. "And I suppose you're right. I guess I've always been that way—expecting trouble. And then, well, the service and the job kind of just enhanced it."

"Do you ever relax?"

"Ah, I think so. I like to read, and that's pretty relaxing. I don't really have all that much free time for much these days. The gym a few times a week and that's about it." She paused. "I hope they have a gym somewhere here. Everyplace has a gym, right?"

Tally laughed. "I'm not entirely sure. I'm just happy there's a grocery store. And of course the hardware store."

"There is that," Rome agreed.

"Well," Tally said with an audible sigh, "I'm afraid your scant moments of relaxation are about to be over."

Rome opened her eyes and sat up straight. "The puppies?"

"Yes, I wanted to let you know that we can't place them. Our options now are to board them here and try to foster them out one at a time or—"

"No, not necessary. I want them. I'm all set for them."

"All right, I figured you'd say that, which is why I wanted to give you a heads-up. We'll move them over to the boarding center in the morning, and when you're ready—"

"No, you misunderstood. I'm ready. I want them. I can be there in…thirty minutes."

"Tonight?"

"Why not. I'm gonna be home all night. Otherwise they're just going to sit around all day tomorrow in a new place wondering what's going on, and the same thing will happen tomorrow night."

"I don't think they'd be all that concerned by the move, but I guess there's really no reason you can't have them tonight." After a beat of silence, Tally continued, "There's also really no reason for you to drive all the way out here. Blake or Margie—I'm not sure which one has kennel duty tonight—can help me get them ready, and I'll drop them off on my way home. Is an hour and a half okay?"

"Yes, I'm…" Rome hesitated. She was supposed to meet Pam for burgers right about that time. It hadn't exactly been a date, and Pam knew about the puppies. She was pretty sure Pam would understand this was an emergency situation. She'd let her know right away. "No, that's good. That's great. I'm leaving the hospital shortly, and I'll be there waiting. If you're sure you don't want me to come out?"

"No, I think this will work out fine. I can go over everything with you and the kids when we bring the puppies, so everyone will be on the same page."

"Great," Rome said. "I'll see you soon. And Tally? Thank you for this. You don't have to worry."

The silence over the line had Rome gripping the phone hard and holding her breath. Was Tally going to renege? Had she suddenly decided she couldn't trust Rome after all? Rome kept waiting for Tally to decide Rome was the person she believed her to be, the person who attempted to seduce her sister with a date-rape drug, and suddenly want nothing to do with her again. The idea kindled equal doses of fear and rage, emotions she hadn't experienced in years. This time, though, she wasn't furious about being unjustly accused. This was about Tally, and how much she did not want Tally to walk away from her. "Tally?"

"I'm sorry," Tally said abruptly, as if her thoughts had been far away. "I'm not worried. At least not about the puppies. I ought to be more worried for you."

Rome laughed, relief like a reprieve. "I'm tougher than a bunch of furry little buggers."

"We'll find out," Tally said lightly. "I'll see you soon."

"Yes. Okay. I'll be waiting."

When Rome ended the call, she immediately texted Pam. *Really sorry not going to make it tonight. Having a puppy delivery.*

Almost instantly the reply came back. *!!!awesome. NP. Some other time*.

Rome texted back *yes*, and shot to her feet, mentally sorting all the things she was going to need to do before the puppies arrived. And Tally. She'd made one little step closer to convincing Tally to give her a chance to prove she wasn't the person Tally remembered, even if it was just to take care of a bunch of puppies. She didn't ask herself why that mattered so much. Right now she just enjoyed the sweet thrill of possibility.

❖

Rome stood in the middle of the trailer and surveyed the arrangements. As Brody had suggested, she'd found an expandable kiddie gate at the hardware store and was able to block off a four-by-four-foot area at the far end of the trailer opposite her sleeping quarters. That cut down a little on her eating and sitting space, but it's not like she planned to throw a party. She had the big dish for the food and another one for the water and a basketful of a couple hundred toys. She'd also set up the crate along with the puppy pads for the floor. The crate didn't seem big enough for half a dozen puppies, but Tally had assured her that it was. All in all, the setup looked pretty cozy. Had to be better than them spending the time alone at the kennel, anyhow. She was ready, sort of, she hoped.

At the sound of a car pulling onto the gravel parking area in front of the trailer, she checked her watch. She hadn't expected Tally to show quite so soon, but soon was just fine with her. She just wanted to see her. And the puppies, of course.

She stepped outside as five kids piled out of a royal-blue Buick that had to be twenty years old. The driver was a muscular sandy-haired guy with a megawatt smile who looked like nothing in the world could ever bother him. A skinny guy in a plaid shirt and khaki pants with dark, spiky hair shooting every which way was next. He might have been labeled a nerd even without a pocket protector, but he had the casual air of a guy confident in his own skin. The blonde who climbed out of the back Rome remembered from the café—Taylor. Following close behind her was a lithe dark-haired teen with russet-brown skin, round gold-rimmed glasses, and a mass of complicated-looking braids coiled around her head, who looked enough like Pam to be a younger version.

Number five Rome already knew. "Hi Margie."

"Hi Rome," Margie called back. "Blake texted and said the puppies were coming. We're your puppy minders."

Margie proceeded to introduce Dave, Tim, Taylor, and Annika. "We thought we'd get acquainted and meet the puppies. Hope that's okay."

"Hey, it's fine. Good to meet you all, and thanks for volunteering. I guess you're all pretty busy."

The five of them chorused a smattering of "No problem," "I love puppies,"—that from the big jock-looking guy—and "It will be so much fun!"

"Right. So, they should be here soon." Rome wondered if she could fit all these kids inside her house. On the other hand, there was a sort of outdoor flagstone patio area in the fenced-off yard, which she hadn't really thought about using much, but there was a picnic table out there. "Come on in and I'll show you the setup. It's going to be crowded, but—"

She broke off as a pickup truck and Tally's VW Bug pulled in beside the Buick. Blake jumped out of the truck as Tally exited the Bug. She stood by the door looking up at Rome, and for just an instant, Rome forgot about everyone and everything else. Tally looked amazing in jeans, a plain beige cotton sweater, and extremely muddy boots. That wild urge to kiss her came roaring back.

Tally cocked her head, her smile amused. "Hi. Are we late?"

"No. You're perfect." Rome coughed. "Perfectly on time. Hi. You look like you spent your day out in the field."

Tally glanced down at herself. "I can't imagine how you could tell."

She laughed. There it was again, that instant of free laughter, where Tally wasn't thinking about anything except them in the moment.

"You look great. We've got a crowd already." Rome paused as a red Miata pulled in next to Tally's Bug. Pam got out, opened the trunk, and lifted out four giant pizza boxes.

Pam waggled a finger at the crowd and called, "Little help here, if anyone's hungry."

The teens descended on her like locusts.

"Margie," Rome said, "take them out the back door to the table out there. I'll find plates or something in a second."

"Paper towels will work," Taylor said as she passed by. "If you have them."

"I do…I think."

Tally glanced over at Pam and then up to Rome, her expression curious.

Rome schooled her features to hide her surprise. "Hi Pam."

"Hi," Pam said. She'd changed from scrubs, which was the only thing Rome had seen her in before, into dark brown flared pants, a high-necked, body-hugging ochre top, and a cropped caramel leather jacket. "Annika texted me about the puppies coming, and since I knew you'd missed supper, I thought emergency rations were in order. I know this crew is always hungry." She opened the driver's door as if to leave and added, "Good luck with the puppies."

"Wait," Rome called, "you should stay for pizza and see them."

Pam smiled. "Well, if you don't mind."

"Of course not. You brought the food, after all." Rome gestured to Tally. "This is Tally Dewilde, our vet."

Pam walked around her car and held out her hand. "Hi. I'm

Pam. I'm a nurse over at the Rivers. My niece is one of the puppy minders."

"I can see the resemblance." Tally smiled. An attractive nurse from the Rivers. Who seemed to know that Rome had missed dinner. That was interesting. "Hi, good to meet you."

Pam smiled back as the teenagers came back outside and crowded around the truck as Blake extracted the carriers they'd placed the puppies in.

"Hope you like pizza," Pam said.

Tally hesitated. When she got the puppies settled, which wouldn't take very long, she could just leave. But actually, pizza sounded good, and for some reason, she didn't want to leave the impromptu party. That might be the smartest thing to do if she wanted to avoid spending any more time than necessary with Rome, but she'd worked hard at not avoiding the things she wanted by taking the safe route. She'd spent her entire life growing up, making choices that were best for everyone else— except her. Right now, wise or not, she wanted to stay. The almost kiss she wasn't going to think about had absolutely nothing to do with her decision.

CHAPTER FOURTEEN

Tally followed Pam and Rome inside the trailer, which was neat and tidy, even if everything from the stove to the dinette set did look miniaturized. The interior was presently standing room only with six teenagers crowded around Rome at the pen area. Blake and Margie freed the puppies from their carriers and passed them one by one to the other teens, who all cuddled them and exclaimed over them before turning to Rome.

"Which one is this one?" Tim asked.

"That's Bravo," Margie said instantly.

Rome nodded. "Yep. That's her. Bet she was the first one out. She's gonna want to check to see everything is in order first thing."

"Pack leader," Tim observed, handing her to Rome.

"I'd say so." Rome accepted the next puppy, a brown spotted one with a bent ear. "And this one is Hood."

Margie piped up instantly. "Dibs on Hood."

Rome shot her an amused smile. "Okay, sure."

"Who's this?" Annika asked, holding out a white puppy with scattered black patches.

"I'm afraid the rest don't have names yet," Rome said.

"Now's a good time, then," Annika said with a winning smile.

"You sure you don't mind me naming them?" Rome said, looking at the circle of teens.

Dave spoke up. "Hey, yeah, you saved them, after all."

"It's cool," Blake and Margie said in unison.

"Okay, then, that one is Camo."

Annika rubbed her cheek against the puppy's round belly. "Oh my God, that's perfect." She held the puppy up and cooed, "Aren't you just perfect."

Pam murmured, "Uh-oh."

"Are they doing what I think they're doing?" Tally whispered.

"I think so. I wonder if any of their parents know what's coming."

Rome proceeded to name each of them as the teens picked them out, one by one.

"Hey," Dave said, "give me that little one. And we're not calling him runt."

The wiggly pup, mostly tan with pointed ears and coal-black eyes and a tail that never stopped whipping, made its way from hand to hand down to Dave. He picked it up and peered at its belly. "Oops. That'd be a her. Even better." He glanced over at Rome. "What would you say?"

"Looks like a Ranger to me."

Dave laughed and put his nose to the puppy's, who immediately licked his. "Ranger, huh. Yeah, that sounds pretty tough. Don't worry, size isn't everything."

Tim snorted and elbowed him in the side. "Says the biggest guy in the room."

Dave grinned and bumped shoulders with Tim.

"I think we might've a problem here," Rome said, "because we've only got six puppies and there's six of you, and Bravo—"

"That's no problem," Margie said quickly. "Blake and I already settled on shared custody. Hood will live with Blake. I'm the co-parent."

Tim piped up, "And Taylor and I already chose." He pointed to a brindle who looked a lot like Bravo except for the brown scattered through its coat. "That one's mine."

"That one's Lookout," Rome said, pointing to the one Tim

lifted, "and that one"—as Taylor grabbed the final puppy, another brindle, this one more brown than black, and hugged him to her chest—"is Storm."

"Storm," Taylor whispered. "Oh, I can't wait until my purr-faces meet this little guy."

Rome surveyed the teens. "That's all of them. So…am I going to have a whole bunch of distressed parents when they find out there's a new face in the family?"

The teens all looked at each other and laughed. Margie said, "What's another dog. They're like kids, right? When you have one, who cares how many more."

"Yeah, right." Rome grinned and looked over at Tally and Pam and shrugged.

The teens stood around the pen watching the puppies explore their new home as if they had all been transported to some shrine and were witnessing a miracle. Tally and Pam traded amused glances. Pam, who gave off friendly vibes, looked gorgeous with understated makeup and a perfectly coordinated outfit that worked beautifully and still managed to look casual. She made Tally feel frumpy at best. Tally didn't think of herself as vain, but she hadn't grown up among men and women who constantly vied for dominance on every level, including physical, without learning that appearances mattered. She also didn't like to think of herself as jealous and had a niggling fear that that's exactly what she was feeling. And heaven knew, she had absolutely nothing to be jealous about or any reason to care the slightest about Rome's personal life. Not that she actually *knew* there was anything between Pam and Rome. And not that she would be the slightest bit bothered if there was.

Pam chuckled. "It looks like those are matches made in heaven."

"All the way around, really."

"Actually, Rome is pretty clever," Pam said. "Now those kids are going to have even more reason to be over here taking care of the puppies."

"I don't actually think she cares about that," Tally murmured. "She'd take care of them all by herself if she had to go without sleep without the slightest complaint. They've been hers since the second she saw them."

Pam gave her a quizzical look. "Yeah, I can imagine that's true."

Tally drew a sharp breath. She wasn't sure what Pam had seen in her face or heard in her voice, but she didn't like to be read and usually was very good at keeping her feelings to herself. "Well, I'm sure you know that she's incredibly responsible. You work with her, and I imagine she's the same way at the hospital."

"She's definitely that, and clinically sharp too." Pam laughed. "That describes everyone I work with, and I'm not just saying that. I've worked in the ER for ten years, and this new crop of ER docs and PAs are top class. You'll have to come over sometime and see the ER. It's an amazing place filled with amazing people."

"I've met some of them," Tally said. "Val, my boss, is Brody's wife...of course you know that. She invited me to go along to meet some of the Rivers family the other night at an impromptu dinner." She laughed. "Actually, it wasn't exactly dinner. It was more like half a beer at Bottoms Up."

"Oh, that must've been quite an introduction to the family." Pam laughed. "At least you've been indoctrinated properly. So you probably know what I mean then when I say that it's quite an incredible clan."

"I got that after just a few minutes." Tally had to thank Val for that invitation again. She'd obviously fallen into the middle of the ruling family, although her quick introduction to them hadn't struck her as anything like the social elite she was used to. No one assessed her with pointed glances or politely questioned her about her family, her marital status, or her connections. "Did you grow up here too?"

"Actually, no, I didn't," Pam said, "but I've been here since I was a teenager, so I pretty much feel like this has always been home. My father bought land and moved us here when I was just thirteen. He was one of the first people of color to start a farm around here." She laughed. "I was *not* happy at all, but Baltimore was a dangerous place to be then." She was silent for a moment. "My older brother was killed in a gang war, and I think that was the reason that we left."

"I'm so sorry," Tally said. "That's a terrible loss for your family."

"It was especially hard because my mother had died a little over a year before." Pam shook her head. "He threw himself into working the land. I was pretty angry for a year or so, but then I made friends." She shrugged. "I healed, and I think he did too. He's still farming, and I am thankful to him every day for moving us here."

"You never wanted to leave?"

Pam laughed. "Oh, I couldn't wait to see the world. And I did, as soon as I could get out there."

"But you came back."

Pam nodded. "I did. I thought I wanted to go away to college, and he didn't try to stop me. So I spent four years in DC, got my degree, and promptly turned around and came home."

Tally thought about how different that was for her. She got her degree, still entrenched in the entitled world she'd been born into, and couldn't wait to leave. Now here she was, alone in a world where she definitely did not fit. She was past pitying herself, though. "Sometimes we have to leave to know what we want."

Pam gave her a long look. "You're so right. You'll have to tell me sometime how you ended up here."

Tally recognized the time to deflect. Anything she could say about herself would come too close to the past and Rome. "It's a very long story, and right now, I'm for grabbing some pizza before it vanishes."

Pam laughed. "I'm for getting out of this very nice but extremely small trailer. Shall we go join the party?"

"Yes, let's." Tally liked Pam, quite a bit. She could see how Rome would like her as well.

❖

Rome chuckled as Bravo explored the pen, studiously sniffing into every corner. After her tour she came back to the gate, looked up at Rome, and yipped. "Are you satisfied now? Can we put the rest of the pack in there?"

"Yeah, besides, I'm hungry," said Tim, the tall skinny one who looked like he never got enough to eat.

"We probably *should* let them get quieted down," Blake said, his reluctance clear as he gently placed Hood back into the enclosure. "There you go, buddy. You're gonna like it here. And I'll be back soon."

Everyone surrendered their puppies and trooped outside, following Rome. The teens had all grabbed pizza before the boxes had even made it into the trailer and were clearly ready for their second or third courses. They all secured slices and dispersed to various spots on the patio.

Rome managed to snag a couple of pieces and sat down at the picnic table with Pam and Tally.

Pam said, "That's quite a crew you've got there. Puppies and teens alike."

Rome laughed. "I know. Those kids are amazing. I don't know how I'm going to accommodate all of them, but I'm pretty sure they're all going to show up for every shift."

Tally pushed her makeshift paper towel plate aside and laughed. "I think you can pretty much count on it. Once the puppies are a little bit bigger and we've got their vaccinations up to date, you can at least get them outside for a little while. They'll love exploring, and you might get a few minutes of quiet." She glanced around the yard. "The fence is good. Just be sure they can't get under it or through it somewhere."

"Actually," Rome said, "I was thinking I could put a run

inside the yard, if Brody's okay with that. That would be more secure, and there's already a doggie door. I'm working on some plans already."

"It's a good idea," Tally said. "They're going to be way too big to be inside all the time before long. As long as the weather holds, they have some shelter, and someone's here to keep an eye on them, you can let them out."

Pam said, "You should talk to Gina Antonelli—her construction company has done most of the major renovations at the Rivers. Someone on her crew could probably do the job."

"Okay, great. I'll do that," Rome said. "If I can't get to it myself."

Tally rolled here eyes. "Spoken like a true optimist."

"Hey!" Rome said. "Just watch—things are going to be smooth as silk once my troopers learn the drill."

"Uh-huh." Tally's smile was amused and her tone playful.

Rome's heart did that bump-and-run thing again—like she'd just gotten a mega-adrenaline boost.

Pam glanced at her watch. "I'm going to take off. I promised my dad I'd be by tonight."

Rome stood. "Thanks for bringing by the pizza. I'm certain that at least some of them would've perished by now without it."

Pam laughed as she and Rome walked to the trailer. "I'm willing to bet that's their second dinner."

"I wouldn't take that bet." Rome escorted her through the trailer and out to her car. "Sorry about the mix-up with dinner tonight."

Pam leaned on the door of her Miata and smiled. "Nothing to be sorry about. I wouldn't have missed seeing all of them with those babies for anything. The puppies are gorgeous, the kids are fun, and Tally is really nice."

"Yeah, she's terrific."

Pam gave her a long look. "I'll see you at work tomorrow."

"Okay, thanks again." Rome waved as Pam pulled away and turned as the kids all clambered out.

Margie said, "They're all settled for now, so if you've got this, we're going to go over to Blake's and get in an hour of SAT prep."

"I think I can handle it from here," Rome said. "In fact, I think I'm good for the night. They don't need to be fed again tonight, and I've got all the supplies I need. I can feed them in the morning too."

Blake glanced at Margie. "Um, we thought we'd come by maybe around six o'clock for their morning feeding? That gives us time to take care of things at the clinic."

"Not a problem, I'll be up," Rome said. She doubted she could keep them away even if she wanted to, which she didn't. She might not need as much help as they wanted to give her, but those puppies were clearly already spoken for. Orphans no longer. The trailer was going to be a busy place for the next six weeks. She didn't mind, especially if Tally was going to be a frequent visitor. Speaking of whom, she'd left her alone out on the patio, when what she really wanted to be doing was talking to her. Talking…and maybe whatever came after that. "I'll see you in the morning."

"Solid," Blake said. "We all have the schedule, so we've got the rest of the day covered."

"Okay. You've got my number. Whoever stops by, text me the all-clear when you've finished, so I'll know the pups are good."

Everyone nodded. Tim, Dave, Annika, and Taylor piled into the Buick, and Margie climbed into Blake's truck. Once they were underway, Rome walked back into the trailer. Tally stood packaging up leftover pizza in the kitchen.

"Hey," Rome said, "you didn't have to do that."

Tally looked over her shoulder and smiled. "No problem. I found the aluminum foil, and I made packages for each of the different pizzas."

"Thanks," Rome said. "I'm pretty sure that's not in your job description. I appreciate you making a house call tonight."

"I don't mind. It really wasn't out of my way, and I really *did* want to see what arrangements you'd made. After all, I helped procure all the supplies."

Rome laughed. "What do you think? Did I pass inspection?"

"So far, high marks."

Ridiculously pleased, Rome shrugged. "I'm making progress, then."

Tally turned and leaned against the counter next to the minifridge. "You know, all of those kids are taking those puppies."

"I know. Not Bravo, though."

"She's been yours since the beginning. I knew that."

Rome laughed. "That obvious?"

"She's like you—that's why you bonded with her," Tally murmured, watching as Rome took a step closer. The trailer was small and made even smaller by the space that had been designated for the puppies. The only light on inside was the one small convenience light over the tiny kitchenette. Rome's face was shadowed, but her eyes were easy to see, intent and gleaming. Tally's breath hitched. She couldn't pretend not to know what her body was saying. Something in Rome's searching gaze pulled at her, as if Rome was looking deep inside her, past the masks and carefully constructed walls she'd built since childhood to hide her feelings and keep herself safe. Of all people to see past the shields, Rome was the last person on earth she would have picked.

"I don't know what that means," Rome said, "*being like me*. Right now, she might be, though. She's probably a little unsure of her surroundings, maybe feeling a little helpless, and trying really hard not to let her fears show."

"Is that what you feel?" Tally murmured. Was Rome closer now? Had Rome moved? Or had she?

"Let's say I am unsure of my reception and helpless to do anything about what I'm feeling and hoping all of that doesn't show."

"Why is that?" Tally asked.

Rome was definitely closer—only inches away. She looked impossibly gorgeous and smelled like sandalwood, and pizza, and puppy—altogether human and not at all as Tally had always imagined her to be. Tally tilted her chin to keep her gaze locked on Rome's. Rome was only a couple of inches taller, but that was enough. Enough for Tally to feel ever so slightly overwhelmed, and liking the way it felt to be almost out of control.

"The reception part is easy to explain," Rome murmured. "I'm wondering if you'd be open to me kissing you."

Rome brushed her thumb close to but not quite over Tally's lower lip. Close enough for Tally to quiver in her deepest reaches.

"The helpless part is easy too," Rome went on, her eyes never leaving Tally's. "I can't change what I feel. I don't even want to stop it." Rome took a breath and cupped Tally's jaw. "I'm hoping you'll say yes."

The blood rushing through Tally's veins, the desire surging through her limbs, the need tugging at her all screamed *yes*.

Rome waited so patiently, so tenderly.

Tally shuddered. "I can't."

Rome froze for an instant and then stepped back, her hand falling away. "I understand."

Do you, Tally thought. *How could you when I don't? I don't understand anything at all.*

"I should go," Tally said, hurrying toward the door. Rome didn't argue, didn't try to stop her. She rushed to her car, climbed in, and started the engine. She glanced once at the trailer before she backed out. Nothing was visible except the faint yellow glow from the light in the tiny kitchen.

CHAPTER FIFTEEN

Rome left the small light on over the kitchenette in case the puppies were bothered by the dark. She thought about walking down to the other end of the trailer to the bunk, but the little snuffling noises and occasional squeaks from the puppy pile were oddly comforting. She'd gotten used to the sounds of others sleeping nearby—the restless shuffling and murmurs of uneasy sleepers. She hadn't even noticed until the heavy weight of silent darkness surrounded her those first nights in a roadside motel. She hadn't gone home—or back to her parents' town house, more accurately—when she'd returned stateside. She'd called her grandmother to say she was alive and well, declined an invitation to stay with her—the news of which would have traveled through the social network with lightning speed—and driven far enough from the city to feel free of the scrutiny and speculation she'd left once to avoid. That's where she'd been when she'd run across Brody on the veterans' Facebook group.

"I guess if we're a team now," she said to the puppies, "I ought to stay close in case you need something. Maybe that's why I found you, huh? Another team."

She laughed a little and dug out her duffel, pulled out the groundsheet, and spread it out next to the pen. She didn't really expect to sleep much, but she'd bedded down in worse places. At least she didn't have to search for rocks or poisonous creatures underneath her bedding and breathe sand all night. She folded her arms behind her head and stared up at the ceiling. "I screwed things up," she whispered.

The gentle snoring didn't change. Bravo and company, at least, didn't seem concerned.

Rome sighed. She'd made some serious miscalculations in her life, and the biggest ones seemed to center around the Dewildes. First Sheila and now Tally. Who would have figured that, considering the sisters were nothing alike. Neither were her feelings for them. Sheila had been hard to say no to, and that was probably her first mistake. Certainly her biggest. Doing nothing when Sheila started putting out hints they were together had been the wrong approach. She grunted. Now, there was irony for you. The mistakes she'd made with Sheila were exactly the opposite of the mistake she'd just made with Tally. She should have done something about Sheila, instead of hoping Sheila would get bored and move on. And she sure as hell should've waited with Tally. Sure, she was used to making the first move when she sensed that a woman might be interested, and she'd *thought* she'd read the signals right with Tally. But the women she'd been with in the last ten years had been different women, in different times, and in vastly different circumstances. Those had been hurried couplings in the high tension moments when tomorrow was a question mark and tonight was the only time that mattered. Life was that unpredictable then, and waiting seemed pointless.

She didn't *need* to know a woman very well, but she knew them in all the ways that had mattered then—they were her teammates, her fellow soldiers, her sisters-in-arms. She knew a lot about them in one critical way and perhaps nothing in any of the others.

Tally was completely the opposite. She knew a lot about Tally, about her past, about her present, and a lot about how Tally felt about her. Tally had made it really clear.

"Just didn't want to hear it," Rome muttered. The past might be dead and buried for her, but Tally had been crystal from the start that everything about that night and Sheila's troubles afterward was alive and well for her. Why she'd thought Tally would welcome an advance from her she couldn't fathom right now. Sure, she was going by instinct, and instincts in that area had usually served her pretty well. But not tonight. She'd blown it in a big way. She'd just proved Tally right about her.

She turned on her side and stared into the shadows of the puppy pen. A pair of dark eyes stared back. She stretched out a hand and slid her fingers through the gaps in the gate.

"Hey Bravo, are you on perimeter duty tonight?"

A cold, moist nose touched her fingertip. Rome kept her fingers still, and after a moment Bravo licked them. She stretched a little farther and petted the puppy's muzzle. "I'd take you out and let you sleep with me, but I think you better stay with the other troopers tonight. They're going to want you around. But I'll be right out here, so you don't have anything to worry about."

A soft sigh and she felt the puppy lie down.

"One thing is true—I don't walk away from my duty." She kept her hand there and closed her eyes. She didn't expect to sleep, but she had more company now than she'd had on most nights like this. If her dreams were troubled, she was used to that too.

❖

Tally parked, walked directly inside the renovated schoolhouse she now called home, and shed her work clothes while standing in the middle of the bedroom off the main living room and kitchen. She left them in a pile on the floor where they'd fallen, something she never did. She'd always kept her room neat because she didn't like the housekeeper or one of the maids picking up after her. It felt so wrong to expect them to clean up her messes, even though no one else in the family seemed bothered by it. For one bitter moment, she reflected on how easily Sheila expected someone else to fix her messes.

And that wasn't fair. She wouldn't even be thinking that

way if it hadn't been for Rome. If Rome hadn't appeared and somehow made her forget Rome's role in that night and the tumultuous months that followed.

Once in the shower, she leaned back and let the hot water beat down on her. She'd never been impulsive. Not ever. She'd been cautious growing up, understanding that she was expected to be the good child, the non-troublemaking child, the one her parents didn't have to spend any time controlling or making excuses for. That was how she won the occasional smile or absent pat of affection. Sheila had consumed all their energy, dealing first with her outbursts of temper when young, and then her teenage rebellion and her never-ending list of *escapades*, as they called them. Escapades that ran from drinking to drugs to tempestuous relationships that often ended with Sheila spiraling out of control.

Tally turned off the water, stepped out, and briskly dried off. Well, her record was mostly intact. She hadn't been tempestuous tonight either. She'd held the line just like she always had, doing what she knew was right even if it wasn't always what she wanted to do. She stopped short, the towel clenched in one hand. She *had* made the right decision. Hadn't she? Of course she had.

She'd just been taken by surprise when she'd been attracted to Rome. She could admit that. She didn't lie to herself. Rome was attractive. Not just physically, although Tally'd always thought Rome was the best-looking one in the crowd that Sheila frequently entertained. The dark-haired, good-looking, popular Rome—the one everyone, girls and boys alike, had tried to emulate. The one Sheila had insisted was her girlfriend—even though she was still with Justin. Tally didn't question Sheila— she *had* posted that picture of them on Facebook after all.

She'd just been taken by surprise by this older, intense Rome with her well of unexpected empathy and compassion. And yes, by the unmistakable heat in her eyes when she'd looked at Tally. And all right, who wouldn't find that attractive? The attraction of others was always attractive. Rome's desire burned right through to the core of her and ignited a hunger she'd never experienced. She was human. Great. But she also had free will and a brain.

And her brain said *time to step back*. Now she just needed to put some distance between herself and Rome. Whatever unconscious attraction she felt to her would disappear quickly enough. Fortunately, there was no reason for her to actually see Rome again. She could make up some excuse and ask Val to make any stops for the puppies. Time and a little distance would allow her to remember why Rome was someone she didn't want anywhere in her life.

Tally pulled on a loose sleep shirt with the logo of her vet school on the front, crawled into bed, and closed her eyes. Satisfied she'd made the right choice, she willed sleep to come. After a very long time, she managed to block the memory of Rome's fingers caressing her face and finally slept.

❖

During an unusual lull in the ER, Rome wandered down to the flight ready room to see if Brody was around. Other than brief casual hellos to the ER staff coming and going, and talking to the teens who came by the trailer morning and night to see the puppies, she hadn't talked to anyone in two days. Ordinarily she wouldn't mind the minimal contact. Casual conversations were the order of the day in the service—brief half sentences, the occasional good-natured jibe, and fleeting morning-after *see you around*s. No one had much in the way of serious conversations, except in the late hours after a tough mission or a few too many rounds when being alive seemed to open the floodgates. When the hours slid back into routine, everyone carefully pretended the personal conversations had never happened and the business of war went on.

But for the last couple of days, she'd had too much time in her own head when she wasn't busy working, and the thoughts plaguing her were all of Tally. She hadn't expected to see her again but was still disappointed when she didn't. Tally had no reason to come by until, by Rome's calendar, another ten days when the puppies needed their next shots. She was pretty sure when that time rolled around, it wouldn't be Tally but Val coming by the trailer. She'd had a lot of practice dealing with disappointment and failure, but this one was hard to shake. Mostly because she'd messed up with someone whose opinion mattered to her. Making a move on a woman who wasn't interested would have bothered her under any circumstances, but that the woman was Tally made it about a million times worse. She'd simply reinforced exactly what Tally thought of her. That she was a womanizer at best or something far worse. She'd come to terms with what others thought of her a long time ago and couldn't—wouldn't—let this mistake with Tally throw her back into those bleak times. She'd read Tally all wrong, Tally had set her straight. No harm, no foul. She just needed to be done with it. And that meant not dwelling on images of Tally's quick, bright laughter, or the way she looked in the soft evening light, or the way her breath had caught when Rome had touched her face. Distraction, that's what she needed.

And thankfully, she found it.

Brody and one of the medivac pilots, Jane, were lounging in the ready room on a well-broken-in mustard-yellow sofa, where an open box of pizza and a couple of cups of brew sat on a low coffee table. Brody smiled when she saw Rome and motioned to an empty chair that looked like the springs had given up the ghost a decade before. "Come on in and grab a slice."

Jane stood, stretched, and said, "I'm going to try to get some rack time. Hey Rome."

"Hi Jane," Rome said as she eased carefully into the chair and leaned forward for a slice of pizza. She wasn't hungry, but she hadn't had anything to eat since breakfast, and it was the middle of the afternoon. She still had a few hours left on her shift, and fuel was always welcome.

"You look a little ragged," Brody said in a teasing tone. "Those puppies keeping you up all night?"

Rome smiled. "Thanks for the compliment. Can always count on you for a positive assessment."

"That's what friends are for," Brody said.

"The one good thing about those puppies is they do everything together," Rome said, taking a bite of the very good pizza. "They sleep at the same time, they all decide it's time for personal business at the same time, and they get hungry at the same time. And presently, they think getting up at two in the morning to try for food is a good idea."

Brody laughed. "How're the backup helpers working out?"

Rome shook her head. "I don't think you can call them backup when most of them show up together even when I'm there. They just want to spend time with the puppies."

"Your days of solitude are over, my friend."

Rome merely nodded. Brody didn't know how wrong she was.

"Speaking of which," Brody went on in her new relaxed and still slightly unexpected tone, "don't forget about the game tonight."

Rome stared. "What game?"

Brody narrowed her gaze. "Don't try that one on me. Remember, I told you, the game first, and then after, the get-together at our place. Seven o'clock, Central High School gym. You know where it is? Right around the corner from Bottoms Up?"

"Oh yeah," Rome said, letting out a breath. "I don't think—"

Brody cut her off with a wave of her hand. "No excuses. It's a thing."

"And what happens if I ignore the *thing*?"

"Everyone in the village will get the idea that you're antisocial and elitist."

Rome laughed ruefully. That would really make her feel like

the clock had somehow reversed and she was about to wake up in her old life. "Well, I certainly wouldn't want that."

Brody's expression grew serious. "Something wrong?"

Rome let out a breath. Still way too complicated and maybe way too late to explain. Brody was part of her life now—and the past was over and gone. "No. It's all good."

"Okay then," Brody said, knowing, like Rome, from long years of experience when to push and when not to. "So, seven o'clock. Don't be late."

Rome's beeper went off and saved her from committing.

"ER," she said and stood. "I'll be right there."

"Seven o'clock!" Brody called as Rome left.

Pam waited at the desk when Rome walked back into the ER. To Rome's querying look, she replied, "A five-year-old got his finger crushed in the weight machine while dad was working out."

A fairly common injury in toddlers and young children. "Amputated the tip?"

"No, it looks like it's hanging on by a few cells. I figured you'd want to Steri-Strip and immobilize it to try to save it. I put the supplies in there for you."

"Okay, thanks," Rome said, pulling up the chart on her tablet.

"What do you think about getting a burger tonight?" Pam said. "Before the game."

Rome laughed. "You too? Brody just reminded me that the game was compulsory."

Pam laughed. "It's the happening thing. But dinner is optional."

Rome appreciated Pam offering her an easy way out but pushed aside the hesitation. She liked Pam, and she might as well face she was going to the thing. "I've got to get home after the shift and check on the puppies, but I ought to be able to make it back in time for a quick bite."

"I can come by and give you a hand," Pam said.

"It's kind of messy work."

Pam laughed and gestured toward the patient area. "Believe me, nothing's messier than this on a regular basis."

"I guess you're right," Rome said. "Sure, you're more than welcome to come by and see them."

"Great, five o'clock sound okay?"

"I'll text you if I get hung up here," Rome said.

Brody had been right about one thing—she was out of luck if she wanted solitude. Somehow she'd already made more connections than she'd had in years. At least she'd be too busy to think much about Tally. For a few hours.

❖

"I didn't expect you to still be here," Val said as she walked into the clinic at a little after five.

"Oh," Tally said, trying to disguise her surprise at having lost track of the time. Doing exactly what she'd sworn she wouldn't do—replaying every word she said and gesture she'd made that might have signaled she'd *wanted* Rome to kiss her. She'd already freely admitted she'd wanted Rome to kiss her— attracted to the attraction and all that—but, God, had she invited Rome without knowing it and then turned her down? Was she becoming Sheila finally—to the point she was even toying with the same woman Sheila had chased and then scorned?

Realizing Val was staring at her with a puzzled frown, she blurted, "Oh. No! I mean—I just got off the phone with Mildred Porter. I promised I would call her with the results of Hector's glucose from this morning. I just got the results back."

Val sat on the bench inside the back door and pulled off her farm boots. As she reached for her low-heeled brown leather ankle boots, she asked, "How's he doing?"

"He's much better already. His glucose is still a little high, but I think that's probably better than increasing the insulin right now. That will give Mildred *and* Hector a chance to get used to the new diet regimen."

"Sounds like a good idea." Val pulled the scrunchy from her ponytail and shook out her long blond hair. How did she manage to have it look so salon-perfect after a day at work? "I'm heading into town to meet Brody for burgers. Want to come before the game?"

The game? Oh no. Was that tonight?

"Oh." Tally frantically searched for a polite way out. She didn't mind the invitation for burgers, but she definitely did not want to spend a couple of hours watching teenagers she didn't know play basketball. And she didn't really want to be stuck in a social situation where she'd have to pretend to be interested in… anything. Right now, all she wanted to do was concentrate on work and stay far clear of any kind of personal interactions. Even innocent ones.

How to get out of it. She needed to wash her hair? She had to clean the kitchen? She needed to call her mother? She almost laughed out loud at that absurdity.

Val slipped into a gorgeous butter-yellow leather jacket that went perfectly with her dark blue jeans and boots, and gave her a long look. "Something wrong?"

"What?" Tally couldn't say she would be terrible company because she was suffering from a mega-case of guilt and recrimination. Could she? "Oh no. Not at all."

"So burgers?"

"Sure. Yes, great." Tally grabbed her perfectly fine Burberry duster, even if it failed at country chic, and followed Val outside. Besides, if she went for burgers, she'd at least have fulfilled her social obligations and could simply say she wasn't up for anything else. An hour and a simple meal could hardly be complicated.

Chapter Sixteen

Just as Rome stepped from the shower, someone knocked on the trailer door. For an instant, her heart leapt. Maybe Tally... but no, she wouldn't drop in. Might not even come by for a professional call after their last encounter. One of the teens, maybe, or Pam. She grabbed a towel, wrapped it around her torso, and called, "Just a second!"

"It's Pam. No hurry."

Rome could dress in a fraction of a minute after years of practice rolling from the rack to the Humvee in seconds. She was nearly as fast pulling on khakis and a navy and red striped polo shirt, and slamming into her boots. She rubbed the rest of the water from her hair with the towel as she crossed through the trailer and pulled open the door. "Hi."

Pam smiled, her gaze traveling over Rome's body. "Sorry— I'm a little early."

"I'm running a little late. Dad decided to faint when I unwrapped the crushed finger."

Pam bit her lip, holding back a smile, as she climbed the steps into the trailer. "I should have called that one and stayed to help."

"Claudia was assisting. She managed to get him to a chair. It all ended well."

Pam seemed not to have heard as her attention swept to the

pen where Bravo yipped indignantly. "Oh my goodness! Look how big they are already."

Rome shook her head, used to playing second string to the puppy platoon whenever anyone walked in. "I'm not sure, but I think they're on an exponential growth curve. They definitely *eat* three times their weight in food every day."

"All right, let me see if I've got this right," Pam said, pointing. "That one's Bravo, easy to tell. She's always the first one at the gate."

"Yup, she takes her job seriously."

Pam went on to name the other five.

"I'm impressed," Rome said. "I think I might be as hungry as they are. How do you feel about corralling them if I let them out while I clean up in there and get their food ready."

"You mean I'm going to be covered in puppies? Sounds like the worst job I've had all day."

"You might regret that in another minute." Rome opened the gate, and Bravo bounced out like a bullet. Rome leaned down to pet her. "Hi there, Sergeant. How's your squad?"

The other five came out in a tumble of wagging tails, joyful yips, and general chaos. Pam crouched down, laughing, and they crowded around her.

"This will just take me a minute," Rome said.

Pam gazed up at her. "Take your time. This is the most fun I've had in ages." She shook her head. "And I don't know what that says about me."

"Well, whatever it is, that goes double for me." Rome quickly cleared out the makeshift puppy run and replaced everything with clean bedding. "Okay, let's get them back inside. All I need to do is dish out their food and give them clean water. Then we can get out of here."

"Oh, must we? They're having such fun, and they've been cooped up all day." Pam cuddled Camo, who'd managed to wiggle into her lap. "Poor babies."

Rome waved her phone. "According to the duty report... Margie and Blake came by at lunch, and Annika stopped in after school let out. Dave is due to come by after football practice. I'll let him know he doesn't have to come," she said as she texted, "but I suspect he will."

"Oh." Pam looked slightly crestfallen. "Then I guess they aren't starving for company."

"I can add you to the list of puppy duty," Rome teased, "but you'll have to negotiate with the kids for space on the schedule."

Pam stood slowly as Rome placed the last puppy back inside and closed the gate. "I was hoping I'd get an invitation to come back that wasn't just for the puppies."

Pam had changed after work into a soft pale green V-neck top tucked into chocolate colored slim-fit trousers and tan boots. A thin multistrand gold chain drew the eye to the deep V in the sweater. Rome carefully raised her eyes to Pam's. "You can assume an open invitation to visit anytime."

"Good," Pam said softly.

The opportunity was there, as was Pam's invitation to her, and everything about it seemed easy. Uncomplicated. Pam was clear in her signals, easy to be with, easy to talk to, and just exactly what Rome needed to get grounded in the present. And that was exactly why she didn't kiss her. That wouldn't be fair. Those easy kisses and easy uncomplicated sex had worked in the past, in different times, but just like everything else in her past, those times were over. She wasn't in the service anymore, and hookups that were momentary escapes didn't fit in the present. Especially not with a woman like Pam, who deserved a lot more than that even if Pam only wanted casual. Rome's casual at least ought to be focused on her, for her alone, and not some other reason. For sure not to take her mind off another woman. That might change, but for now, the timing was wrong.

"I'll just be a second getting them settled," Rome said.

Pam graciously smiled. "Let me give you a hand."

"I didn't invite you over to work, you know," Rome said.

"I know," Pam said. "The puppies were their own reward. What can I do?"

Together, they rinsed bowls, filled them with kibble, made sure the puppies had toys and water, and secured the pen.

"What do you think," Rome said as they walked outside. "Take two cars?"

Pam stopped next to her Miata. "I think probably two cars makes sense."

"Right, okay. I'll see you there." Rome followed Pam to the village and parked next to her in the lot beside Bottoms Up.

"The place looks busy already," Rome said as she walked to the tavern with Pam.

"Friday night before a game? We'll be lucky to get a table."

Pam was right. They managed to grab one of the few empty tables, and Pam said, "It's bar service. What will you have?"

Rome pulled out one of the two chairs. "I'll get it. Beer and a burger?"

Laughing, Pam nodded and sat down. "Got it in one. Draft is fine. Medium on the burger."

"Be right back." Rome put the food order in, got a receipt with their number on it, and carried two drafts through the increasingly large crowd at the bar back to the table. "Here you go."

"Thanks," Pam said, sipping the beer.

Rome hit the problem head-on. "Can I just say—it's a timing thing. Believe me, it's not you."

"You don't need to explain. I'm more than happy to spend time with you." Pam raised a brow. "Although I am a little surprised."

"Well, hell. I'm way out of practice—sorry if I'm sending the wrong signals here."

"No, you're not." Pam smiled. "But I'm a little surprised *I'm* reading them wrong. So just to be clear, you're single?"

Rome laughed. "Very and pretty much always."

"That's another surprise. How did that come about?"

"Really long story, but to make it a short one, I joined the Army when I was nineteen. That's where I got my medical training. And then I spent a while in the Middle East."

"Nothing before that? No childhood sweetheart?"

"Ah, no," Rome said a little wryly. Sheila's face immediately filled her memory, and she hid a wince. "I dated, but there was no one serious."

"I imagine that was your choice," Pam said.

"Right again. What about you? Single?"

Pam sighed. "I am. And there was someone, in college. She wanted to pursue an acting career in LA. After two and a half years, we called it quits. I already knew that wasn't a life I wanted, and no way was she going to come to cow country, as she called it." She shook her head. "My father's an organic food producer. We don't even have cows."

"At least you knew what wouldn't work."

Pam lifted a shoulder. "Since then casual, and not very often. This place is a little small for that."

"The village, you mean?"

"Mm, that. And then there's the hospital. The grapevines are so thick, it's hard not to get tangled in them."

Rome chuckled. "No matter how big a hospital is, it's a little small where those things are concerned."

Pam laughed. "You got that right." She reached across the table and touched Rome's arm. "So, we've established the no strings and no recently broken hearts. Am I reading right that there could be some interest? I'll say I have some, and taking things slow is fine."

Searching for an answer that made sense, other than *I seem to be hung up on a woman who couldn't be less interested*, Rome caught movement out of the corner of her eye and paused.

Brody stood by their table and said, "Hey, I know Pam's coming to the game, so I won't have to twist your arm any longer." She grinned at Pam. "Make sure this one gets over to the house afterward too."

"I'll do what I can." Pam smiled. "Hi Val. Hi Tally. Planning to go to the game?"

"I…" Tally's gaze traveled from Pam to Rome and quickly skipped back to Pam. Maybe she would've said no if she hadn't seen Pam's hand on Rome's arm. A cold wash of reality flooded through her. Rome certainly wasn't wasting any time establishing her place in the community. Still the same charismatic force she'd always been. Well, Tally had a life to build here, and sitting at home avoiding Rome wasn't going to accomplish that. If she was going to live here, and she damn well was, that meant bumping into Rome from time to time. She would simply have to remind herself that what Rome did was of no matter to her.

"Yes," Tally said brightly. "I wouldn't miss it."

❖

"Are the burgers here really good? I don't eat much meat, so when I do…" Tally said as she sat down with Brody and Val at one of the last open tables across the room from Rome and Pam. If she angled her chair just a little, she wouldn't have to watch them talking and looking like the attractive couple they undeniably were. She wasn't so petty she resented someone else's pleasure. She just didn't want to watch.

"They really are," Val said. "I actually don't eat much in the way of meat either, but these are from one of the local farms that feeds organic. Pam's dad supplies the feed to most of the organic farmers in the region, so I can vouch for the quality. If you're ever going to have a burger, this is the place."

"All right, I'm convinced."

"Beer with that?" Brody asked as she stood.

"Sure." Tally wasn't about to swim against the tide. Maybe in time she could actually acquire a taste for beer. Like so many things here, new challenges. "Somehow I don't see Pam as a farmer."

Val laughed. "I doubt Pam does either. As I recall, she did

her share of chores, like every farm kid, I'm sure, but she was born and mostly raised in the city. She went away for college too and still has a lot of city in her."

"Yes," Tally said softly. Pam would be just the kind of woman Rome would be attracted to—smart, lovely, and polished. She turned her chair just a little more to move them out of her line of sight. To be polite. And to avoid the irrational emotional response to seeing them together that she did not want to think about.

"So," Val said as she leaned back in her chair. "Impressions of the new situation?"

"Complicated," Tally said without thinking.

"Oh. Problems?" Val sat forward, looking concerned.

Tally felt heat rise to her face. Just because she was fixated— and how she hated that word!—not everyone was talking about Rome. "Oh God. No, work? Absolutely not. It's everything I hoped it would be and more."

"Good," Val said, visibly relaxing. "I have to say I think we're a great team. The staff loves you, at least two patients have stopped me when I was in town to tell me what a great job you did with their babies, and well"—she raised a shoulder—"partnering with someone is a lot like being in a relationship. At least in a small operation like mine. It's family."

Tally drew a breath. Family. Nothing about living and working here resembled her memories of family. "I know what you mean, but I'm not sure how good I'll be at that."

"I think you're already great at it." Val added carefully, "I'm happy to be a sounding board, and I really hope we'll be friends, but I don't expect us to be sisters. You're entitled to your private life at all times."

"Sisters," Tally said, shaking her head. "Believe me, that's the last thing I want."

"Sorry if I got too personal," Val said.

"No, you didn't." Tally chided herself for slipping. She never, ever revealed personal information to strangers. But then Val wasn't a stranger, was she. She was someone who'd already become important to her. She took a deep breath. "I'm sorry. I am having a little bit of a hard time adjusting."

"I'm not surprised," Val said. "This has to feel like another planet to you."

"You know, it does and it doesn't. The intimacy is new. Everyone knowing everyone else. The easy way people seem to pull other people into their orbits. I grew up in a very social environment, but there were incredible barriers too. If you scratched the surface of the web of social connections, you'd find all kinds of agendas and secrets plans...or rather, machinations." She shook her head. "My mother was planning where I'd go to preschool practically before I was born—and it just went on from there."

"I suppose the same thing goes on here, perhaps on a slightly smaller scale." Val laughed. "Maybe not over the same kinds of things—there's not the pressure to climb the social ladder as you've likely experienced. The economics of small rural towns foster a fair amount of interdependency. If we don't at least try to work together, we might not survive. But you'll find your fair share of family feuds—take that from someone who grew up in the middle of one—and, unfortunately, the occasional small-mindedness and bigotry that crops up everywhere."

"I definitely didn't expect a fairy-tale world when I moved here," Tally said, smiling. "And I want to make this work. More than I can tell you."

"Then we're going to do just fine. And I promise not to drag you to *too* many village events if you'd really rather not."

"I thought," Tally said slowly, "when I got here life would be a blank slate. I would rewrite myself and everything about me." She glanced across the room toward Rome and Pam. "Seeing Rome after all these years was so unexpected. *She's* so unexpected. So much for my plans to start fresh. Maybe that's impossible. It's all been a little confusing running into my past, but I've sorted it out now."

"That's good to hear," Val said.

"And thank you for not asking."

Val shook her head. "That's another one of the good things about living in such a close community. People's private business stays private unless they decide it won't be. Oh, sure, everyone likes to gossip a little bit. Up to a point. But digging into affairs that don't concern you? Not so much."

"There really isn't anything to tell," Tally said and, as she said it, realized how true that was. Telling, retelling, obsessing over events that could not be changed and had nothing to do with the present was pointless, a lesson she needed to remind herself of more often. She *would* remember. Knowing that, believing that, eased some of the weight inside her. "I do have a secret, though."

Val regarded her seriously. "Oh?"

Tally leaned forward. "I've never liked beer."

Val cast a glance to where Brody threaded her way through the crowd with three foaming glasses of draft beer. "Just let her down gently."

Tally laughed and found herself almost able to forget about Pam and Rome across the room.

CHAPTER SEVENTEEN

Tally followed Val and Brody to the high school and parked the Bug next to a long line of yellow school buses in the crowded parking lot. Some of them had the name of a town she didn't recognize on the side. They must have carried the team or maybe the students from the competing school tonight. She'd seen the buses picking up kids throughout the countryside on her way to the clinic in the morning and been surprised the first time she witnessed small children happily hopping onto the buses on their own after a hurried wave to the parents who waited with them by the side of the road. The idea of that amount of freedom left her a little envious. She'd never ridden a school bus. Her parents or one of her friends' parents had driven them to Brearly until she'd been old enough—meaning a teenager—to take the subway with friends or ride with someone who had a car. Sheila had never let her ride with any of her friends, of course. Tally was too young and would just be in the way. As if four years created a social chasm never to be crossed.

"Did you ride the school bus when you were growing up?" she asked Val as the three of them walked inside. The lemon-yellow halls were brightly lit and tiled in serviceable gray and white vinyl squares. The rumble of many voices grew louder with every step.

Val laughed. "It was that or walk five miles—no, thanks. Why?"

"Oh. I never did."

Brody chuckled. "Then you missed some of the many courtship rituals reserved for school bus riders the world over."

Tally glanced at Val. "Sorry?"

Val rolled her eyes. "Depending on the age, Brody could be referring to being hit with a wad of paper blown through a straw or to a note passed from hand to hand asking *Do you like Brody?*"

"Except," Brody said, "you never answered. You were too hung up on Flann."

"Really?" Tally asked. "There's a story I'd like to hear."

"That was high school. Having a crush on one of the Rivers sisters was almost a requirement." Val slipped an arm around Brody's waist. "And for your information, I always thought *you* were the hottest of them all."

Brody grinned. "I *knew* it."

Tally wondered what it would be like to love someone you'd known for so long—to be *in* love with someone you'd grown up with. The ache that crept up on her caught her by surprise. As did her instant thought of Rome and what life might have been like for all of them if that night had never happened. To her relief, they reached the gymnasium, and the wave of noise and blazing lights made not only conversation but coherent thought nearly impossible. The bleachers that rose from courtside halfway to the vaulted ceiling and extended the full length of the room on each side looked full.

"You weren't kidding about the whole town being here," Tally shouted to Val. "I hope you got reserved seats!"

"Same thing. Over there," Val said, waving, "it looks like Flann and Abby have saved us a place."

Tally obediently followed Val and Brody along the narrow path between the bleachers and the gleaming basketball court and gingerly threaded her way up the stands, trying valiantly not to step on anyone or fall into the gaps between the rows. When she reached the six inches of open space between Val and Abby Remy, she carefully wedged herself in.

"Hi," Abby said. "You made it."

"Hi," Tally said. "I can't believe how many people are here."

Abby laughed. "Between parents and grandparents of the players, the students and most of their families, plus the school staff on both sides, you've got a good chunk of two towns squeezed in here."

"I understand the competition is pretty heated."

"There are definitely age-old rivalries, beginning so far back most people can't even remember what started them. It's pretty good-natured, although occasionally some of the parents get a little overinvolved."

Tally wasn't surprised by that. Although her parents never came to her field hockey games, and she wasn't really in the running for a sports scholarship, the parents of the girls who were could sometimes be super aggressive. "How about the kids?"

"I think their coaches do a really good job teaching them good sportsmanship. Of course, they're teenagers. Boys and girls alike can get a little *enthusiastic*, shall we say."

"I know Blake has been looking forward to this," Tally said.

Abby nodded. "The coach didn't give them the starting five before tonight, so we're not sure how much he'll be playing—if at all."

"I have to say I don't know a lot about the game. Basketball wasn't exactly a big sport, at least at my school."

"Let me guess, private girls' school?"

"All the way," Tally said. "Not really by choice—it was just what everyone did. Everyone my parents knew at least."

"Mm," Abby said, "I know what you mean. Private schools tend to lean more toward field hockey, lacrosse, tennis, and the like. I was golf. You?"

"Field hockey. Not good enough for college competition, though." Tally felt a little more comfortable every minute. Abby, well everyone, seemed so easy to talk to. Why was that? She didn't feel the slightest bit of competition or appraisal from anyone. So refreshing, and she knew, not being naive, that of course underneath the surface all kinds of ambitions and rivalries existed in this village just as they existed anywhere else. But she hadn't had any close acquaintances, let alone friends, since high school, and hopefully that would change.

"I managed *not* to end up at an all-girls school," Abby said, "much to my disappointment at the time." She laughed. "But it all worked out. I have Blake, and that's changed my whole life. We moved here, and I met Flann. Blake has made great friends. I can't imagine being anywhere else."

"Like you," Tally said, "I think this move might be the best thing I've ever done."

Abby's brow rose. "Well, you've certainly picked the polar opposite place to settle."

"In some ways, yes," Tally said. "But then, people are people."

Abby laughed. "You've got that right. Between the family free-for-all the other night, the game tonight, and the party after at Val and Brody's, you'll be getting a pretty good look at a lot of the town."

"Oh, that night at Bottoms Up was a great introduction to your family."

"And there are more of us." Abby tipped her head toward a man in a white shirt and navy tie with a full head of dark brown hair seated beside a woman with thick auburn hair shot through with silver in casual hunter green slacks and a floral patterned sweater. They sat one tier down in front of Flann. "That's Flann's parents right there, sitting next to Harper and Presley. I think you've met all the sibs already. The only members of the extended family not here yet are Val's cousin Courtney, who's probably still at the hospital, and her fiancée Bennett, who's over with the team. She's the team doctor. They should be at the party later, though."

"Looking forward to meeting them." Tally laughed. "I was just putting all the names to faces when I had to leave early to give Rome a hand with gathering the puppy supplies."

"Yes, I understand I'll be having a new addition before too long."

"I was wondering how all the parents were going to take this. We really didn't plan it."

Abby laughed. "Oh no, I'm sure you didn't. Those five—six now that Annika has joined the crew—are perfectly able to make all the necessary plans themselves."

"They're an awfully good bunch," Tally said.

"The best. Oh look—here we go." Abby's attention switched to the far side of the gym as the crowd began to stomp and clap. She grasped Flann's hand. "Here he comes."

The players came out from opposite ends of the gym, the home team in maroon and blue, the visitors in green. Tally picked out Blake right away. He was half a head shorter than most of the players but clearly had been putting in serious time in the gym. She felt Abby's tension even though they weren't touching. She suspected every parent was a little anxious and tried to imagine how Abby would feel each time her son was in a new situation. She couldn't remember her parents ever being protective of her or worried about how she would manage in a new social situation. But to be fair, she'd worked very hard not to give them any reason to worry.

Now that her choices were her own, she could look back at her younger self and see that she'd survived without any serious damage. And as she did, the past faded ever so slightly, and along with it, the pain. If only she could find a way to put Sheila and Rome—

Beside her, Val leaned over and said, "You'll probably be a little lost trying to follow all the plays, but the important thing is that our team puts the ball into the basket one way or the other. That's really all you need to know."

Tally laughed. "I think I can follow it that much."

Just as the teams were coming onto the floor, Brody called, "Hey, Rome, over here."

Tally watched Pam and Rome climb their way up through

the bleachers toward their group. Rome's eyes met hers for an instant, and Tally flushed. Rome nodded slightly, and that small recognition made her pulse jump. Hopeless. She was absolutely hopeless. Thankfully, Pam and Rome ended up sitting one row down and on the far side of Brody. She wouldn't have to talk to them or, better still, watch them together.

❖

Brody leaned down and said in Rome's ear, "Was starting to worry you wouldn't make it!"

"No way," Rome half shouted above the clapping and chanting. "I got paged from the ER. I'm second call, and they might be getting patients from a multi-car pileup on Route 7. If they do, I might have to go in."

Brody frowned. "Jane's flying tonight. I switched call so I could be here for the first game."

Brody looked uneasy, and Rome understood why. Jane and Brody most often flew together—they were a unit. Brody would want to be there if Jane was making a run, especially a night run when weather and visibility were always more unpredictable.

"If I hear anything more," Rome said, "I'll let you know."

"Thanks."

Rome turned back to the activity on the floor, but her focus was still on the row behind her where Tally sat on the far side of Val. Studiously ignoring Rome. She shouldn't have been surprised to see her. After Tally walked in with Brody and Val at the tavern, Rome assumed Tally would be at the game. She'd had almost an hour to prepare for the moment she saw her. She'd actually looked for her as soon as she walked into the gym so she wouldn't be caught off guard again. She *hadn't* been prepared to see Tally walk into the tavern. But then she never seemed to be prepared for that moment when she first saw Tally, no matter where they were. The world seemed to pause for an instant and sound disappeared, the people she was with faded into the background, and all she knew was Tally. She'd never had that experience before, but she knew instinctively what the surge of emotional overload signaled. She was in trouble and no point denying it. She wanted the one woman who would never want her.

Fortunately, the teams were on the floor warming up, and she could at least focus on that and try to ignore the urge to look over her shoulder to see if Tally was possibly looking her way. Her puppy crew sat a few rows down from her, closer to courtside, all five of them already cheering loudly for Blake. Rome had played plenty of pickup ball while deployed and didn't need to watch long to see Blake was a strong all-around player. From the patterns they were running in warm-ups, it looked like Blake was playing point guard. Basketball wasn't her sport, but the team looked good working together—nice crisp lay-ups, accurate passes, and a couple of shooters, including Blake, hitting three-pointers from all over the court. The other team's players were all bigger and looked pretty good warming up, but they traded size for quickness.

"Ought to be a good game," she remarked to Pam.

Pam leaned closer to be heard. "This is the team we beat last year to go to State. They're holding a little bit of a grudge."

"That might explain the noise level," Rome said with a grin.

Pam laughed. "They've got most of their starters back, and our team is a little younger. And of course, Blake is brand-new since he transferred in."

"He looks pretty comfortable out there," Rome said as the ref signaled it was time for the tip-off.

The game got off to a good start, and with the home-court advantage and the crowd spurring them on, the Ravens were up by ten with a minute and a half to go in the second quarter. Blake had played all but a few minutes, and he had eight points, including two three-pointers, and a handful of assists. He passed off when other players had a better shot and took his own with confidence when he had the opening.

The game was physical, with a fair amount of jostling, especially in the paint, but that was to be expected. The competition was clean until the moment one of the two players guarding Blake made a grab for the ball as Blake brought the ball downcourt and pretty deliberately elbowed Blake in the face. His muttered, "Faggot," was audible too. Blake went down and half the people on the home side of the court got to their feet, screaming for the foul. Rome stood with everyone else, Pam's hand clamped to her forearm.

"Oh no," Pam murmured as Blake failed to get up.

"God damn it," Rome heard someone behind her growl and turned to see Flann Rivers on her feet and about to push her way down through the stands to the gym floor. Abby grabbed her arm and said with preternatural calm and quiet command, "Wait, Flann. Ben is on her way out there right now."

Flann paused, stone-faced, her eyes blazing. She linked her fingers with Abby's and stared down at where Blake had now pushed himself up to a sitting position. Rome picked out the tall, blade-thin, dark-haired woman in navy pants and a pale blue shirt who crouched down next to Blake as the likely team doctor. The basketball coach in a maroon polo and khakis leaned over with a hand on Blake's shoulder, talking to him. Thirty seconds passed, and Blake got slowly to his feet and was escorted by the team doctor over to the bench where several other people—probably trainers—crowded around. The home crowd roared in support along with quite a few shouts of *Eject him! Eject him!* Blake's team formed a knot of grumbling, adrenaline-fueled temper. The ref walked over to the opposing team's coach, spoke to them, and the coach, grim faced, nodded and signaled to the player who'd knocked Blake down. The players' shouts of protest could be heard across the floor when the ref called a technical foul. When the player tried to push his way past his coach toward the ref, still shouting, the ref's arm shot out, pointing to the back of the gym, indicating the player had been ejected from the game.

Pam murmured, "What *is* it with people. I hope Blake isn't hurt."

"He took a pretty good shot, but he got up pretty quick." Rome shook her head. "Is he gay, or was that just the slur du jour?"

"I don't know if he's gay," Pam said. "He's trans. I suppose that could be behind all this. I can't imagine being Abby or Flann right now. *I* want to go down there and shake sense into that other boy!"

"Harder to sit still for it," Rome murmured. She didn't actually know that from personal experience, because her parents had only wanted to bury her problem. She couldn't completely blame them, since Justin and Sheila's story contradicted hers and, with Tally's statement, had left her looking guilty. But they hadn't even *asked* for her side. She shrugged off the old and mostly faded hurt. "The guy's a jerk, and he's out of the game. That won't be forgotten right away by anyone watching."

Ben, who'd been examining Blake, turned, looked over to where the Rivers family were all poised to move at any instant, and said clear enough for anyone watching to understand, "He's okay."

"I'm willing to bet the team comes out on fire now," Rome said, and her bet proved true. The home team won by twenty points. As the crowd rose and began to leave the gymnasium, Pam said, "I want to talk to Abby for a minute. Are you coming over to Brody and Val's?"

Rome said, "If I can. I might get called in—I'm waiting to hear. Sorry."

"I'll look for you," Pam said with a smile. "If you can't make it, I'll see you tomorrow."

Rome nodded and started down through the stands.

"Are you planning to escape?" Tally said as she and Rome reached the floor at the same time.

Rome turned, got hit with the first paralyzing wash of

attraction, desire, and sheer happiness at seeing her, and said when she found her voice, "I have a legitimate excuse—several. I'm second call and waiting to hear from the ER. And I think the puppy-care crew will want to stay around here to see Blake. I was planning to text them and tell them I've got the duty."

"I think I envy you," Tally said. "Those are legitimate reasons to duck the gathering."

Rome didn't hesitate. "I could use a hand with Bravo Company—if you don't mind missing the party."

Tally's searching gaze was unreadable, but her answer was clear enough. "I don't mind at all. Let's go."

Chapter Eighteen

I'm parked down at the end, toward that row of school buses," Tally said as she and Rome filed out of the school amidst the boisterous crowd. She'd managed a minute among the crowd of Rivers family members gathered on the gym floor at the end of the game to tell Val she was skipping the party. Val had smiled at Rome and nodded to Tally and said not to worry, there would be others.

As they broke free of the throng in the parking lot and turned down one of the aisles between the trucks and cars, Rome said quietly, "If you change your mind on your way over to my place, just shoot me a text."

Tally shook her head, not looking at her. "Why would I do that?"

"You're not the impulsive type," Rome said lightly, "so if—"

"What makes you think that?" Tally turned to face Rome. The long lot adjacent to the school was illuminated in a hazy yellow glow emanating from lights atop tall, curved silver lampposts every twenty feet or so. Enough to make out Rome's surprised expression. "That I'm not impulsive?"

Rome seemed to take a moment to answer. Tally liked that about her. She considered what she would say, and that made Tally feel as if what she'd just asked actually mattered to Rome. That *she* mattered.

"It wasn't meant as a criticism," Rome said slowly. "I think of you as being very deliberate—careful but not necessarily cautious. Grounded." Rome raised a shoulder. "I was hoping you'd accept my invitation to come over, but I was a little surprised. I'll understand if you change your mind, but I sure hope you don't."

"Grounded," Tally murmured. "Maybe you should have said *stuck*."

"Stuck?"

"Mm." Tally laughed softly and had an image of herself throwing off the mantle of her mother's expectations and her sister's needs. To listen to her heart instead of her head. Just this once. "Never mind. I don't plan to change my mind."

She walked on to her Bug and said as she slid behind the wheel, "See you in a few minutes."

She didn't close the door, looking up at Rome to reply. Rome's heart stutter-stepped, and she braced an arm on the curved roof as she leaned down. Tally's eyes widened but she held Rome's gaze. Rome could have kissed her then, wanted to, but half the town was walking by. And she didn't want a quick kiss in the dark. She wanted something more. "I think I neglected to add I also think you're amazing, accomplished, and astonishingly attractive."

Tally laughed. "Nice save. And...thank you."

Rome let out a breath. "I'll see you at the trailer."

Tally nodded, closed her door, and watched in her rearview mirror as Rome walked briskly away. Feeling just a bit wild and not even questioning why she wasn't questioning herself, Tally started the car and followed the line of traffic out to the street, which, considering the long line of vehicles, was probably the closest this place ever got to rush hour traffic. The few minutes' wait added to the buzzing in her middle that had begun as anticipation and quickly grown into an agitated mix of excitement and impatience. She drove the few miles to Rome's, taking care not to speed. Her mind was surprisingly and luxuriously clear. Rome had asked her, quite clearly, to ditch the party and come home with her. Her immediate, uncensored response was *Yes, I'd like that.* And to hell with the usual cautions and considerations. She was an adult, free of any commitments. And if she wanted a woman—to *go home* with a woman, she meant—then she didn't need to ask permission or explain to anyone.

She waited in the Bug until Rome pulled the Porsche in alongside her, got out, and came around to her car.

When she got out, Rome said, "There isn't a whole lot that needs doing. Pam and I fed them earlier, so they mostly need a little bit of people time and a cleanup of their sleeping area. It won't take more than a minute. I've got some wine, if you'd like some while you wait."

"That would be great," Tally said as Rome held the door open for her and she climbed the two metal steps inside. "I'm sorry if I disrupted your plans with Pam."

"We didn't have any set plans for later tonight," Rome said carefully. She wasn't sure exactly what Tally was asking or how much she wanted to know, but she added, because *she* wanted Tally to know, "It wasn't a date, just friendly colleagues getting together after work."

The lights were dim inside the trailer again, with just that little light over the kitchenette that threw everything into soft shadows. Even the softness of the light couldn't alter the striking contours of Rome's face, though, and Tally marveled once again at how much more beautiful the older Rome, the woman she had come to know, was than the memory of her she'd carried for a decade. "I wondered. Pam's very nice."

"She is," Rome said. "And I'm glad we're going to be friends—she and I."

"And are we?" Tally asked. "Going to be friends?"

"Pam asked me something interesting," Rome said in a ruminative voice, as if she was recalling something from a dream.

Tally leaned back against the kitchen counter, the same position she'd been in the last time they were alone together. She'd never seen Rome this way—so open and vulnerable. Or maybe she just hadn't wanted to see. "What was it?"

"She asked me if there was anyone serious in my life, past or present."

Tally drew a breath and waited. The answer to this could change...perhaps *would* change...everything. At the very least it might send her out the door with sanity, or insanity, restored.

"I told her that there wasn't. And then she asked about teenage loves."

Tally tensed. Sheila? And as soon as she thought it, she dismissed it. She knew, without knowing exactly how, but absolutely certain that wasn't the case.

"I told her there wasn't." Rome took a breath. "I wasn't altogether honest."

"This surprises me," Tally said, refusing to jump to conclusions. "If someone had asked me to describe you, I would've said *honest*."

Rome visibly shuddered, and the movement, so unguarded, struck at Tally's core. Rome wasn't so controlled after all, and she'd been hurt. Just weeks earlier, she would've dismissed the wave of sympathy with an angry mental shake, but she believed it now.

"What is it?" Tally said.

"Hearing you say that means a lot to me."

Tally sighed. "We haven't exactly done a good job of communicating so far, have we?"

"What do you mean?" Rome asked.

"First impressions can often be deceiving—if a person is very good at deception or projecting an image that isn't really who they are inside. But sometimes, depending on the circumstances, that first glance is the most accurate." Tally paused, hearing her own words echoing back to her. Was it possible she'd met two very different women, one that night so long ago and the other the morning Rome appeared with the rescued puppies? Was that what all the sleepless nights had been about, bringing her to that truth? She smiled at Rome's puzzled expression. "Never mind. You first. You were about to tell me about past sweethearts?"

Rome shook her head. "I guess I wasn't exactly clear either. I told Pam the truth, that there wasn't anyone and hadn't been anyone serious in my life. What I didn't tell her was that I was serious now about someone who didn't actually know it."

Tally's heart did a crazy kind of drumroll inside her chest. She needed to stay ahead of her emotions for just a few more minutes. "Part of the reason I said yes when you asked me to come over tonight is that we never seem to see each other alone, and I need to apologize to you."

"Why? I was about to tell you I was sorry too," Rome replied.

Tally frowned. "About what?"

"When you were here the last time," Rome said, "I came on pretty strong. I'm sorry I pushed. You shouldn't have had to say no. I'm sorry for any discomfort I caused you."

Tally closed her eyes and took a long breath. When she opened them she met Rome's gaze. "That's just what I was about to say. The last time I was here, I was guilty of sending mixed signals. I *wanted* you to kiss me, just like the first time in the car, but part of me wasn't ready. I know it sounds like I was playing games with you, but I wasn't, not intentionally. That's not who I am. So I'm sorry." When Rome started to protest, she touched the tips of her fingers to Rome's mouth. "*And* I'm sorry if I made you feel like you had upset me. There's certainly no need to apologize."

Rome ran a hand through her hair. "I can't believe I've gotten so bad at this. Hell, no wonder you weren't sure. Talk about garbled messages. I could have just said I really wanted to kiss you and let you answer."

Tally reached out, gripped the fabric of Rome's shirt with both hands, and gave her a tug forward. She came instantly until their bodies nearly touched. Lifting her head to meet Rome's eyes, she said, "I don't want you to be sorry. And I'm answering now. I really want you to kiss me."

Rome groaned, a deep soft rumble in her throat as her hands came to Tally's shoulders. Her grip was gentle and sure, her fingers splayed on Tally's back, each tantalizing point of pressure kindling heat like a breeze on smoldering embers.

"Now?"

"Now would be a very good time," Tally murmured, just as Rome's mouth covered hers.

She wasn't a novice at kissing, but she'd never experienced a kiss that felt capable of satisfying her for hours. Rome's mouth was hot, her kiss soft and teasing, as if Rome was learning her through the slow glide of her lips over Tally's, there and then gone again. Tasting her with a barely-there tug of her teeth, as if sampling her essence. Tally pressed closer, the sudden ache in her breasts demanding contact, the pressure deep inside reaching for the echoing need in Rome's body. Rome's grip tightened, and Tally wrapped both arms around her waist, cleaving to her. The kiss went on, deepening, until they both explored, hands skimming restlessly over back muscles, smoothing and searching, their breath, their beings, seeking.

After an endless moment, Rome straightened, her hands clasping Tally's sides, thumbs spread against her abdomen. "I've been thinking about that since I looked up and saw you that first morning in the clinic."

"Funny," Tally whispered, pressing close, her lips against Rome's throat. "I have too, but I didn't let myself know it at first."

"Are you sorry now?" Rome whispered, and Tally thrilled to the hunger in Rome's voice.

"Not a bit."

"Can you feel how much I want you?" Rome's fingers trembled as she stroked Tally's cheek. "When I touch you, I'm lost. You've captivated me from the moment we met..." She laughed, a hollow aching sound that pierced Tally's heart.

"Then what? What hurts you?" Tally said.

"If we had just met that day in the clinic," Rome said, "I'd want you in my bed right now, so I could slide my hands all over you, so I could show you with kisses, with words, with everything I am how much I want you. How I think of you when we're part, how I imagine us lying together, your mouth on me, mine on you. What it would be like to wake up in the morning, to feel your breath against my skin, to make coffee and bring it to you in bed. To have the chance to show you all over again in the light of day how knowing you has opened something inside me, shown me a place I've never been before. But we didn't meet that morning in the clinic, and we can't pretend we did."

Tally pulled back, a cold fire racing through her blood. "What are you saying?"

Rome framed Tally's face and kissed her softly, an endless aching kiss that so plainly said good-bye that Tally's heart bled. When Rome stepped back, Tally didn't try to hold her.

"I've tried to outlive the past, to outrun it in any way I could," Rome said. "The journey hasn't all been bad. It's brought me here, taught me the skill that gives my life meaning. But we can't ever completely leave the past behind, especially not us. And I don't want just one night with you."

"And if I said I want more than that, too?" Tally asked.

"She's your *sister*. Your family knows me. Will she forgive you if you're with me? Will they?" She slid her hands to Tally's shoulders, gently holding her away. "Will you be able to forget that night and believe I'm not that person?"

"Are we always going to be the prisoners of our past, then?" Tally asked.

"I don't know," Rome said. "I only know that I'm falling in love with you and there's no going back. And if ultimately the past wins? I'll lose everything. Everything."

Tally took a long shuddering breath. "I've thought a lot of things about you in my life, but never, never *once*, did I think you were a coward."

"Then maybe you don't know me as well as you thought," Rome whispered.

Tally edged around her and walked to the door. "Good night, Rome."

She didn't look back as she walked out.

❖

Rome stood in the shadows of the pale yellow light, listening to Tally's car start up and drive away. The hollow ache in her chest expanded to an emptiness that stole through her like a lethal infection. Tally was right. She was a coward. She'd pushed Tally away, fearing an abyss a thousand times greater than the one swallowing her now if she took Tally to bed, and in the morning, Tally realized what she'd done. She didn't doubt Tally's word when she'd said she only cared about the now. She said that *now*. But Rome needed more than now—she needed a tomorrow she could count on. She wasn't falling in love with Tally, she was already in love with her. Losing her after letting her in, after letting herself hope, would be more than all the losses she'd faced in her life, a loss she didn't think she'd have the strength to survive. She ran a hand over her face and closed her eyes. Maybe she'd always been a coward. She didn't have the courage to find out.

A whine followed by a sharp bark brought her out of the dark. Bravo stood at the puppy gate, her paws resting as high up as she could go. She peered at Rome and barked again. An indignant, accusatory bark. One that said, *I'm still here.*

"I hear you." Rome retreated from the pain and did what she was good at, what had always saved her. She went to take care of her squad. She let the puppies out, and they raced around while she cleaned their quarters and replaced the chow. As she wrangled them back inside, a vehicle pulled in, crunching over the gravel in front of the trailer. Rome closed the puppies behind their gate, her heart pounding. She might be strong enough to make sure her path didn't cross Tally's in the future, but she'd never be strong enough to turn her away from the door. And nothing could prevent her from opening it. She pulled open the door, the hope she couldn't quite kill surging through her.

"Oh," Blake said, "sorry. I didn't think you'd be here."

Rome drew a deep breath. "That's okay. Come on in."

"I, uh, thought I'd check on them." He'd changed into jeans, high-tops, and a white T-shirt under a red hoodie.

"Just you?" Rome asked.

"Yeah," Blake said, sounding uncharacteristically uneasy.

"Sorry if you're missing the party. I sent a group text to let you all know you could skip the duty tonight."

"I got it. I just didn't feel like going." Blake's expression brightened at a sudden cacophony of puppy sounds as the puppies rushed over to the gate again.

Rome reached in, pulled out Hood, and handed the puppy to Blake. "I think this is the one you're looking for."

Blake buried his face against the small wiggling body for a moment and breathed deeply. When he raised his head, he smiled wryly. "Yeah, thanks."

Bravo barked impatiently until Rome picked her up. Holding Bravo to her chest, she tilted her head toward the back door. "Want to sit outside? Still pretty warm out there. The rest of them will probably quiet down if they can't see us."

"You don't mind?" Blake said softly.

"Nope," Rome said. "We're good. Come on."

The night sky was clear and dark with a scattering of bright stars, a sky not unlike that in the desert. They sat at the table behind the trailer side by side, puppies in their laps.

"Congratulations on the win," Rome said after a few moments of silence. "I thought you looked good out there."

"Thanks," Blake said.

"How's your face? You took a pretty good shot."

Blake gave her a crooked grin. "Hurts a little. My parents agree I'm going to have a shiner."

"The guy was a jerk," Rome said. "But you know that, don't you?"

"Yeah," Blake said with a sigh. "I've sort of been expecting it…at some point…" His voice tightened with the first sign of anger. "I get tired of it, you know?"

"I *don't* know," Rome said, "not exactly. I've run into some bigots, for sure, who gave me some grief over being queer. Not the same, but I can imagine."

"Well, you get what it's like. It upsets my parents too."

Rome got the picture then. "Your parents love you. They can handle it."

"I wish they didn't have to."

"They feel the same way about you. Love is like that—it goes both ways. The good and the bad."

"It's a big responsibility," Blake finally said. "The love thing."

"Sometimes almost more than you can handle," Rome said quietly.

"My teammates were all angry about it. I don't want to make trouble for the team."

Bravo stirred and whined a little in her sleep, and Rome stroked her until she relaxed again. "That's what being part of the team is all about. You look after each other, you watch each other's backs, and when somebody goes after one of your own, you close ranks. They handled themselves tonight. So did you."

"I can talk to my parents about most anything," Blake said, "but sometimes I worry I'll just make them worry more."

"I don't know them real well, but I work with your mom. I can tell you a hundred percent that nothing you tell her—and I bet that goes for Flann too—will be something they don't want to hear."

Blake let out a breath. "Yeah. But sometimes I don't want to talk."

"They probably know that too. And luckily, Hood there will always listen."

Blake laughed and scratched the puppy's ears. "That's what I figured. Sorry I barged in."

"No, I'm glad you did. Sometimes listening helps as much as talking."

Blake didn't ask her what she meant, and she didn't feel any need to explain. They sat in silence a few minutes longer, and then Blake stood. "I better get home. Thanks."

Rome didn't ask him for what—they understood each other in that moment. "Anytime."

With the puppies back in the pen, Rome stood at the door as Blake pulled out and drove away. She didn't expect to sleep much and tossed her bedroll next to the puppies again. She curled on her side and slipped her fingers through the gate. Bravo came over and nosed her hand.

"Just so we understand each other," she murmured, "I'm not going anywhere."

She should have remembered love wasn't always so simple.

CHAPTER NINETEEN

"Hey, Rome," Brody called as Rome crossed the parking lot toward her Porsche. She stopped and waited for Brody to jog up next to her.

"How about a burger and a beer," Brody asked. She was still in her navy-blue flight suit and had probably just come off duty. Rome hadn't bothered to change into street clothes and still wore her maroon scrubs. She didn't plan to leave the trailer once she got home and didn't expect to see anyone since she'd taken puppy duty, so why bother changing?

"Uh…" Rome said, stalling to formulate a reasonable excuse. "Wasn't really planning on going out in public. Not really dressed for it."

"That's not a problem. If you hadn't noticed, hospital duds are practically high fashion around here." Brody raised a brow. "I kind of get the feeling you've been avoiding me for the last couple weeks. Something I said?"

Rome laughed. "Yeah, everything."

Brody grinned. "Seriously, problem?"

Rome shook her head. "Not so you'd notice. Been busy with the pups, settling in, that sort of thing."

That sounded weak even to her, but she hoped Brody would just let it go. They knew each other well enough to read the *don't go there* signals, although Brody had changed since she'd reentered civilian life. Not in a bad way, except at moments like this, when Rome would have preferred the don't ask, don't tell attitude toward most anything personal she'd enjoyed while active duty to Brody's low-key but insistent efforts to get her to open up. She could pretend she hadn't been avoiding anyone for the past few weeks, but they both knew that was BS.

And Brody seemed hell-bent on finding out why.

"I saw you made it to the last few games, but you cut out pretty fast after," Brody said.

"You know I've never been much for socializing." Rome pointed a finger. "You were the one for the all-nighters while I was in the rack when the sun went down."

"Not every night," Brody countered. "Besides, that was then, but this is now. Hanging with your friends for an hour here and there isn't exactly socializing." Brody shrugged. "I need the company anyhow. Val's out on a call, and she took Honcho with her. The house is too damn big and quiet when they're not there."

"And there's the little matter of you being a lousy cook?" Rome said dryly.

"That too." Brody grinned. "So, if you don't want burgers, we can hit that new Thai place. They're supposed to be good."

"I wouldn't mind a beer." Rome figured there was no way she was shaking Brody, and hell, if Brody wanted company, she owed her that. For countless moments over the years when Brody's steady presence had helped Rome find her own balance in the midst of the insanity that was war, and for getting her this job once she'd made it out the other side. They *were* friends, and that counted. "Let's do the tavern."

"Excellent. I've been wanting to drive the Porsche."

Rome laughed. "I don't think I suggested that."

"Well, I can be the designated driver," Brody said.

"I'm going to have one beer with food," Rome said. "I hardly need a driver." She tossed Brody the keys. "But be my guest."

"All right. Let's go."

The ride from the hospital through the village to Bottoms

Up took five minutes, or would have if Brody hadn't headed the other direction out of town.

"You lost?" Rome asked.

"Nah. But I figure if I got a chance to drive this, I might as well see what it will do."

"Should have seen that coming," Rome muttered and settled back to enjoy the view.

Brody was a good driver, and they still had an hour or so of light left with mostly empty roads. Pretty pleasant to just ride along and not have to worry about ambushes or IEDs.

"You want to talk about it?" Brody said.

"Not so you'd notice," Rome replied. She *had* been avoiding Brody and almost everyone else since the night Tally had been over to her trailer. She'd picked up a few extra shifts, so when she wasn't working or looking after the puppies—who had doubled in size and had four times the energy—she didn't have too many hours to fill. Or to think. Pam had casually asked her if she wanted to get together for dinner again a week or so ago, and she'd said she'd take a rain check. Pam, ever gracious, had said that was fine and to look her up whenever she felt like some friendly company. Gentle emphasis on friendly. Rome didn't think she'd damaged that potential friendship and was glad for it.

Other than Brody, she had no personal connections with anyone, so it was easy to avoid Tally or even having to try to be good company with anyone else. When one of the puppy crew showed up when she was home, they were mostly focused on the pups and easy conversation otherwise.

"Okay. Just tell me this," Brody added after a moment, "in general terms, are you the asshole?"

Rome laughed. She couldn't help it, even though the idea stung—Brody was so on the money. When she couldn't stay busy enough to keep from thinking, she beat herself up, wondering if she'd made a huge mistake. "Is this like one of those things where people write in to some Reddit and tell strangers all about some stupid thing they've done, and then ask Am I the Asshole?"

"Well sort of, except, you know, I'm your best friend, so I might not call you an asshole." Brody concentrated on negotiating a series of tight switchbacks and then shot her a grin. "But then again, I might. So? What's the deal?"

"I think I might be the a-hole here, but I don't plan on publicizing it."

"You want to fix it?"

"I don't see how I can," Rome said after a minute.

Brody grunted. "Since when did you quit without even trying?"

"Since I..." Rome blew out a breath. "Did you ever want anything, *anyone* so much that it scared you?"

She half expected Brody to laugh at her, but Brody just nodded, a faraway expression replacing her usual devil-may-care grin. "Yeah, once. When I first laid eyes on Val and every minute since. So you telling me you're in love? Cause that's pretty much the universal feeling that you get, when it's the real deal. Like scared down to your boots, right? Along with feeling that you don't deserve her, that you'll screw it up. And if you do, you'll never make it out the other side of the dark?"

"Yeah."

"So that's the problem? You're twisted up over someone?"

"You're not going to let this go, are you?"

"I'm not actually even poking very hard," Brody said. "So maybe that means you want to talk about it."

Rome rubbed her face with both hands. "Believe me, this is one thing I don't want to talk about. I've spent the last ten years trying to forget it."

"You lost me."

"When I was nineteen years old," Rome said, "I was accused of slipping a girl G at a party so I could talk her into having sex with me. I nearly went to jail, and it tanked my college sports scholarship. Pretty much finished most everything for me."

Brody stiffened. "Jesus. Who would say something like that? The girl?"

"Tally."

Brody pulled into a turnoff and cut the engine. "Tally? Our Tally? Tally Dewilde, my wife's new soon-to-be partner, said that about you?"

"Yeah, but it's worse than that."

"How exactly could it be worse?" Brody asked, a lethal edge to her voice.

"She accused me of giving it to her sister."

"Oh man. How could that happen?"

"A house full of teenagers, partying hard, with a lot of substances rolling around. It looked to Tally like that's what happened—that I gave her sister the Liquid X—and that's the story that stuck."

"And you couldn't prove it otherwise?"

"It was one of those he said, she said things—literally. Her sister's boyfriend backed Tally's story—and Tally did see me with her sister, alone, in a bedroom. No way to prove what really went on that night, other than what Tally believed she saw. What she *still* believes she saw."

"But," Brody said slowly, "something happened between the two of you since you met again, just the same."

"For me at least," Rome said, "while I wasn't paying attention. Like I just blinked and all the pieces fell into place—what I was feeling for her."

"Yeah, it happens that way too."

"So, now you know the story."

"I figure there's a lot more to it, but you don't have to go through it all again. Man." Brody shook her head. "Is that how you ended up in the service?"

"Yeah, like a lot of people. I needed to start somewhere else where nobody knew me."

"I know, me too. I knew Val, you know, in high school."

"I figured that," Rome said, glad to have the topic shift from her. "But you didn't date?"

"It was complicated, the family situation on both sides. And Val, she was like this princess, and I was pretty much a nobody."

"I can't see her thinking that way."

"Who said she thought that way?" Brody shook her head. "Sometimes the way we see things isn't the way everyone else does."

"You're trying to tell me something, but I think it's too deep for me." Rome tilted her head back against the seat. "What it amounts to, though, is Tally and I have too much history that can't be undone."

"Maybe you should think about the possibility that the two of you aren't the same people anymore." Brody started the engine. "And now let's go have that beer."

Rome didn't think it made any difference now what she believed about the past or the present. She feared whatever she might have shared with Tally was already lost.

❖

"I didn't expect to see you here this late," Val said as she poked her head into Tally's office. "Something come up? If you don't leave soon, you'll miss the game tonight."

"Oh no, nothing's going on, but I'm not planning on going to the game." Tally pushed the paperwork she'd been doing to one side. "I told Margie she didn't need to come in tonight. I took care of the evening kennel work." At Val's questioning expression, she waved to the stack of charts on her desk. "And I had some billing to finish up, so I'm just going to stay until that's done."

"You've been spending a fair amount of extra time here. Are we loading up your clinic schedule too much? There's no planning for emergencies, but if they're double-booking you at the front desk, we can—"

"No," Tally said quickly. "Not at all. The schedule is fine. I just don't like to get behind, especially"—she laughed a little—"especially with the things I don't really like to do."

"Uh-huh. The paperwork never ends." Val hesitated. "If you're sure the workload's okay. We can make adjustments."

"Absolutely not necessary," Tally said. "Actually, work is my favorite thing most days."

Val settled into one of the two undeniably uncomfortable chairs across from Tally's desk, looking as if she planned to stay awhile—game or not. The last thing Tally wanted to do was talk about much of anything, and especially not why she was practically camping out at the clinic as many hours a day as she could. Val was the boss and, more than that, someone she was coming to count on as a friend.

"The puppies are due for their second round of shots this weekend," Val said offhandedly. "I can't believe how quickly time is passing and how big the little critters have gotten."

"I know. They'll be ready to go home soon."

"I think so. You haven't been by to see them lately, have you."

Val made that a statement and not a question. Probably it was obvious that she'd been avoiding a visit to Rome's trailer. The two of them had actually managed *not* to end up sitting near each other at the last two basketball games, as if they'd arranged it. Since they hadn't spoken since *that* night, as she thought of their last personal interaction, which happened whenever she couldn't keep her mind occupied with something else, Rome wasn't any more eager to speak to her than she was to bump into Rome. The avoidance was mutual, and she had to admit that stung. Rome's message that their almost-relationship was over came through loud and clear. Since she had her pride, she'd been careful that Rome didn't see her occasional glances when she hadn't been able to help herself from taking a few peeks during the game. She wasn't sure she was happy or not that Rome came into the gym just before the game started, sat by herself, and left as soon as the last buzzer sounded. Someone else's unhappiness did not please her, especially not Rome's. She might be angry with her, and a lot more than a little hurt, but the last thing she wanted was for Rome to be hurting. Which certainly made staying angry with her a lot more difficult.

"I take it that's intentional," Val said.

Tally came back to the moment with a start. "I'm sorry?"

"You're avoiding Rome and not the puppies. On purpose, I take it."

Tally squeezed the bridge of her nose and briefly closed her eyes. With a sigh, she met Val's sympathetic gaze. "I'm assuming it's only super obvious to anyone who knows us—or are we headlining the town news circuit?"

"Not that I've heard from anyone," Val said. "I may have mentioned to Brody that I thought you and Rome might've had some kind of falling-out, but no information was forthcoming."

"Does that mean Brody doesn't know or she doesn't share?"

"If I had to use one word to describe Brody—other than incredibly sexy—I'd say loyal. I imagine Rome is much the same. They've shared things that no one else can ever really understand, and that's a bond that neither one of them would ever endanger."

"I wouldn't have minded," Tally said quietly, "if Brody had mentioned something to you. I imagine that's what happens between couples." She shrugged. "I wouldn't actually know since my parents rarely spent enough time together to actually converse."

"No long-term attachments for you, then?" Val asked.

Tally shook her head. "Nothing romantic, no. A few relationships that I never expected to go anywhere long-term, and neither did anyone else."

"Sometimes, it doesn't have to be long-term or even a long time together for you to know it's the real thing," Val said quietly.

"Was it that way with you and Brody?" Tally wasn't sure if

she was diverting the conversation from her and Rome or hoping to find some clarity on what to do about the tangle they were stuck in.

"Yes and no." Val got a small smile that made Tally's heart ache as she imagined Val thinking about some very special moment. No matter how much she delved into her past, she wouldn't find anything—or anyone—that made her feel like that. Not until recently. Not until Rome.

"I've known Brody since we were in high school," Val said. "She was the dark, mysterious Rivers. You know she's part of the family, right?"

"I thought there was something extra special between her and the rest of the Rivers clan when I saw them all together, but they all seem to treat anyone with any kind of connection like family."

"True," Val said. "And the nicest part of that is they mean it."

"So I guess Brody didn't notice you way back then?"

Val laughed. "According to Brody, she certainly did, but I couldn't see it or was too silly to take her noticing seriously. But lucky for me, I got a second chance. When Brody showed back up here after the Army, *I* most definitely noticed."

"Second chances," Tally said softly. "They don't come along very often, do they? Especially when we've made a mistake."

"Is that's what's going on between you and Rome?" Before Tally could reply, Val went on to say, "You don't have to see the two of you together for more than five minutes to tell there's chemistry. More than chemistry. Connection. But something went astray, I take it."

"Some unfinished business," Tally murmured. She'd always been so certain, so absolutely certain. If she hadn't been, she never would've said what she'd said about Rome. She never would've believed it, for all these years. But she *knew* Rome now, knew her in a way that went against everything she'd believed about her. Something, somewhere, was wrong, and she needed to know what. For her peace of mind, and fairness to Rome—and just maybe, if she was very, very lucky, another chance for them would come along. Tally sat forward, suddenly energized. "Would you mind very much if I switched weekend call with you?"

"You need some time off?" Val asked.

"Yes, just until Monday. I know I haven't been here very long, and I know it probably sounds…not very professional, but—"

"Tally," Val said firmly, "you're the most professional vet I've had working with me here at the clinic since I started. I've had plenty of short-term help, and none of them I wanted to keep. Now that I found you, I'm not letting you get away. *You* are a keeper."

Tally laughed. "I'm so glad. I'll be back on Monday, I swear."

"Take however long you need. Nothing is seriously wrong, is there?"

"Only something I should have taken care of a long time ago."

"Then I hope it all goes well," Val said. "Just don't forget you have a place here when you're done."

"Oh, I can promise you that. I have a lot of reasons to come back."

CHAPTER TWENTY

A ll right, come to order," Rome said to the rambunctious tumble of puppies roiling around the trailer. Most of them gave her a curious glance and went back to the business of chewing on each other, attacking imaginary shadow prey, and hunting for morsels of stray food. All except Bravo, who, as always, watched her intently.

"So, this morning we're having a very special visitor, and—" She broke off at the sound of a car pulling in. Her pulse kicked up, even as her conscious mind warned her not to expect Tally to be glad to see her. Even so, this should be Tally's turn to make house calls, and Rome'd had a restless night working out what she would say to her. Not that anything she might come up with could rewrite the past, but she could at least get up the guts enough to ask for a chance to prove she was not that person. Somehow. After how she'd screwed things up the last time they were together, she might already be too late, but she could hope. Some part of her, despite everything she'd endured at home and in the desert, had never quite learned *not* to hope. The sharp rap on the door got all the puppies barking, and her mouth went dry. She swallowed hard. Right. Last chance. Don't blow it.

"Just a second," she called, hurrying to the door and trying not to step on any of them while diverting the throng of puppies rushing for freedom. "Bit of a jailbreak going on here."

Val called back, "No problem. I'll catch any stragglers who manage to escape."

Rome caught her breath. Val, not Tally. Tally hadn't come. Why was she surprised. And now she still had a mission to carry out. She straightened and said in her best alpha voice, "Listen up, the bunch of you. Back away from the door."

Hood and Camo sat obediently with the expectant expression that announced they were waiting for cookies. Bravo went still and watched her, waiting for the next command. The other three gamboled off, totally unaware of anything other than whatever shiny object had just caught their attention.

"Coast is clear if you move fast," Rome said, opening the door a few inches.

Val slipped inside, closed the door behind her, and took a look around. "I can see they've taken over."

"They're way too active to keep penned up. Fortunately, there's not much at puppy level they can actually destroy."

"Oh, you'd be surprised. Wait'll they start teething."

Rome winced. "I suspect they'll be gone way before then. The crew has been asking just about every day when they'd be able to take them home."

"I'd give them a week after this round of shots," Val said. "By then they ought to be pretty safe to be around strange animals and out in the world in general."

"They'll be glad to hear that." Rome grabbed Lookout, who was busy tugging on the corner of the doormat. "It'll be pretty dull around here without them, though."

"Any problems with any of them?" Val asked.

"As far as I can tell, they're all perfect. They eat like champs, and they're all active and smart." Rome snagged another puppy before it could escape down the hall to the sleeping quarters. "Other than these three, who can't seem to respond to any orders."

"That does sound like a serious condition," Val said, just a bit of a smile racing across her face.

Rome smiled. "Could be worse. Which one do you want first?"

"Let's take Bravo. She'll be less anxious if she knows what's going on."

"Okay." Rome sat on the narrow bench seat under the window and said, "Bravo, come."

The puppy ran to her, and Rome lifted her onto her lap.

Val laid out the syringes on the small dinette table and picked up the first one. "This isn't going to bother her."

"She'll be fine," Rome said but couldn't help tensing as Val came closer. "She's scary smart, so just tell her what you're going to do."

"Of course she is," Val said softly. "She's responsible for all of them. Aren't you, Bravo? I'll be done in just a second. One quick little jab. There."

Rome set her down. "You think she's going to have a problem when the others leave?"

"It's possible. She's used to being with the whole group, and she's used to taking care of them. With you gone a good part of the day, she may have a little trouble adjusting."

"Well, hell." Rome pushed her hand impatiently through her hair. She hadn't thought about what losing her pack would mean for Bravo, and she should have. She still had a hole inside where her squad used to be. And now with Tally gone, the shadows had grown. "I can't very well tell one of the kids they can't take one."

"There are plenty of puppies and dogs out there who need homes."

Rome rubbed the bridge of her nose. "Right. Should I take Bravo with me when I go pick one out?"

"If you wait a week, she can go."

"Okay. I guess that's the plan," Rome said.

"It's a good one," Val said. "A kind one."

Rome glanced at Bravo. "Sometimes you've got to get used to new recruits. It'll be fine."

"How about you," Val asked casually. "Will you be fine? Big change for you too."

"Bravo and I will work it out." Rome studied Val. She worked with Tally. Maybe Tally talked to her. Weird, but she didn't mind. "I thought Tally would be on call this weekend. Did she ask you to come in her place?"

"No." Val picked up the next puppy and handed him to Rome. "She had to go out of town for a few days."

"Oh. Right." Out of town. Business? Didn't seem likely. Visiting family? No. She couldn't see Tally going home right away, not from what she'd said about her family and their criticisms of her career choice. She could be visiting friends. Or she could be away for the weekend for personal reasons. With someone else. There was no reason to think Tally wouldn't move on. Probably as quickly as she could. "Right. Makes sense."

"Does it?" Val said as she switched puppies yet again. "How's that?"

"Oh, nothing," Rome said. "Just talking out loud."

"I notice you haven't been to any of the parties after the games on Friday nights. We missed you out at the Rivers Homestead last weekend."

"Yeah, Brody called me on it too." Rome didn't bother with any of her tired excuses. "I just haven't felt too sociable."

"I understand," Val said. "These get-togethers can be loud, noisy, and nosy."

Rome laughed. "I didn't say any of those things. Especially not about any of the Riverses and their gatherings."

"Tally hasn't been around much either."

"Probably just busy getting settled in."

"Mm." Val finished the last puppy, stood, and stretched. "I imagine that's what it is."

"So, when you see her, just tell her—"

"You could probably tell her yourself," Val said. "As you're likely to bump into her almost anywhere in town or at the games, or would, if you weren't actively trying not to."

Rome raised her brows. "You know, Brody has already hit me with this."

"Well, good. I hope whatever's going on gets sorted out."

Rome blew out a breath. "Yeah, I'm not sure that's possible."

Val paused at the door. "I'm willing to bet that Brody didn't agree with you on that either."

"You'd win the bet."

"Good. You should listen to her. And Rome, don't be so quick to think you've got it all figured out. You can't always do it all alone." Val stopped again with the door partly open and looked back. "Have a good weekend."

"Thanks," Rome called as Val let the door close behind her. "I think."

She scooped Bravo up and said, "Let's talk about what we're going to do."

Bravo, at least, would not tell her she was the a-hole. Even if maybe she was.

❖

At three thirty in the morning, Tally lay awake in the hotel on the edge of Central Park, listening to the once familiar noises of the city—the blare of horns and the muted swell of hundreds of voices from the packed streets on a Saturday night—sounds that made for odd but somehow comforting company. She couldn't sleep, hadn't really expected to, but at least she could relax a little, which was more than would have been possible if she'd been spending the night in her parents' guest room. Nothing about her brief visit there had struck a chord of belonging. She didn't have fond memories of living there. It had taken leaving for her to realize that for more than half her life, she'd existed in a narrow world defined by the expectations and desires of others. And now that she'd left, had finally broken free and left almost everything behind, she was a stranger there.

The still village nights, absent of traffic sounds, with only the occasional barking of a neighbor's dog, the faraway yipping of a coyote pack, and the rare rumble of a truck engine going by had become more familiar than anything she'd known all her life.

The noises of home.

She sat up on the side of the bed and looked out the window at the brightly lit New York skyline. She could stay here with her endlessly circulating thoughts, rearranging the pictures of her past into a new reality, or she could get in the car and drive home. Home. She knew where that was now.

After a quick shower, she dressed in jeans, button-up cotton shirt, and flats, shoved her computer and bits of electronics into her overnight bag, and headed to the elevator to check out. Once on the road, she had the fanciful thought that the straight, mostly empty Thruway north was an arrow directing her home. She turned the heat on rather than stop and pull out the light jacket she'd packed against the cooler nights that had descended in early November. She didn't even feel particularly guilty eating the M&M's she'd picked up in the hotel on her way out. A little sugar would help keep her awake, that and her favorite playlist. She followed the white lines into the dark and refused to think about the last day and a half again. Nothing would be solved alone.

The sun was just starting to make an appearance as she drove into the village and pulled into the convenience store lot to fill up her tank and grab coffee. The brunette behind the counter smiled as she came in. "Morning, Dr. Dewilde. Out on a call?"

"Hi Connie," Tally said. "No. Just up early. How's Gunner?"

"Oh, he's a lot better now. All the swelling went down right after you got that tooth out."

"Good. Tell Rob and the kids I said hi."

"Sure thing. Say, we've got Hot Pockets that I just put out in the food rack. There's a cheese and broccoli…if you don't want the sausage."

"Cheese and broccoli. Sure. Sounds great." Tally hesitated for second. "You know what, why don't you give me two of those while I grab two cups of coffee."

"You got it." Connie got a little smile, as if she suspected Tally was up to something special.

Not exactly accurate. More like a potentially disastrous idea.

Nope, no time for second-guessing now. Don't think, don't analyze. Just get in the car and go. Tally listened to her own best advice—a new but welcome habit—swiped her credit card, wished Connie a great day, and drove in the opposite direction from her house toward the mobile home park. The small pull-off in front of Rome's trailer was empty. Her stomach clenched as she drove in and parked. Rome wasn't home. Maybe she was already too late.

Before she conjured up several possible explanations, all of which were guaranteed to overload her already frayed emotions, she needed to take a breath. And have some coffee. She really wasn't thinking about this very clearly. Or actually, she was thinking far too clearly, and all her thoughts cut at her. She sipped the coffee and contemplated the Hot Pocket. It actually smelled pretty appetizing, which said a lot about the state of her nervous system. She could leave a note on Rome's door. Now, that was silly. She could text her. No, that would be embarrassing if Rome was somewhere else…with someone.

That started another train of circular thoughts, which she quickly squashed. What she needed now was to stay out of her head until she could get all of it out. At last.

Just as she decided she should probably stop lurking in front of Rome's trailer, the Porsche rumbled in beside her. She glanced over as the engine quieted and met Rome's gaze. She wasn't sure what she'd expected. She hadn't actually thought about what she'd do if Rome really didn't want to see her again. If she had, she wouldn't be here at all. *Impulsive.* Not her. Not the old her, at least. But everything was changing now, wasn't it.

Rome nodded, and even with the windows between them,

Tally swore she could detect the heat in her gaze. Or maybe she just wanted to imagine that she saw it.

She rolled down her window as Rome got out and strode around the front of the Porsche to her door. "Hi."

"Hi," Rome said. "Are you going to get out?"

The husky sound of Rome's voice and the fierce intensity in her eyes were all that Tally needed. She knew exactly what to do.

"I am," Tally said, "if you're inviting me in."

"Anytime," Rome said. "Anytime you want."

Tally smiled to herself, grabbed a cup of coffee, and held it out the window. "Here, this is for you. I also brought breakfast."

Rome laughed and looked at her as if she didn't quite believe what she was seeing. Or hearing. "Did you? That's good, because I don't have a lot to eat, and I'm pretty hungry."

Tally grabbed the bag with the Hot Pockets and got out of the Bug. "Cheese and broccoli Hot Pockets, compliments of Stewart's. Does that work?"

Rome still looked a little incredulous. "Absolutely. Sounds fabulous. Come on inside."

Tally hesitated by the front fender of the car. "I probably should have called or texted or something."

"Why?"

"Well, it's almost seven o'clock in the morning, and you might've been sleeping or you might have had company or—"

"Stop right there." Rome gently grasped Tally's shoulders, leaned down, and kissed her. A kiss so light it might have been a whisper. A kiss that coursed through her like lightning.

"I don't have company," Rome said. "I haven't had any company since before I met you—a long time before. And I'm sorry I didn't ask first before I kissed you, but I'm really glad to see you."

Tally found it a little hard to speak for a second, but then said steadily and calmly, which took some effort, "Stop right there. You don't have to ask. Invitation is always open. But before you do that again, and I don't ask you to stop, I need to talk to you."

Rome grimaced. "I know—I need to talk to you too. Let's have some coffee and Hot Pockets and talk."

"Are you sure it's okay? I mean, now?"

"I just got off work. I'm still wired after a busy night, and I wouldn't've gone to sleep right away." Rome took her hand. "And believe me, there's nothing more I want than to see you."

"I don't know how you always manage to say the thing I need to hear," Tally murmured. Rome's hand, so warm and firm, filled her with a sense of rightness.

"I have no idea what I'm supposed to say," Rome said. "All I know is I've missed you. More than that. I've been walking around with a big hole inside."

Tally closed her eyes. "I know. Me too. I'm sorry."

"I think that needs to be my line, but can we go inside?" Rome tilted her head toward the trailer. "They can hear our voices."

Tally slowly became aware of the world beyond Rome. Now she heard the puppies. "Oh God. Right. The coffee might have to wait. I can come ba—"

"Don't even think about going anywhere." Rome tugged Tally's hand. "They'll be fine once we're inside, and they see us. Annika texted me an hour ago that she was here and took care of their morning needs. I told the squad to let me handle the mornings, but I can't really keep them away. Any excuse."

"I'm not surprised." Tally gripped Rome's hand harder. "I haven't been able to think about anything except you since I left the city."

"Come inside with me."

"I would like that very much," Tally whispered.

CHAPTER TWENTY-ONE

J ust give me a minute to give them all some chewies," Rome said as she held the door for Tally. "That will keep them busy for a little while."

"Look at them," Tally said, laughing, as she followed Rome inside. The puppies, just about eight weeks by her estimation, tumbled over each other to get their paws up on the barrier amid an avalanche of barks.

"Yeah. They're outgrowing this place pretty fast." Rome passed out dental chews to each of them. "Val gave the go-ahead for them to go home with the crew at the end of the week."

"It's going to be awfully quiet around here without them," Tally said.

"I don't think I'll mind too much, but I think Bravo might." Rome shrugged as the pack settled down to work on their chew sticks. "We've got some ideas about that too."

"I'm sorry I've been out of touch—"

"I'm just glad you're here now." Rome gestured to the rear of the trailer. "I think if we want to talk, though, we ought to get out of their line of sight before they finish. There's not much room back here, but it'll be quieter."

The compact bedroom at the rear of the trailer held a double bed on a frame that took up most of the space below built-in shelves and cubbies where Rome had stored a few piles of clothes. Multiple windows made the space feel larger than it actually was.

Rome ran a hand through her hair. "Sorry, the only seating room is on the bed."

"That's fine." Tally sat down near the end of the bed and put her coffee on the window shelf as Rome turned a pillow around and propped it behind her back at the opposite end.

"I've been working out what I wanted—*needed*—to say all the way here," Tally said, "but first, I need to ask you a question."

Rome sipped her coffee and nodded. "Go ahead."

"All the times that I've brought up what happened with Sheila, and how I felt about it, and what I thought about it, you never told me your side of the story. Why is that?"

Rome blew out a breath. "Okay, well, let's start with an easy question."

"I'm sorry, I know this is hard—"

"No, it's not that. It's just…" Rome shook her head, looking frustrated. "If I thought there was anything that I could say that would make a difference, don't you think I would have? Don't you think the one thing I've wanted since the moment this happened was to find a way to make everyone believe that I didn't—not that night, and not any other night—give Sheila any kind of drug at all?"

"But you knew that she took them," Tally said. "I didn't know that."

"She wasn't the only one," Rome said, "and I didn't think that was really the issue."

"You didn't try to make her look responsible."

"Tally, nothing was provable." Rome shook her head. "Not even what I was accused of doing, except for…"

Rome looked away, but Tally heard what she didn't say. "There was no proof except for what I said about you. My statements were what made you look so guilty."

"You told the truth as you knew it."

"And you never contradicted me. You never accused me of not telling the truth. Why not?"

"I turned around that night and saw you in the doorway. You saw me alone with Sheila and she was…not right. That's the truth of it."

"And I believed what everyone said you were doing," Tally replied.

"Why wouldn't you? And nothing's changed," Rome said. "*Nothing*. You saw me with your sister. Sheila and Justin both made statements that I was the one to bring the drugs, to give them to her, and there I was, alone with her. The conclusions were clear."

"I know," Tally said, "and I came here today to tell you…" She took a deep breath. She was taking a chance that what she was about to say wouldn't destroy any possibility of their being together. But Rome deserved to hear it. And she needed to say it.

Rome sat forward and took her hand. "Tally, there's no point to this. I can see that this hurts you and—"

Tally pressed her fingers to Rome's mouth. "Listen."

Rome closed her eyes. "All right."

"I went home this weekend," Tally said. "I went home to find out the truth."

"And did you?" Rome asked softly.

"I did." Tally reached for Rome's other hand. "Let me get this all out, at last."

Rome nodded. "All right."

"When I got home," Tally said, "my parents were surprised to see me. Actually, they were mostly annoyed because I had shown up without letting them know I was coming, and they were hosting a dinner party that night. I assured them I wasn't planning to gate-crash." She laughed and shook her head. "I only stopped there before heading to Sheila's apartment because I felt I owed it to them to let them know I was going to talk to her. I knew she would call them as soon we spoke, and I wanted them to be prepared for the fallout. As it turned out, I didn't have to drive to her apartment after all. She was spending the weekend with them because of the party that night."

Tally let out a breath. "Anyhow, this is what happened when I finally found my sister."

Rome's fingers slipped through Tally's, linking them. "I'm listening."

Sheila was in her old bedroom in a pale blue dressing gown and lounge slippers, obviously having just gotten up, although it was already after noon. Clothes lay strewn over a bedside chair and window seat and several pairs of shoes littered the floor. The vanity held a collection of makeup bottles and lotions. If Tally hadn't known better, she'd think Sheila had never left home.

"Tally," Sheila said with just the slightest false note of welcome in her voice. "What are you doing here?"

"Hi," Tally said. "Sorry I didn't let anyone know I was coming. It was kind of spur-of-the-moment."

"Well, I hope you brought party clothes, baby. Mother is doing one of the holiday things already. You know she likes to be the first on the circuit so everyone else will have to compete with her."

"I just found out about it. I don't think I'll be going, though."

Sheila pursed her lips. "You really should. I've seen the guest list, and believe me, there are quite a few interesting names on there. You remember Elliott McIntyre? He'll be there. He's recently divorced, and I'm sure desperate not to be single for long." She flicked a wrist dismissively. "He's had a little trouble in the business area, so I'm not inclined to consider him."

"Ah, I know I haven't seen you in a while, but have you forgotten my interest doesn't run to men in that regard?" Tally asked.

Sheila scoffed. "Oh, that doesn't matter. They have so much

to offer, even if it's not financial—all that male privilege is worth a little compromise in the bedroom. There are plenty of ways around that, after all."

"Right, okay. Well, I don't want to get in your way, but I need to talk to you about something important."

Sheila looked over her shoulder as she began sorting through her overfilled closet. "Are you pregnant?"

"No, not even close. Do you think you could sit down for a minute and listen?"

Sheila huffed and sat on the edge of her bed. "All right, but I don't have a lot of time to chat. I still need to do my makeup and figure out what I'm going to wear tonight."

Tally said, "You know I'm living upstate now, for my new job."

Sheila rolled her eyes. "I know. That's not going to last. Whatever will you do up there."

"Actually, I really like it. But that's not what I wanted to talk to you about. Rome Ashcroft is working at the hospital in the village."

Sheila's eyes narrowed. "Roman Ashcroft? How bizarre. I haven't heard that name since she disappeared from...everywhere."

"She was in the service, and now she's a PA," Tally said. "We've gotten to know each other very well."

Sheila stared. "The two of you are friends."

"Yes. And—"

"What has she said about me?"

Tally expected the question, because of course, everything was always about Sheila in Sheila's mind. "Not a single word."

"Really. She didn't ask about me?"

"No. And she's never talked about that night either."

"Oh, that," Sheila said with another wave of her hand. "Really, that's just so old news that it's ancient history. And who cares about that any longer."

"I do," Tally said. "I want to know what really happened that night."

"What difference does it make now?" Sheila glanced at her watch. "Everyone has forgotten it, and why wouldn't they. It was nothing."

"Nothing," Tally said softly. "Rome Ashcroft being accused of drugging you, attempting to assault you, that's nothing?"

Sheila laughed. The laughter was cold and brittle, like ice cracking on the surface of a frozen lake, a snap with dangerous undertones. "I told you. No one cares about that anymore. No one even remembers it, and besides, no one believed it then except you."

Tally caught her breath. "What do you mean?"

"You were the one that spread the story. If it hadn't been for you, nothing about the party would have ever come out. Justin wouldn't have broken up with me and I wouldn't have had to settle for Aron just to show everyone I couldn't care less what Justin did. I wouldn't be just another divorced thirty-year-old now. Everything that's happened has been your fault."

"My fault," Tally said.

"You were the one that started all the fuss. You were the one that made the accusations, and once you did, well, there was nothing to do about it except go along with it. Everyone heard what you said, and once some idiot called the fucking police, what were we supposed to do?"

"Tell the truth?" Tally asked.

"Why? You already had the perfect explanation for everything. Yes, we were drinking. So what? Everyone was doing it. No one cared about that. But you had to bring up drugs, and that was a much more serious problem. Justin didn't want anything to do with it. He was going to law school. So, of course, it had to be Roman's fault."

"But it wasn't, was it," Tally said, filling with terrible dread. All of it had been her fault. She'd been the one to make the accusation.

"Roman?" Sheila snorted. "Who barely ever touched alcohol, let alone drugs like G? Of course you'd be the only one to believe that it would be her. God, how naive could you be."

"And you—all of you—were willing to let her life be ruined?" Tally fought down the horror threatening to suffocate her.

"Well, I couldn't very well point fingers at any of my friends, could I? Involve my fiancé…" She shot to her feet. "The fiancé who wouldn't stand by me, who was so afraid that his father would take away his trust fund and his support for law school that he walked out on me."

"Where did they come from?" Tally asked. "The drugs?"

"Oh, I don't know. Someone always brought something. The whole point was to make everything feel better—especially the sex. And I knew if I texted Roman and said I was in trouble, she'd come." She laughed again. "And she did. Only by then, well, I'd maybe had a little too much."

"She never said anything about you texting her."

"Who would have cared?" Sheila said. "I was the victim. And there was a perfectly good explanation for everything, which you provided. But really, why bring it all up again now?"

"Because I ruined someone's life," Tally said.

"Oh God, don't be so dramatic," Sheila said. "Everyone survived. Everyone always does."

"Not everyone lives on lies."

"Still naive, I see." Sheila threw off her robe, unconcerned about her nakedness, and strode toward the en suite. "I'm going to bathe and get ready for the party. You can look through my closet. There's probably something in there you can wear."

"I won't be staying for the party," Tally said.

"You'll be sorry that you missed it."

"I don't think so. Good-bye, Sheila."

Tally took a deep breath and met Rome's gaze. "If I hadn't been there that night, none of what happened to you after would have ever occurred. I am so sorry. I know that's inadequate, and I won't blame you if you hate me after this."

Rome took Tally's other hand when she tried to pull away. "Wait. Your turn to listen."

Tally shuddered, and Rome moved a little closer. "I don't hate you. I could never hate you. And I don't hold you responsible for anything that happened that night."

"How can you say that after what I just told you?"

"Tally," Rome murmured, cupping Tally's cheek. "You were fifteen years old. You saw what you believed you saw, and everyone else supported you. It wasn't just you alone. And you have to let it go now. It's over. it's done."

"I know, but everything that's happened to you since is my fault."

Rome brushed her thumb over Tally lips. "Everything *good* that's happened to me is because of you, then and now. But mostly now. I love you."

"I…" Tears filled Tally's eyes. "I love you too."

CHAPTER TWENTY-TWO

Tally," Rome murmured, sliding her arm around Tally's waist and pulling her closer.

Rome kissed her, and the shadows surrounding Tally's heart faded like the gray sky of dawn with the morning sun. She gripped Rome's shirt in both hands to keep her from escaping. "I feel like I've finally found you, and I'm almost afraid to believe it."

"You can, I swear," Rome said. "I don't want to be anywhere without you. I will never go unless you tell me to."

"Never," Tally whispered and clasped her hands behind Rome's neck, watching her eyes, those so expressive eyes that always told her so much, as she kissed Rome back. What she saw—the tenderness, the desire, the want—echoed the storm building inside her. "We have a little bit of a problem right now, though."

"No, we don't," Rome said. "Not anymore. Not now that I'm holding you. Not now that I can say I love you." Rome kissed her again, a deep, thorough kiss that left Tally breathless. "Whatever's troubling you, we'll deal with it."

Tally laughed softly. "First of all, you are not allowed to kiss me and then stop."

Rome feathered another kiss against the corner of her mouth. "I wasn't planning on stopping. Just a slight intermission for a sit rep. What's wrong?"

"There's the problem of the six in the other room."

"They've been fed, watered, and cleaned up. They can wait for anything else."

"Have you ever tried to make love with six puppies barking?" Tally said, slowly unbuttoning each button on Rome's shirt. When her fingers brushed against the skin at the base of Rome's throat, Rome shuddered. Heat rushed through her, the feeling of power and wonder making her head light. She rested her forehead against Rome's. "Because there's no way we are stopping. I love the way you feel. I adore your body. I love you."

"We're not stopping, not now, not ever." Rome gently tugged Tally's shirt up and rested her fingers against Tally's middle. "There's nothing that compares to being with you."

Tally caught her breath. Just that little touch stirred urgency so overwhelming she wasn't sure how she'd keep her sanity. "God, I want you."

Rome groaned, a hungry sound that fired Tally's need even higher. Rome pulled her back onto the bed until they were lying face to face, her fingers busy opening Tally's jeans as Tally tugged at her shirt.

"Oh," Tally gasped, "I think I broke a button off."

"I don't care if you rip it to shreds," Rome said, hooking a thumb in Tally's jeans to push them down. "I want you naked."

Somehow, through the haze of pounding need, Tally managed to help get her clothes off while Rome tore hers off and tossed them aside. She wanted to glory in the sight of Rome's body, but Rome rolled onto her back and slid her thigh between Tally's.

"Oh," Tally cried, astonished at the the exquisite pleasure. She wrapped her arms around Rome's shoulders and kissed her, demanding what she had no more words for. Skating over the softness of her lips, darting, teasing, tasting, she drew one leg up the back of Rome's, needing to touch her everywhere she could.

Rome kissed her back, deep and sure, and cupped her breast in her palm. When she gently squeezed, Tally moaned. Rome's thumb brushing her nipple to piercing tautness ignited showers of pleasure that brought her to the peak of arousal.

Tally pushed against Rome's shoulders. "Touch my clit. I'm so close."

"Soon," Rome murmured, her kisses trailing down, skimming down Tally's throat until her mouth was against her breast.

On a cry, Tally arched, Rome's mouth a furnace driving her. Rome's palm against her middle, her fingers caressing closer and closer to where her body demanded relief, brought the tension between her thighs to the bursting point. She dug her fingers into Rome's shoulders, trying to hold on, trying to hold off.

"You're going to make me come," Tally cried.

Rome rolled over onto her back and pulled Tally on top of her, her thighs still between Tally's. "Look at me. Look at me now. See how much I want you."

So close, so close. Tally forced her eyes open. Rome's were dark pools of hunger and need. Her vision hazed as her body took over. She slid along the warm, smooth skin of Rome's thigh, reaching, reaching, reaching for the crest. Rome cradled her breast, her thumb on her nipple like a spark to a flame. She exploded, dazzling bursts of pleasure driving a cry from her throat as her back arched. She rode the waves of release until she went limp with exhaustion and pressed her face to Rome's neck.

"So good." She sighed. "You make me crazy."

Rome chuckled. "Prepare to be crazy on a regular basis, then."

Even without looking at her, Tally could see the satisfied smile. She adored that her pleasure pleased Rome. "That's quite a statement."

Rome brushed her lips over Tally's ear. "Consider it a promise."

Tally gathered her strength and leaned up on an elbow. "I have to look at you. I have promises to make too. But first I need to see you, touch you." She caught her breath and murmured, "Taste you."

"Please," Rome whispered.

Tally smiled and traced the planes and valleys of Rome's body. Rome was gorgeous everywhere. Long, toned, with a faint triangle of tan still at her throat, a reminder of the desert that had yet to fade. She kissed the hollow there and delighted when Rome sucked in a breath. She decided then and there that she'd keep kissing her just to make her do that again. To her delight, everywhere she kissed and stroked as she strove to touch every inch incited a shiver or a groan, and her heart trembled at the gift.

"I could touch you for hours," she murmured as she shifted over Rome's thigh and settled between her legs. "I could spend a lifetime right here."

A few minutes later, Rome threaded her fingers through Tally's hair. "If you do that much longer, you're going to make me come."

Tally looked up, her cheek against the inside of Rome's thigh. "Then be prepared for more of the same. Like I said, a lifetime."

When Tally took her into her mouth and felt Rome's pleasure flood through her, she knew her heart had come home.

EPILOGUE

Four months later
High School Boys Division 2 Championship Game

"Looks like everyone is here," Rome said, reaching for Tally's hand as they threaded their way up the bleachers. Val, Brody, Flann, and Abby sat on the top row, just above Edward and Ida, who each held a grandchild—Carson's son Davey and Harper and Presley's baby daughter Toni—flanked on each side by Margie and the childrens' parents.

Abby waved and pointed to the empty spaces next to her.

"Thanks for saving us seats," Tally said as she and Rome squeezed in. "The seller's attorney was late, but the deal is done."

"That's great," Abby said. "It's such a fabulous place. I'm so happy the owner decided to sell it."

"And it's got a really good yard for the dogs," Rome said.

Brody looked over her shoulder at them and said, "How's Charlie doing?"

"He's great. Settled in like a seasoned trooper."

"Still can't believe you picked a dog that's going to be fifteen pounds soaking wet," Brody said with a chuckle.

"We didn't pick him, Bravo did," Tally put in. "He follows her everywhere, so we're not worried about letting them outside together. Bravo would never let anything bother him."

"Dogs," Tally murmured to Abby. "I heard Margie and Blake discussing a companion for Hood."

"Since the day Hood came home with him," Abby said. "It was only a matter of time."

"Is Blake nervous about tonight?" Tally asked.

"He's been pretty quiet about it," Abby said as the crowd noise picked up and the two teams came out onto the floor for warm-ups. "This game is what they've all been working toward all season. If they win, they'll go to State."

"Then I guess we'll all be going," Tally said. "They've been doing so well all year. And Blake has been great at point."

Abby tugged her lip. "It's a lot of responsibility for him, but he really loves the game, and he loves being part of the team."

"By this time next year he might be deciding on what college team to play for." Tally wouldn't have imagined in her wildest dreams that she'd now be an ardent high school sports fan. Between the boys' and girls' teams—basketball, football, field hockey, and soon baseball and softball—something was going on almost every weekend and some weekday nights. She and Rome made as many as they could, and the gatherings after. Her life before coming here, which she rarely thought of in between the rare thinly veiled commands from her mother to be available for some critical social function—which she politely and routinely refused—now seemed colorless and flat, much like a landscape devoid of depth or color.

She squeezed Rome's fingers, leaned close, and murmured, "I love you."

Rome turned from her discussion of the latest flight schedule and smiled. "I love you back."

The whistle blew and the game started. Both teams played hard, physical basketball, and when the buzzer rang, cheers filled the auditorium. The Rivers family—by blood or choice—stood to add their voices to the tumult. Teammates crowded around Blake, who turned and looked up toward them with a wide smile.

Rome slipped an arm around Tally's waist. "He's found his team for sure."

"You always know when you've found the place where you belong," Tally said.

Rome pulled her close for a kiss that said, *I know.*

About the Author

In addition to editing over twenty LGBTQIA+ anthologies, Radclyffe has written over sixty-five romance and romantic intrigue novels, including a paranormal romance series, The Midnight Hunters, as L.L. Raand.

She is a three-time Lambda Literary Award winner in romance and erotica and received the Dr. James Duggins Outstanding Mid-Career Novelist Award from the Lambda Literary Foundation. A member of the Saints and Sinners Literary Hall of Fame, she is also an RWA/FF&P Prism Award winner for *Secrets in the Stone*, an RWA FTHRW Lories and RWA HODRW winner for *Firestorm*, an RWA Bean Pot winner for *Crossroads*, an RWA Laurel Wreath winner for *Blood Hunt*, and a Book Buyers Best award winner for *Price of Honor* and *Secret Hearts*. She is also a featured author in the 2015 documentary film *Love Between the Covers*, from Blueberry Hill Productions. In 2019 she was recognized as a "Trailblazer of Romance" by the Romance Writers of America.

In 2004 she founded Bold Strokes Books, one of the world's largest independent LGBTQ publishing companies, and is the current president and publisher.

Find her at facebook.com/Radclyffe.BSB, follow her on Twitter @RadclyffeBSB, and visit her website at Radfic.com.

Books Available From Bold Strokes Books

A Degree to Die For by Karis Walsh. A murder at the University of Washington's Classics Department brings Professor Antigone Weston and Sergeant Adriana Kent together—first as opposing forces and then as allies as they fight together to protect their campus from a killer. (978-1-63679-365-8)

Finders Keepers by Radclyffe. Roman Ashcroft's past, it seems, is not so easily forgotten when fate brings her and Tally Dewilde together—along with an attraction neither welcomes. (978-1-63679-428-0)

Homeland by Kristin Keppler and Allisa Bahney. Dani and Kate have finally found themselves on the same side of the war, but a new threat from the inside jeopardizes the future of the wasteland. (978-1-63679-405-1)

Just One Dance by Jenny Frame. Will Taylor Spark and her new business to make dating special—the Regency Romance Club—bring sparkle back to Jaq Bailey's lonely world? (978-1-63679-457-0)

On My Way There by Jaycie Morrison. As Max traverses the open road, her journey of impossible love, loss, and courage mirrors her voyage of self-discovery leading to the ultimate question: If she can't have the woman of her dreams, will the woman of real life be enough? (978-1-63679-392-4)

A Talent Within by Suzanne Lenoir. Evelyne, born into nobility, and Annika, a peasant girl with a deadly secret, struggle to change their destinies in Valmora, a medieval world controlled by religion, magic, and men. (978-1-63679-423-5)

Transitioning Home by Heather K O'Malley. An injured soldier realizes they need to transition to really heal. (978-1-63679-424-2)

Truly Enough by J.J. Hale. Chasing the spark of creativity may ignite a burning romance or send a friendship up in flames. (978-1-63679-442-6)

Vintage and Vogue by Kelly and Tana Fireside. When tech whiz Sena Abrigo marches into small-town Owen Station, she turns librarian Hazel Butler's life upside down in the most wonderful of ways, setting off an explosive series of events, threatening their chance at love…and their very lives. (978-1-63679-448-8)

The Accidental Bride by Jane Walsh. Spinsters Miss Grace Linfield and Miss Thea Martin travel to Gretna Green to prevent a wedding, only to discover a scandalous passion—for each other. (978-1-63679-345-0)

Broken Fences by Jo Hemmingwood. Former army sergeant Seneca Twist has difficulty adjusting to civilian life until she meets psychologist Robyn Mason and has a place to call home. (978-1-63679-414-3)

Never Kiss a Cowgirl by Ali Vali. Asher Evans dreams of winning the National Finals Rodeo in Vegas, and Reagan Wilson wants no part of something that brings back the memory of what killed her father. (978-1-63679-106-7)

Pantheon Girls by Jean Copeland. Cassie Burke never anticipated the detour life is about to take when a meeting with a prospective client reunites her with a past love and reignites the star-crossed passion they shared twenty years earlier. (978-1-63679-337-5)

Roux for Two by Aurora Rey. For TV chef Chelsea Boudreaux and hometown boy Bryce Cormier, love proves as tricky as making a good pot of gumbo. (978-1-63679-376-4)

Starting Over by Nance Sparks. Jennifer has no idea if she can mend Sam's broken soul after the sudden loss of her wife, but it's never too late for starting over. (978-1-63679-409-9)

Three Wishes by Anne Shade. A magic lamp, a beautiful Jinni, and a cursed princess make for one unbelievable story. (978-1-63679-349-8)

Undiscovered Treasures by MJ Williamz. For Cyl and her friends Luna and Martinique, life's best treasures often appear when they're not looking. (978-1-63679-449-5)